VULTURES

A JOHN MILTON THRILLER

MARK DAWSON

PART I

VENICE

1

John Milton took out his phone and looked down at the screen. The single blue dot showing the position of his stolen AirPods was half a mile away from him. He kept his eyes on the phone, watching as the dot moved slowly, weaving its way from Piazzale Roma toward San Marco, one of the city's most exclusive neighbourhoods.

Milton had never been to Venice before, and, so recently after being in Siberia, it felt like another world; the labyrinth of canals, the sense of history, and the feeling that everything, eventually, would be submerged beneath the water of the lagoon created an almost dreamlike sensation. There was a bustling, chaotic energy here, too; it was a place that thrived on its own peculiar rhythm, untethered from the rest of Italy. Milton found that he liked it very much.

He fell back into step, eyes up, looking for anything that might help him identify who had his AirPods and, perhaps, the jacket that had been stolen from the café at the same time. He turned a corner and caught a glimpse of the Grand Canal between the shoulders of two buildings. The morning cast the city in shades of gold and grey, the water sparkling beneath a sky that had started to bruise with a threatened storm and the reflections of the nearby palazzos.

The dot on his screen crossed the Ponte di Rialto and moved to a side street, slipping into a tangle of alleyways. Milton reached the bridge and followed, pausing at its central portico to take in the view of the canal as gondolas and vaporetti glided below. The neighbourhood closed in around him as he descended to the opposite bank, the streets narrowing into winding passages. There were art galleries and boutiques on either side of him, not all of them yet open for the day despite the time being just past noon.

He glanced at the map: the dot was just ahead.

Milton had arrived in the city yesterday and had taken a room in a cheap hotel in the Cannaregio district. He'd been tracking the AirPods ever since they'd been stolen in Paris. He knew, of course, that it would have been easier to buy another pair, but he had nowhere else to be and decided that following them was as good a reason to choose his next destination as any. A normal person might consider his behaviour obsessive, but he'd never cared about what other people thought. There was a principle involved; Milton didn't intend to do anything other than retrieve his property and perhaps have a stern word with whoever had stolen them from him, and if by so doing he made it less likely the thief stole again? That would be another benefit to taking the trip.

Milton had been occupied with his business in Ukraine and then Russia and had forgotten all about the AirPods until he had finally extricated himself from the situation with Lilly Moon; it was as he'd parted ways with Ziggy Penn and Alex Hicks in Lappeenranta that he'd tried to listen to music and remembered that the case that ought to have been in his pocket was gone. He'd opened the Find My app to see that whoever had the AirPods was in Barcelona. He booked a flight for the next day, but as he checked into his hotel that night, he'd seen that the AirPods had moved. Fascinated, Milton had watched as the dot slid across the city to the airport, and then, when he'd checked back again four hours later, it had scooted all the way across the Mediterranean and mainland Italy and settled in Venice.

And so Venice it was. He'd cancelled his Spanish booking, changing it for a seat on the seven-forty evening Iberia flight to Marco Polo. He'd landed at just before ten and decided that he would grab some sleep before dealing with his business in the morning.

He turned a corner and saw a crowd of people gathered in a campo outside a typically grand Renaissance building. The building stood by the canal, its pale stone walls weathered by years of salt and sun.

He looked at the map again.

The dot had stopped moving outside the building.

Whoever had the AirPods was somewhere in the crowd.

Milton zoomed in on the map and read the label: the building was the Scuola Grande di San Teodoro. He Googled the name: it was a sixteenth-century hall that had since become a venue for concerts, galas, and now, it seemed from the second search result on the page, a seminar for a cryptocurrency called TrueCoin.

The crowd shuffled forwards, climbing steps polished smooth from centuries of use, and filtered through a large doorway flanked by Corinthian columns. Milton joined the back of the queue. The crowd was diverse, with a mixture of young and old waiting to go inside. Conversations buzzed in a variety of languages: Italian, English, German, and others Milton couldn't identify. Some of the attendees were dressed in sharp business attire, while others were more casual; everyone seemed eager. Half a dozen men and women at the door were scanning digital tickets before sending the guests inside.

Milton reached the front, and one of the staff members—a young woman with a pierced septum—smiled at him. "*Biglietto?*"

"Sorry," Milton said. "My Italian is very bad."

She switched to English. "Ticket?"

He spread his hands. "Afraid I don't have one."

The woman was wearing a T-shirt with 'TrueCoin' written across it. "You need a ticket if you want to come in."

"Can I buy one now?"

"We're sold out," she said. "Sorry."

"Can I ask what it's about?"

"What?"

He pointed. "Inside."

"Cryptocurrency," she said. "It's all online."

The man behind Milton was getting agitated, so Milton stepped aside. He watched as the queue filed through the door, he was still interested in finding out who had his property, but he found his curiosity had been piqued even more by the event.

There was a coffee shop on the other side of the campo that would offer a decent vantage to observe the attendees when they emerged outside once more. He'd wait there, enjoy an espresso, and see what he could find out about TrueCoin.

2

Marco Caruso shifted uncomfortably in his seat, his fists clenched tightly in his lap. The hall was packed and buzzing with excitement and anticipation. The chandeliers overhead cast a golden glow over the crowd, and he looked around to see a host of eager faces. He'd been like that not long ago, but not anymore. He'd seen through it all: the high-energy music, the glossy brochures, the staff members who answered the questions of potential investors with messianic zeal.

Marco knew better: it was all a trick.

TrueCoin's polished veneer made him sick.

He looked up at the stage. Valentina Rossi wasn't there yet, but the MC was winding up the warm-up speakers, and Marco knew they'd wheel her out soon enough. She was the star attraction, after all, the reason so many people had paid a hundred euros just for a ticket and the chance to invest thousands more. Marco thought of his parents, the savings they'd poured into the scam because of him. His sister had invested the payment she'd been given when she was made redundant after Marco told her she could double it. His brother-in-law had maxed out their credit cards to buy more. He'd trusted TrueCoin and had sold the dream to others, and now the weight of his guilt felt like it would crush him.

And that wasn't even considering what the scam had cost him and his wife.

The speaker, Riccardo Moretti—he proudly declared himself the only Platinum affiliate in Italy—wrapped up with a flourish, his voice rising as he proclaimed the limitless potential of cryptocurrency in general and TrueCoin specifically. The crowd erupted into cheering and applause.

Marco didn't join the ovation; his jaw was locked tight, and he stayed in his seat. He knew he had to do something, but now that he was here—surrounded by the converted—he was having second thoughts. They were all here because they wanted to change their lives, and they wouldn't respond well to anyone who tried to tell them that the edifice at which they were worshipping was built on sand. Marco knew all about confirmation bias; he'd been just the same until the scales had finally fallen from his eyes.

He drew in a breath, trying to ignore the knot of discomfort in his gut.

He couldn't just sit here and let these people be fed the same lies he'd believed.

"And now," the MC announced, his voice ringing out through the hall, "the woman who has inspired us all with her vision and leadership. Please welcome Valentina Rossi!"

The applause went up several notches as Valentina stepped onto the stage. She was as dazzling as ever, her long black dress shimmering under the lights, her hair perfectly styled. She waved to the crowd, her smile radiating warmth and confidence.

Marco's stomach churned with disgust. The smile was as fake as everything else about her.

"Good evening, everyone," she began, her voice warm and confident. "Let me start by thanking each of you for being here tonight and for placing your trust in TrueCoin. It's your belief and commitment that drive us forward every single day. What we're building together is more than just a financial innovation—it's a gateway to true freedom."

She paused, her gaze sweeping across the room, her smile radiating sincerity.

"For far too long, so many of us have felt stuck—stuck in jobs we hate, routines that wear us down, lives designed to benefit others while leaving us behind. But with TrueCoin, we've created something *extraordinary*. A chance to break those chains. A chance to take control of your future, your finances, and to achieve the life you've always dreamed of living."

The room was silent, every face turned toward her, captivated. Valentina leaned forward, her tone intimate, as though she were speaking to each person individually.

"Picture this: waking up every morning not just getting by but *thriving*. You pick up your phone, open the TrueCoin app and look to see that your coins have appreciated in value *again*. You bought them for a hundred euros each—maybe you bought them *today*—but now they're worth two hundred. It's true passive income—they make money while you sleep. That's the promise we're delivering. TrueCoin isn't just a cryptocurrency—it's a lifeline. It's your chance to step off the hamster wheel, to escape the grind—to truly *live*."

The crowd erupted in applause once more.

"And this is just the beginning. We're creating a legacy—not just for us, but for future generations. So let's keep pushing forward. Let's keep growing. Together, we're not just changing the game—we're creating a whole *new* one."

The applause swelled, filling the room as Valentina raised her arms slightly, basking in their approval.

She is so good.

Marco knew she was full of shit, but he still felt the same flutter of excitement.

He felt a surge of anger.

He couldn't let her continue.

He *couldn't* let these people fall for the same lies.

He pushed his chair back; the legs scraped loudly against the marble floor. A few heads turned, but Valentina's voice carried on, unwavering.

He stood, his knees shaking, and shouted, "This is a scam!"

The hall fell silent. Valentina froze mid-sentence, her smile faltering for a split second before she regained her composure. Security guards stationed at the back of the room began moving toward him.

"It's all a lie!" Marco yelled, his voice growing stronger as he found the confidence to speak. "You're stealing people's money—destroying lives!" He pointed at Valentina. "You... you're a fraud!"

"Sir," one of the guards said, reaching him now, "you need to leave."

"I'm not leaving until everyone here knows the truth!" Marco shouted as loudly as he could. "They don't care about you or your money—just their own greed!"

The guards grabbed him by the arms. Marco struggled against them, his anger boiling over. "You're all being scammed!" he yelled to the crowd desperately. "Don't trust them! Don't give them another cent! They're thieves. They're *vultures*!"

The crowd murmured, and, just as he'd feared, they started to boo.

But not at Valentina or TrueCoin...

They were booing at *him*.

Valentina stepped forward, smiling, her hands raised palm-out and her voice calm. "I'm so sorry you feel that way," she said. "But I promise you, TrueCoin is here to help people, not hurt them. We can talk about this privately, if you'd like."

"Liar!" Marco spat. The guards began dragging him backwards toward the exit, his heels scraping against the floor as he resisted. "*Liar!* Don't believe her! She's lying to all of you!"

Valentina kept smiling. "Let's give this gentleman some space," she said. "We'll sort this out."

Marco continued to struggle as the guards hauled him out of the hall and into the bright daylight outside. They let him go on the steps of the Scuola, shoving him hard enough that he stumbled down them and into the campo.

"Go home," one of them said. "And don't come back."

Marco steadied himself, brushing off his jacket. "You're just as bad as she is," he said, glaring at the guards. "You should be ashamed."

The guards ignored him. They turned and went back inside, the heavy doors closing behind them. He stood there for a moment, breathing hard, his heart racing. The adrenaline was fading, leaving him drained and weak. He looked around at the tourists in the square, many of them watching him, oblivious to what had just happened.

Marco felt a sharp pang of despair.

Had anyone in the room even heard him? Would it make any difference?

He pulled out his phone and dialled Carlo. The call rang twice before it was answered.

"It's me," Marco said, his voice still hoarse.

"Are you okay?"

"I did it. I called her out."

"And?"

"What do you think? Her hired monkeys threw me out."

"Did anyone listen?"

"I don't know."

"You tried," Carlo said. "You took a stand. That's more than most people do. And if one person has second thoughts, that's enough."

Marco nodded. "I know."

"Come to the meeting."

"I don't know if I have the energy."

"Come," he insisted. "It'll do you good. You need to unload it all. You know how bad it feels when you shoulder it all alone."

"I know."

"And there's someone here I want you to meet."

"Who?"

"Someone who might have some good news. I'm not going to say anything else—you need to come and listen to her for yourself."

Marco looked at his watch. The meeting was at the Istituto, a twenty-minute walk away. And Carlo was right: it *would* do him good.

"All right."

He ended the call, took out the case with the second-hand AirPods he'd bought on eBay and put them into his ears. He selected the new album by Måneskin and tapped play. He could grab a coffee from the café across the campo and walk. The exercise would do him good. Help him to get rid of some of the stress he could already feel settling into his shoulders.

3

Milton sat at a table in the campo, his espresso cooling in front of him. He had an excellent view of the Scuola and knew, from the Find My app, that his AirPods were still inside. He'd be able to follow whoever had them as soon as the event ended and the attendees came back outside.

He had time to kill and spent it researching the company that had put on the event. TrueCoin's website presented itself as a 'revolutionary force in cryptocurrency.' Their smartly designed homepage boasted slogans about financial freedom and independence, promising a 'once-in-a-lifetime opportunity to build generational wealth.' The company claimed to be on the cutting edge of blockchain technology, offering seminars and investment packages that would help ordinary people break free from the constraints of traditional banking. The founder, a glamorous woman called Valentina Rossi, was featured prominently in promotional videos, delivering rousing speeches about empowerment and opportunity. The website was peppered with testimonials from smiling investors who claimed their lives had been transformed. Professional photographs of her were everywhere.

Milton sipped his espresso, his gaze fixed on the venue's entrance. The buzzwords and promises might dazzle some, but he'd been around the block enough times to know not to trust something that appeared too good to be true. Something didn't feel right. He knew, of course, that the subject—cryptocurrency—might just be something he didn't understand. Milton thought of what Ziggy would say if he knew he was interested in crypto. Milton knew absolutely nothing about it, and some of the language on the website might as well have been written in Sanskrit for all the sense it made. Ziggy would have laughed, called him a dinosaur, and then taken great pleasure in explaining it to him in such a way that a child would understand.

The thump of a door banging open caught his attention. He looked back to the entrance, where two burly security guards were hustling a young man outside. The man stumbled as he was shoved forward, catching himself just in time to avoid falling. His cheeks were flushed, his gestures animated as he turned back to shout at the guards.

"You're as bad as she is. You should be ashamed."

The double doors slammed shut.

Milton watched as the man took out his phone, put it to his ear and then called someone. He finished the conversation, replaced the phone in his pocket and pulled out a small white case. He opened the lid, took out a pair of AirPods, and pressed them into his ears. He lingered outside the venue for a moment, pacing back and forth. His hands were clenched into fists, and he muttered under his breath as though replaying the argument he'd just lost. Finally, he gave a frustrated shake of his head and set off across the square.

Milton opened the Find My app. The small dot that represented his missing AirPods blinked on the screen and then moved with the young man.

Milton rose from his seat, leaving a few euros on the table, and followed at a comfortable distance.

They headed south, crossed the Grand Canal at the Ponte dell'Accademia; the walkway was crowded with couples and families snapping photos. Milton weaved through them, keeping the young man in sight.

He reached the opposite bank and turned down a series of side streets, the shopfronts giving way to residential buildings and narrow alleyways. The hustle of the tourist-heavy areas faded behind them, replaced by the muffled sounds of daily life: the clink of dishes from an open window, the faint hum of a distant motorboat.

They walked for another five minutes until they reached a modest building with a faded sign that read Istituto Canossiano. The young man pushed open the heavy wooden door and disappeared inside.

4

Valentina Rossi leaned back against the plush leather seat of the Hotel Cipriani's private launch, the hum of the engine blending with the lapping of water against the bow. The city unfolded around her, its silhouette crowned by the domes of St. Mark's Basilica and the lights of the palazzi lining the Grand Canal. The boat, impeccably maintained, was a sanctuary after the noise and bustle of the event. She had been treated like a rock star, hustled backstage and then taken straight to the dock. They'd been pursued by paparazzi, but the parasites couldn't follow them onto the boat, and Valentina had watched behind her as their cameras flashed in an attempt to capture an image of her. It was ridiculous, and she still hadn't grown used to it.

An attendant came back to where Valentina was sitting and offered her a glass of Spritz. She took it, thanked him with a smile, and sipped it as they approached Giudecca, the Cipriani's dock coming into view. A team of uniformed staff awaited her arrival, their smiles warm as they helped her disembark. The scent of fresh flowers wafted from the reception as the concierge opened the door for her.

"Signorina Rossi," he said, "welcome back. How was your event?"

"Very good."

She was tired and strung out and hoped he would take the hint that she wasn't interested in a conversation. He did, wishing her a good afternoon and then stepping to the side so she could continue into the lobby.

Valentina had grown used to an itinerant lifestyle over the course of the last six months; every week saw her speaking at another conference in another country, with the only constant being the five-star luxury to which she retreated at the end of the day. Just the last three weeks had seen her appearing at events in the United Kingdom, France, Spain and now this extended stay in Italy, where it all began. The team took care of the arrangements, including the best suites at the best hotels. She had stayed at the Ritz in London, the Hôtel Plaza Athénée in Paris, the Majestic in Barcelona, the Armani in Milan, and the Hassler —perched atop the Spanish Steps—in Rome.

The Cipriani, though, might have been the best hotel she had ever visited. It enjoyed an idyllic location at the eastern tip of Giudecca, one of Venice's quieter and more exclusive islands, and offered a tranquil vista across the lagoon, with St. Mark's Basilica and the Doge's Palace visible from the balcony of her suite.

She was looking forward to a quiet afternoon in the spa, but as she approached the lobby, her heart sank as she saw Niko. He was standing with the man who had introduced her onstage earlier. She couldn't remember his name. He was tall and slim, with salt-and-pepper hair meticulously combed back, and wearing a tailored suit that was very obviously expensive. Valentina had no doubts about his wealth, but, if she had, they would have been dispelled by the €50,000 Rolex on his wrist. She couldn't remember his name.

"Valentina," Niko said, "Riccardo wanted to say hello."

"Thank you for introducing me," she said, smiling at him. "You were very generous."

"Not at all," he said. "I meant every word. The impact you're having on people's lives is..." He paused, as if searching for the word that would suitably express his admiration. "Well, it's incalculable."

"Riccardo is too modest," Niko said. "He's helping people, too."

"I'm just an affiliate."

"Not just *any* affiliate." Niko put a hand on Riccardo's shoulder. "His network is responsible for recruiting more investors than anyone else in all of Europe."

Valentina smiled again. "Then I think you're being too kind. You're making just as much of an impact as I am."

"Hardly."

Niko took her arm and started to guide her toward the bar.

"I invited Riccardo for a drink," he said.

She was a little too slow to prevent the frown that creased her brow. "I'd love to," she said. "But I'm a little tired."

Niko raised an eyebrow. "Not too tired for a glass of champagne," he said, smiling. "I insist. They have a very nice bottle of Salon Blanc de Blancs on ice for us."

Niko pointed over to where a table had been reserved for them; the top of a bottle was visible in an ice bucket.

She sighed. "You know how the events take it out of me."

Niko kept the smile, but there was a steeliness behind it

that Valentina had learned not to ignore. "Just one glass," he said. "I think Riccardo deserves it, don't you?"

She felt the pressure on her elbow. "Yes," she said. "Of course."

"I'd love to talk to you about how things are going in Italy," Riccardo said. "It's been amazing, obviously, but I think there's scope for so much more. The enthusiasm after the event today was all the evidence I needed to see. I've already had another three hundred signups through my network."

"Well done," Niko said. He put his hand on Riccardo's shoulder and gently turned him toward the table. "Go and grab a seat. Valentina and I just need a quick chat, and then we'll be over."

Riccardo dipped his head and, taking the hint, made his way into the bar.

Niko waited for him to move out of earshot before turning back to Valentina. "Are you all right?"

"Just tired."

"You weren't at your best," he said.

"I didn't have a great night's sleep."

"It's fine." He smiled warmly. "He's right about the impact you're having. We're making a difference. The people who saw you speak and decided to invest will look back on today as a life-changing moment. You *do* know that, don't you?"

"I know." She shrugged. "I'm just tired."

He put his hands together. "Just one drink and then you can make your excuses. Okay?"

"Of course," she said.

5

The Istituto Canossiano was—according to its website—'a religious house, part boarding school and part holiday home.' It stood by the canal, its yellowish walls weathered by years of salt and sun. Rows of tall, arched windows lined the façade, each fitted with deep green shutters that popped against the faded plaster.

Milton approached the open double doors that led inside from the canal. The website reported that the Istituto had three conference rooms, and the location of the pulsing blue dot appeared to be in the room directly to Milton's right.

Milton went up to the open door and looked inside. The room was large, filled with rows of seats facing a low stage and podium. Sunlight filtered through tall windows draped with blue curtains, throwing soft light across a chequered floor of cream- and rust-coloured tiles. The room was half full, and as Milton waited at the door, a man got up and climbed up onto the stage.

Milton slipped inside and crossed the room to the empty

row of chairs at the back. He sat down, nodding an acknowledgement to the woman who turned to look back at him, and then settled down to listen as the meeting began.

6

Marco took his usual seat at the front of the room. He reached up to pluck his AirPods out of his ears and took a deep breath. The organiser of the meeting took his seat on the small stage. His name was Carlo, and Marco had first met him online in a support group for TrueCoin's victims.

Most of the people in the forum had lost money to the scam, but Carlo's story was particularly grim. His 'investment' had cost him his house after he remortgaged it to release funds he'd hoped would double or triple. It wasn't even as if he had been greedy. Carlo had been desperate to save his family business: a small woodworking shop that had been in his family for three generations. The business had been struggling for years, overtaken by larger companies with cheaper, mass-produced furniture, and the pandemic had delivered the final blow. Carlo had been certain the promised returns from TrueCoin would provide the lifeline he needed to pay off debts, keep the workshop afloat, and pass it on to his son. Instead, his outcome was the same as all the others: he lost everything. His shop had closed, and with it went his family's legacy and his son's future.

And yet, despite everything, Carlo was one of the most positive people Marco had ever met. He'd replied to Marco's first tentative posts in the forum, offering sympathy and advice. Their conversations had graduated to phone calls and, a week later, coffee. Carlo had set up the group to offer face-to-face support to those who needed it; he told Marco about the meetings and urged him to come. It wasn't because it would bring him any closer to getting his money back—although they all clung to the hope that it might—but because it would help him to find people who could relate to the ordeal he had suffered, and, as he often said, 'a problem shared was a problem halved.'

Marco looked around the room, guessing there were forty or fifty people there. Some sat hunched forward, hands clasped, heads low. Others leaned back with arms crossed, staring blankly at the stage. He tried to read their expressions: an elderly woman with a lined, careworn face was looking at her feet, her knuckles white as she gripped the arms of her chair; a few seats down, a younger man whispered to the woman next to him, his face grim, his mouth set in a hard, bitter line.

Carlo cleared his throat and began. "Good afternoon, everyone. Thank you for coming. I wrote on the website that this meeting will be in English. I hope this is still okay."

A murmur rippled through the group.

"I know this is not... perfect," he said, "and my English is maybe not so good, but I hope you understand why it is important. I have very good news. As you know, I was looking for lawyers to help me for many weeks. Every time, they say the same thing: the case, it is too difficult, to fight

TrueCoin is too hard because they are powerful. The money, it is... how you say... impossible to find, hidden in offshore accounts and fake companies. They say it is like catching smoke. I hear this many, many times. I don't need to tell you —this was very hard for me. I was ready to give up. But then, a firm from London, they contact me. They know about TrueCoin already—for months. They work for a person in London who lost millions. And this person, they have the money to fight. They look at our forum, and they start to build a case. First in the UK, but now, they want to go all across Europe. I meet them last Friday, and for the first time in a long time, I feel hope. I ask them if they want to send someone here, to speak with us." He smiled. "And they say yes." Carlo turned and gestured toward the woman standing to Marco's right. "Isobel—please, come."

The woman—Isobel—must have been in her early thirties. She was striking, with dark, wavy hair that framed her face and fell just past her shoulders. Her features were sharp and refined: high cheekbones, a straight nose, almond-shaped eyes. She wore a tailored navy suit, its crisp lines complementing her slender, athletic frame, and a white blouse beneath it. She got up and walked to the front; she carried herself with an air of determination, and there was warmth in her expression as she turned to smile.

"Hello, everyone," she said. "My name is Isobel Turner, and as Carlo says, I'm a lawyer. I was due to be here today with an Italian lawyer I'm working with, but he wasn't able to come, and rather than let everyone down and cancel, I asked Carlo if it would be okay if we spoke in English—I'm afraid my Italian is very basic, so I'm grateful that everyone is making the effort and humouring me." She smiled again, and Marco could feel himself warming to her.

"I'm a partner in Turner, Evans and Hargreaves. We're

known for our expertise in litigation and corporate investigations, and we've built a reputation for taking on complex cases that other firms don't want. My senior partners specialise in international arbitration and financial fraud litigation, and my own practice usually involves cross-border disputes, white-collar crime, and digital fraud. I'm telling you that so you can understand why this particular case is of interest to me. I became aware of TrueCoin six months ago when we were approached by a potential client who said he was unable to sell his coins and worried that the scheme was a scam. We looked into it and quickly concluded that he was right—it most certainly is a scam. We decided that we'd take on his case and see what else we could find out."

A ripple of interest swept through the group. Marco leaned forward slightly in his chair.

"We brought a group claim against TrueCoin in London. The claim is still in its early stages, but we've managed to secure a provisional hearing date later this year. The biggest challenge so far has been unravelling the web of offshore accounts and shell companies they've used to obscure the flow of money. But we've made progress on that front, too—we've partnered with financial forensic experts who are helping us trace the funds, and we're confident that we can establish a clear pattern of wrongdoing. We've also filed injunctions to freeze identifiable assets within the EU, but TrueCoin has been clever in moving its operations out of jurisdictions where such actions are enforceable. This kind of case often involves a moving target. It can be frustrating, but it's not something about which I have any ultimate concern—we'll get them eventually."

Marco looked around the room and saw that his own enthusiasm was shared by everyone else.

"I realise that there are hundreds—thousands—of victims of this fraud, so we're making efforts to find as many of them as we can. We're building group actions around Europe, and we're combining it with an aggressive press campaign that we think will knock them off balance. We have journalists ready to write about what they've been doing. That's why I'm here. Obviously, TrueCoin started in Rome, and a lot of their European infrastructure is in Italy. And of course, they're here in Venice at the moment, running events to get more people to sign up. I've brought my team with me to see if there's anything else we can dig up that might be useful in the claim. I know many of you feel hopeless after what's happened, but I want to assure you that there *is* a path forward. It won't be easy, it won't be quick, and there's no guarantee of success, but it is possible."

"What kind of case are you building?" someone asked.

Isobel glanced at the questioner. "Fraudulent misrepresentation and breach of contract and violations of EU consumer protection laws. We're working to establish a clear paper trail to prove it."

"Isn't that what Carlo just said is impossible?" a man in the back asked sceptically.

"Difficult," Isobel conceded, "not impossible. We've engaged professional corporate investigators, and they're working to identify the individuals behind TrueCoin and uncover vulnerabilities we can exploit in court. They're following the money trail, untangling the shell companies, and digging into the company's history. Every piece of evidence we find brings us closer to building a better case."

Marco raised his hand. "What happens if we win? Will we get our money back?"

Isobel hesitated. "It's hard to say. If we can trace the money, then yes, there's a chance we could recover some of it. But even if we can't, there's value in holding these people accountable. Exposing them for what they are. Making sure they can't hurt anyone else."

The room fell silent for a moment as the weight of her words settled over the group.

Another man spoke up. "But even if we do all that, they'll still be rich, won't they? They'll just keep moving the money."

Isobel nodded. "That's a risk. But I know one thing for sure—if we do nothing, they'll think they're untouchable, and they'll *definitely* keep doing it. They're counting on us to give up. They want us to think it's too hard, too expensive—too risky. But if we don't stand up to them, no one will."

A murmur spread through the group: hesitant, uncertain, but with a flicker of optimism.

"The more of us, the better," Carlo added. "The case, it will be stronger. Yes?"

"Absolutely," Isobel said. "Hence me being here. I can answer your questions, listen to your stories, and help you decide if joining our Italian claim is the right choice for you."

Carlo gestured for Isobel to take a seat at the table in the corner, and she did so, pulling out a small stack of forms from her briefcase. "I'll be here all afternoon," she said. "If you want to talk, come and say hello. I can take your details now so I can see whether or not you'd be suitable. There'll be a formal meeting tomorrow where I'll go through the admin of adding new claimants—my Italian colleague should be there, too."

Marco watched as people began to shift in their seats, murmuring among themselves. There had been false dawns before, and there was scepticism in the room, but Isobel had made an impact. She'd given them the suggestion that something might be possible, and, for a room full of people who had been tricked and robbed and then ignored, that wasn't nothing. It almost felt like hope.

7

Marco lingered. He'd spent most of the meeting staring at the scuffed linoleum floor, preferring not to contribute. He'd told himself he would take up the invitation to stay and speak to Isobel, but it seemed as if everyone wanted to do that, and after waiting for twenty minutes, he decided he'd rather go home. He was halfway out the door when Carlo intercepted him.

"Don't go just yet," he urged.

"The kids have been with Chiara's mum all day," he said. "I can't—"

"Is another thirty minutes going to make any difference? Come on—I know she wants to talk to you."

"You told her?"

"A little."

That had been over half an hour ago, and now Marco felt trapped by his indecision. He was torn between the urge to go and the faint hope that staying might do something to help. He'd been annoyed at Carlo, too, worrying that he'd used his story to impress upon Isobel how much her help was needed. He hated it when people did that.

Hated it. He didn't want to be the desperate case, the one crying out for sympathy and special attention and pity. He'd much rather fix the problem himself, and for the last few months, that was what he'd tried to do. And then he remembered: it hadn't got him anywhere, and even if it did mean pulling on her heartstrings, would that really be so bad if it meant that he could finally see progress in getting his money back?

There were three of them in the queue now: a man called Francesco whom Marco had spoken to at the last meeting, then Marco and, behind him, a man he'd never seen at the meetings before. The newcomer was in late middle age and had piercing blue eyes and a calm but vaguely unsettling presence. He was leaning against the wall, his posture relaxed, but there was something about him that made Marco's skin prickle.

He looked at his watch: it was late, and he knew his mother-in-law would want to get home. He'd just started edging toward the door again when Francesco looked at a message he'd just received on his phone, muttered something about being late for an appointment and left the line; suddenly, Marco was next.

"This is Marco," Carlo said, clapping Marco lightly on the shoulder.

Reluctantly, Marco stepped up to the desk.

"Hi," she said. "I'm Isobel."

"Hi."

"Marco speaks good English," Carlo said.

"I'm sorry about all that," she said. "My colleague should've been here, and you could all have spoken Italian."

"It's fine. Like Carlo said, I can speak it—I studied in America for a year."

"Carlo tells me you've got a story to share."

"We all do," Marco said. "I'm no different than anyone else."

"Maybe not," she said. "He also told me you went to the TrueCoin seminar today."

He sat down. "It was the same as all the others I've been to."

"How many people?"

"Three hundred," he said. "Give or take."

"Can I ask you something—just out of interest?"

He nodded.

"Do you know what the average investment is for the clients we're representing?"

"I don't know."

"Guess."

"Ten thousand," he offered.

"Fifty. Fifty thousand. There are whales—big buyers who drive up the value—at the top who skew the average, but it'd still be a lot even without them. Think about how much money they would've stolen today. Three hundred victims at fifty thousand each—that's fifteen million." She eyed him. "We need to stop them."

Marco hesitated, his gaze flicking toward the door again. Isobel softened her tone, perhaps sensing his reluctance.

"I know how hard it is to talk about this. I know you've had a very bad experience, and I'd like to help, if I can."

"You think you can do something about it?"

"Yes," she said. "We're already a long way down the road. We've got an excellent team on it. They're digging into the company, trying to uncover who's really behind it."

"Can I ask who your client is?"

"We have lots of clients now, but the first—the one who brought it to us—is a very wealthy man back home. It's not the money that he lost that has upset him—he can afford to lose it. His pride is hurt that he's been tricked, and—more than that—he's seen the effect they're having on people who don't have his wealth. He wants to see them shut down, and, in time, we will. But to make that happen, we need people like you to come forward. And I know this will sound crass, and I'm sorry about that, but the emotional stories are the ones we *really* need. We've encouraged several newspapers to run stories on the company, but what they're all after is the *hook*. The human angle that shows it's not just men like my client who have suffered. And then, if we can build up public sympathy, we'll make it more likely that we can get some government attention. The more noise we make, the harder it'll be for the authorities to turn a blind eye."

Marco nodded slowly. He was aware that the man with the blue eyes was still behind him, but it didn't matter. He'd shared his story before, and he had nothing to hide.

"Okay," he said. "What do you want to know?"

"Let's start at the beginning. Tell me everything—when you first heard about TrueCoin, what drew you in, what happened after."

What the hell, he thought. *Why not?*

He took a breath. "It started with the ads. Facebook, Instagram, YouTube—they were everywhere. And Valentina. She was on all of them, and she made it sound like she understood what it's like to struggle. Like this was the answer."

Isobel took notes. "And you went to one of the seminars?"

"Me and a few friends. It was in December—totally packed. Valentina was there. She was incredible. She made it feel real, like it was huge, something we'd be stupid to pass up. I invested everything I had—thirty thousand euros.

It felt like a once-in-a-lifetime opportunity, and I really needed to make money quickly."

"Why's that?"

Marco hesitated, swallowing hard; he was sure Carlo had already told her why, but she wanted it in his own words. "I was diagnosed with cancer last year. A spinal sarcoma. They caught it too late for chemotherapy, but there was a treatment—an experimental treatment, immunotherapy—that they thought might buy me two or three years. The hospital told me it wasn't covered under our insurance, and we'd have to pay for it ourselves. Sixty thousand... We didn't have anything near that." His voice cracked. "I was ready to forget about it and go with whatever they could give me, but my wife had heard me talking about TrueCoin, and she insisted we give it a try. She got more money from her family, and we bought in."

Isobel's expression shifted, sympathy mingling with a sharper edge of anger on his behalf. "That's a terrible position to be put in. I'm so sorry."

He laughed bitterly. "I'm just getting started. Three months after my diagnosis, Chiara—that's my wife—started having problems. There was muscle weakness, and she was slurring her words. At first, we thought it was stress, but then she went to hospital and had tests, and they told us she has motor neurone disease." He paused, looking away and laughing bitterly. "We've got two kids—a boy and a girl, six and eight. They don't understand what's happening, and I don't know how to explain it to them. They think I might have another year, if I'm lucky, and my wife might get another five or six. I *have* to have that money back. It's too late for me now, but I can use it to make the house suitable for her before she needs it."

Isobel's pen hovered over her notebook, but she didn't write. "I can't imagine how hard that must be."

Marco realised that the man behind him in the queue—the man with the blue eyes—was listening intently to what he was saying. It didn't matter.

"We've got nothing. We gambled everything and lost. And I don't even know if I'll live long enough to make it right."

Marco dropped his head into his hands, his shoulders shaking as he struggled to regain his composure.

Carlo put a steadying hand on his shoulder. "You're not alone."

"That's right," Isobel said. "You're not. And we're going to do everything we can to help."

8

Marco unlocked the door to his apartment and stepped inside, closing it gently behind him. He was late. He slipped off his shoes, his legs heavy with the exhaustion that had been dogging him for weeks. Today had been more physically and emotionally draining than he'd anticipated. The meeting with Isobel had been encouraging, but he wasn't sure what to make of it yet.

"Papà!"

His children thundered across the hallway, and Marco braced himself as they launched themselves into his arms. Pietro, his eight-year-old, hugged his waist tightly while six-year-old Sofia clung to his leg.

"Shouldn't you be in bed?" he said, his voice softening as he ruffled Pietro's hair and scooped Sofia up into his arms. She giggled, planting a kiss on his cheek. For a moment, their warmth chased away the tiredness. "Have you been good for Nonna?"

"Yes," Pietro said, his tone slightly too enthusiastic, and Marco raised an eyebrow.

"Mostly," his mother-in-law, Anna, called from the kitchen. She appeared in the doorway, wiping her hands on a dish towel. "They've been a handful."

"Thank you," Marco said, setting Sofia down. His mother-in-law's face was kind but tired, the lines around her mouth deeper than he remembered. "I don't know what we'd do without you."

Anna waved a hand dismissively. "Go say hello to Chiara. She's been resting, but she's awake now. I'll get ready to go."

Marco nodded. He gently nudged the children toward the living room. "Go pick a book for bedtime, okay? I'll be there in a minute."

He made his way down the narrow hallway to the bedroom, where his wife was propped up on the bed with a pile of pillows behind her. Chiara looked even more delicate than usual, her hands resting limply on the blanket draped over her legs. She managed a tired smile when she saw him.

"You're home," she said.

"I'm home," Marco said, leaning down to kiss her forehead. "How are you feeling?"

"About the same," she replied. "Tired, but that's nothing new." Her eyes searched his face, and she frowned. "You look pale."

"I'm fine," he lied, sitting on the edge of the bed. "Just a long day. I'm sorry I'm late."

"It's okay—my mum's been great."

"I just told her I don't know what we'd do without her."

"I know," she said, shuffling back a little to make herself more comfortable. "I told her, too. Did you go?"

"Yes."

"And?"

"I stood up and told them what I thought, but they threw me out."

She laughed. "Did anyone listen?"

"They heard me," he said. "They couldn't not—I was shouting. But whether anyone will actually pay any attention…? I don't know. I doubt it. Most of them will already have made up their minds."

"And after that?"

"I went to Carlo's meeting. I wasn't going to, but he called and said I should come. I think it was probably the right thing to do. There was a lawyer there—from London. She's putting together group claims against them all across Europe, and she wanted to know whether I'd like us to be included in the Italian one."

"And? Should we?"

"I can't see a downside. I don't want to get our hopes up, but I left feeling more hopeful than I have for weeks. Months, probably."

"What was she like?"

"She seems smart. Determined. She's got a team working on it. Get this—she said she has investigators digging into them, too. It felt like it might be something."

Chiara gave a long yawn, and Marco was reminded just how tired she looked. She had some days that were better than others, but when the MND was at its worst, she could be in bed for days; he'd only exacerbate things if he kept her awake longer than necessary.

Chiara gave him a faint smile, and he squeezed her hand gently before standing.

"I'll go put the kids to bed."

Pietro and Sofia had pulled several books off the shelf and were debating which one to read. Marco crouched down beside them, letting them each choose a story. They climbed into their shared bed a few minutes later, snuggling under the covers as Marco sat between them with the books in hand.

He started to read, his voice as soothing as he could make it, but felt the usual pang of guilt. He couldn't help the feeling that he'd failed them—failed Chiara—by falling for TrueCoin's lies, and now he was scrambling to make up for it. But as he looked at their sleepy faces and saw how much they trusted him—how much they *needed* him—he chided himself for even *thinking* about giving up. He couldn't. He had to keep trying.

When the children were finally asleep, he returned to the bedroom, where Chiara was still awake, her eyes fixed on the ceiling.

"They're down," Marco said, sitting beside her. "You didn't tell me about your day."

"I didn't feel like getting out of bed," she said, her tone light but weary.

"Then don't. You get worse when you push too hard."

"The lawyer," she said. "Do you think it might work?"

"I don't know. Maybe. It's hard to say right now. But might as well try."

Chiara nodded, her eyes glistening. "You know I don't blame you."

"I know."

"We both went into it with our eyes open. It wasn't just you. I wanted it just as much."

He kissed her hand, his throat tight. "I know." He stood and pulled his T-shirt over his head. "I'm tired, too. I think I might get an early night."

9

Milton watched as the man who had introduced himself as Marco went inside the building and turned to climb a flight of stairs. Milton idled at the end of the street, his eye on the building; he saw movement in one of the windows on the second floor and saw the young man as he reached to the side and tugged on a cord to close the blind. His silhouette turned and then disappeared, retreating into the room.

Milton had followed him from the meeting. Carlo and Isobel had motioned for him to come forward once Marco had finished, but Milton had said he was running late for another appointment and would have to go. Isobel had said that she would be in a café nearby tomorrow morning to take down the details of those who wanted to be considered for the group claim, and she'd invited him to come so he could share his story with her; Milton had said that he would.

He had gone outside, finding Marco as he made his way to the vaporetto stop. He had waited discreetly, far enough away so Marco wouldn't notice him.

Milton followed when Marco boarded the water bus, staying toward the back while Marco sat near the front, staring out at the canals. The city was alive with its usual evening hum: the soft splash of water against stone, the murmur of voices from restaurants and bars, and the faint strains of music drifting from open windows.

The water bus weaved through the canals for twenty minutes before arriving at a quieter, more residential area. Marco disembarked, and Milton followed at a distance, making sure to remain unobtrusive. This part of Venice was less polished. The buildings were still the same faded ochre, but here the plaster peeled away in large patches, revealing the crumbling brick beneath. Laundry lines crisscrossed narrow alleyways, and the faint scent of algae and seawater hung in the cool night air.

Marco's apartment was in a three-storey building tucked into a quiet *calle*. The stucco was cracked, and a patch of graffiti had been painted over but was still faintly visible, a ghostly message beneath the fresh coat. The wrought-iron gate at the entrance was slightly ajar, and Milton noted the rust across its hinges. The neighbourhood was silent save for the occasional sound of a dog barking or the muffled clinking of dishes from a ground-floor window.

Milton hung back, finding a spot in the shadows of a recessed doorway. He watched as Marco climbed the stairs inside, his silhouette visible through the frosted glass of the stairwell window. When he reached the second floor, a light flicked on briefly before the blinds closed, cutting off Milton's view.

The area around him was quiet. Most of the windows were dark, though a faint glow spilled from a few, their curtains drawn tight. A narrow canal ran alongside the street, the water rippling gently in the moonlight. Across from the apartment, a wooden bench sat beneath a streetlamp that cast a pale circle of light onto the cobblestones. Milton crossed the street, taking a seat on the bench where he could keep an eye on the building without drawing too much attention.

This wasn't a wealthy neighbourhood. The residents hadn't yet been driven out by relentlessly rising rents and the crush of tourism, but Milton could see the signs of strain. The streets were clean but worn, the buildings tired but not neglected. It was a place for people who worked hard and lived quietly.

Milton adjusted his position on the bench, withdrawing into the shadows a little more. He stared up at the window where he had seen Marco and allowed his thoughts to drift. He might not understand TrueCoin or cryptocurrency, but he had helped enough people since leaving the Group to have developed an eye for those who needed him.

Isobel might have offered Marco hope at this afternoon's meeting, but the legal process was slow and success far from guaranteed. It was apparent that TrueCoin had stolen millions from its marks, and Valentina Rossi and the others behind it would disappear into the ether at the first sign of trouble.

Would the lawyers be able to find them?

Maybe.

Would they be able to claw back the money that had been taken?

That seemed unlikely.

Would Milton?

It was hard to say without knowing more, but he had access to tactics the lawyers did not, and, in his experience, they were often a *lot* more effective.

He stood and turned, retracing his steps back to the

canal. The Twelve Steps of AA required Milton to atone for the things that he'd done, and since many of those against whom he had transgressed were no longer alive to receive his penance, he'd decided to help others. Lending a hand to people like Marco had become Milton's calling. It wasn't much and could never balance out his sins, but it was *something*; better that than numbing himself with booze until he didn't know up from down, stumbling from violent encounter to violent encounter until someone put him out of his misery. He looked for those who found themselves facing situations they couldn't handle alone, and Marco, Carlo and the others certainly met his criteria.

Milton had a lot to learn about who was responsible for what had happened to them, but he had settled on one thing: he wanted to help, and he would.

10

Milton had booked a room at La Locanda dei Naviganti—the Sailors' Inn—a hotel in the Cannaregio district. It was a quiet, working-class neighbourhood, not dissimilar to Marco's, and it suited Milton and his preference for a lower profile. The hotel was an old building with a faded blue sign above the narrow entrance. The lobby was dimly lit, with cracked floor tiles and mismatched furniture, giving it a rustic charm that was a million miles away from the modern hotels that Milton had researched before choosing this one. The walls were hung with black-and-white photographs of Venice in the forties and fifties, showing gondolas and fishing boats making their way up and down the canals.

The hotel was owned by an elderly couple, and the wife was behind the desk. She smiled at Milton and asked if he had everything he needed; Milton thanked her, said the room was perfect, and started up the stairs.

He unlocked the door to his room and slipped inside, closing it behind him. The room was spare and functional: a single bed against the wall, a small desk—cluttered with the leaflets he'd picked up when he'd been out for a walk—and a narrow window that overlooked the canal below.

He tossed his jacket onto the bed, pulled the chair away from the desk, and sat down, taking his phone out of his pocket and opening Google.

He typed 'TrueCoin' into the search bar and scanned the first two pages of results. The company's website came up first and then a series of flattering articles. It took Milton clicking through four pages of results before the first negative story appeared. It was obvious that TrueCoin had paid for some very effective online-reputation management. Milton had seen Tristan Huxley launder his own reputation the same way, and Ziggy Penn had explained how it worked: companies hired digital marketing firms to flood search engines with positive content—press releases, blog posts, sponsored articles—designed to bury anything critical. The trick wasn't just creating new content but using high-traffic sites to host it, ensuring it would always rank higher than independent voices with something negative to say. As a result, anyone doing a casual search would see only the polished exterior, never the cracks underneath.

He clicked to open the first negative result and was taken to a forum where disgruntled investors were gathering to share their complaints. Their posts were a mixture of frustration, desperation, and fury. Some users described how they'd invested their life savings, only to find themselves locked out of their TrueCoin accounts without explanation. Others shared warnings about customer support being unresponsive or outright dismissive. One user claimed to have traced some of the company's financial transactions to offshore accounts, but their findings had been met with threats of legal action when they tried to go public.

Milton sat back and realised that, if he was going to help,

he'd need to understand a little more about cryptocurrency: how it worked and what TrueCoin was offering. He opened a new tab and—thinking how hilarious Ziggy would find the prospect of him trying to wrap his head around something like this—he found a website that promised to explain it.

Cryptocurrency, the site explained, was a form of digital money designed to operate without relying on a central authority like a government or a bank. Milton nodded to himself: so far so good. Instead, he read, crypto used a decentralised technology called blockchain, a digital ledger spread across a network of computers. Each transaction was recorded on the ledger, making it nearly impossible to alter without the consensus of the entire network. The allure of cryptocurrency lay in its promise of anonymity, security, and the potential for massive returns on investment.

Milton had heard of Bitcoin, of course; it had been the pioneer, launched as a response to the global financial crisis. Since then, thousands of other cryptocurrencies had emerged, each claiming to improve on the original concept. Many of these so-called 'altcoins' were legitimate, but just as many were speculative ventures with little substance. TrueCoin, it appeared, fell into the latter category.

Milton skimmed through an overview of how people typically acquired cryptocurrency. Investors either bought coins through online exchanges or participated in Initial Coin Offerings, where a new cryptocurrency was launched with the promise of early-bird discounts and exponential growth. The risks were enormous. Without regulation, many ICOs were outright scams, luring investors with flashy websites and celebrity endorsements, then vanishing with the money.

TrueCoin was marketing itself as 'the next Bitcoin.' It

offered promises of stability, rapid adoption, and guaranteed returns, which Milton now understood were red flags. Legitimate cryptocurrencies couldn't promise fixed returns; their value was entirely market-driven.

The website also explained how scammers exploited the technical complexity of cryptocurrency. They used esoteric terms to confuse investors, creating the illusion of a cutting-edge opportunity. The TrueCoin scam was evidently in full swing. People were being convinced to invest in a coin with no real-world use or underlying technology, their funds funnelled into shell companies and offshore accounts, never to be seen again.

Milton sat back. It'd been obvious before, at the meeting, but it was even clearer now: this wasn't just about people losing their savings, it was about manipulation, greed, and the exploitation of hope. TrueCoin was preying on those desperate for a way out of financial struggles, offering them a lifeline that was nothing of the sort. He thought about Marco and the others who had been drawn into a web of lies and concluded, again, that the direct approach—his specialism—would yield much faster results than anything a well-meaning but law-abiding *avvocato* could manage.

11

Milton set his alarm for five the following morning. He rolled out of bed, took a quick shower in the communal bathroom, and dressed in the running gear he'd bought before hunting his AirPods yesterday. He descended the stairs to the lobby and stepped outside. The first hints of dawn were creeping over the rooftops, soft grey light spreading over the canals. The streets were empty, and the only sound was his footsteps echoing off the stone walls and the occasional splash as water lapped up against the gondolas moored nearby.

Venice was quiet here. As Milton ran, the sounds softened and changed; the gently lapping water was replaced by locals heading out to go to work or taking children to school. A woman in a long coat brushed past him; he heard snatches of Italian, laughter echoing from a doorway, the low murmur of voices; he caught the smell of fresh bread and frying garlic.

He jogged through Cannaregio, the air crisp and damp, carrying the faint scent of salt and moss. Venice was a different place at this hour: almost meditative in comparison to what it would become later. He crossed a small bridge, the canal below glassy and still, reflecting the buildings on either side. He passed darkened cafés and shuttered shops, their doors lined with peeling posters and scrawled graffiti.

He turned down an alley and followed it toward the Grand Canal. He picked up his pace, feeling his muscles warm as he ran along the canal, the Ponte di Rialto looming in the distance, arching gracefully over the water. The early morning vendors were just setting up their market stalls nearby; they unloaded crates of fish and other produce, voices low in the morning hush.

Milton continued south toward San Marco, crossing quiet squares where pigeons clustered around fountains and statues. The basilica's domes rose ahead. He slowed as he reached the edge of the lagoon, breathing in the cool, briny air. Across the water, the island of San Giorgio Maggiore was bathed in the soft glow of the rising sun, its bell tower standing tall against the pastel sky.

He paused, hands on his hips, gathering his breath. Isobel had said that she'd be in the café near the Istituto from ten onward, and Marco had said that he would be there; Milton didn't want to be late and miss him. He took a moment to stretch out his legs and then turned and retraced his steps back to the hotel.

12

Valentina Rossi woke to the hum of the air conditioning and the gentle smell from the little parcel of jasmine that housekeeping had left on her pillow last night. The curtains, heavy velvet, muted the morning sun, but a sliver of golden light slanted through a gap, throwing a warm stripe across the white sheets. She lay still, staring up at the ornate ceiling. This was the part of the day she looked forward to the most: the quiet before the pantomime.

She swung her legs over the edge of the bed, her feet sinking into the carpet, then crossed to the window and opened the curtains. The spectacular view of the lagoon greeted her, the water sparkling under the early morning sun. Gondolas and water busses glided along the water, and beyond them, the domes of St. Mark's Basilica rose above the city. Valentina stood quietly, her hands resting on the window frame, trying once again to accept the new realities of her life. A hotel like this would have been so far out of her reach last year that it was almost a joke to find herself here now. The suite was €5000 a night; that would have been enough to pay for three months' rent for her two-bedroom flat in Rome.

She exhaled, as if that might release the knot of anxiety that had lodged itself in her chest.

There was a soft knock at the door. "Signora Rossi," a voice called. "Your breakfast."

She wrapped her silk robe around her more tightly. "Come in."

The waiter opened the door and entered the room, pushing a gleaming silver trolley. She'd placed the order last night: a carafe of freshly squeezed orange juice, a pot of coffee, and a selection of pastries. Valentina thanked the waiter with a smile, signing the receipt, and then settled into the small dining area by the window. She sipped the coffee, savouring the rich bitterness, and nibbled on a croissant.

She took out her phone and opened the itinerary for the day. They were flying to Rome at midday, and the car was due to collect her at ten. Before then, though, she had to record videos for TikTok and Instagram. The team had sent over the script late last night, but she hadn't looked at it yet. She opened it as she absentmindedly twisted a lock of her blonde hair around her finger. "Empowering lives through financial freedom," the script began.

She sighed. The lines were always the same. It was dull and repetitive, but they would expect her to deliver the message with the same sparkling enthusiasm that had come to be her trademark.

She finished her coffee and got up, going into the bathroom to prepare. She showered and then washed her face with cool water, went through her skincare routine, and brushed her hair until it shone. The steam from the shower had fogged up the mirror, so she wiped it clean with a towel, staring at her reflection. Her green eyes stared back, unwavering but weary. She forced herself to smile, watching as the practiced expression transformed her face.

Showtime, she told herself.

Showtime.

13

Milton took out his phone, typed 'TrueCoin conference' into the search bar, and waited for the suggested videos to populate the screen. It didn't take long before he found one that looked promising: Valentina Rossi speaking to a packed arena in London a year earlier. Milton clicked play, and a woman walked onto the brightly lit stage. The audience applauded wildly, hundreds of people standing on their feet, cheering her on as if she were a rock star.

Valentina paused at centre stage, a confident smile curving her red-painted lips. Her hair was pulled back, and a necklace glittered around her throat. She looked out at the crowd and let the applause swell. She let them cheer for another thirty seconds before raising her hands to indicate they should stop.

"Thank you," she said, speaking in English with a gentle Italian accent. "Thank you all for being here. I know some of you have travelled from far and wide, taken time away from your families, from your jobs, to be part of this incredible moment."

Milton watched, fascinated. She paced the stage, her gestures broad and welcoming. There was something magnetic about her presence that Milton had only seen once before: the insanely telegenic governor of Florida who had crossed Milton's path in San Francisco just after Milton had left the services of the Group.

"I want to talk to you about something that'll change the world. Something that will redefine the way we think about money, about freedom, about opportunity. I'm talking about TrueCoin—the future of finance."

The crowd burst into applause again. Valentina paused, and Milton noted the way she held herself; there was an effortless confidence that drew people in. She was calm and composed, seemingly convinced of the truth of the message she was delivering.

She spoke for half an hour, and then the video came to an end. Milton closed the app and put his phone aside. He leaned back, his eyes fixed on the wall, and thought about what he'd seen.

Valentina was good.

She had the unwavering confidence that could make anything sound like the truth.

He looked at the time and saw that he was going to have to get a move on if he wanted to be there at the start of Isobel's gathering. He grabbed his jacket, put his phone and room key in his pocket, and hurried downstairs.

14

An hour later and Valentina was ready. Her makeup was flawless, and she'd picked out a white blouse and tailored black trousers, an outfit to suggest confidence and professionalism. She set up the ring light and tripod in the corner of the room and adjusted the angle of the camera on her phone, ensuring the lagoon was visible through the window behind her. The backdrop was perfect: serene, aspirational, unattainably luxurious.

She tapped the record button, her face brightening as she slipped into her on-camera persona.

"Hello, everyone!" she began, her voice warm and engaging. "I'm here in the stunning city of Venice, staying at the iconic Cipriani, and I can't help but feel grateful for the life I'm living today. I mean, just look at this view!" She turned her head and gestured out of the window. "I woke up to this incredible scene this morning, and it reminds me how far I've come. Because this kind of life isn't just a dream anymore—it's my reality. And it's a reality that wouldn't have been possible without TrueCoin. It's not just about financial growth—it's about freedom. The freedom to travel, to experience the world's most beautiful places, and to do it all on my own terms."

Her tone softened, taking on a more personal quality.

"Venice has always been one of those cities that feels like magic. You've got the gondolas on the canals and the elegance of places like this. It's the kind of experience that used to feel out of reach. But now I've been able to make these moments part of my everyday life."

She leaned forward slightly, as if sharing a secret.

"I know what you might be thinking—'That's great for you, but could it really work for me?' The answer is yes. One hundred percent yes. That's the beauty of TrueCoin. It's designed to help any one of you, regardless of your background or expertise, take control of your financial future and unlock the kind of lifestyle you've always dreamed about."

She gestured toward the luxurious suite.

"You all know my story. I didn't come from a life where this kind of thing was possible. I know what it's like to feel stuck, to feel like opportunities are passing you by. But I discovered a way to change that, and I want the same for you. Whether it's travelling the world, staying in incredible places, or simply having the financial freedom to say yes to the things that matter most, TrueCoin can make it happen."

Her smile brightened as she reached the bottom of the script and the emboldened call to action.

"That's why I'm so excited about our upcoming seminar in Rome. We'll be diving into everything you need to know about crypto and how it can help you achieve your goals. I'll also be sharing some incredible success stories—people just like you who've seen their lives change because they grabbed this opportunity with both hands. From young professionals looking to grow their savings to families working toward a better future—this isn't just about numbers on a screen; it's about real people, real dreams, real opportunities. And that's why I'm so passionate about what we're building together. If you haven't signed up yet, don't wait. Click the link in my bio and reserve your spot today."

Valentina tapped the stop button, her smile fading the moment the recording ended. She sat still for a moment, staring at the screen. The video had come out perfectly—her tone, her expressions, the backdrop, all exactly as planned—but the hollowness in her chest remained.

She uploaded the video, tagging it with hashtags provided by the team:

#FinancialFreedom

#TrueCoinSuccess

#InvestInYourFuture

Within seconds, the likes and comments began stacking up.

She got up, went to the open window and looked out over the lagoon. She closed her eyes and wondered how much longer she could keep this up.

15

Isobel Turner had arranged for everyone who wanted to be considered for the group claim to meet at the Imagina café near the Istituto, and Milton made sure he was there with five minutes to spare.

He dallied outside for a minute until he saw Marco make his way along the busy street. Marco went into the café, and Milton followed, the clink of glasses and murmur of conversation wrapping around him as they stepped inside. It was an unostentatious kind of place: no frills, no gimmicks, just rows of wooden tables, a counter lined with neat stacks of cups, and a barista who barely glanced up as they entered. Milton saw Isobel and some of the others from the meeting at a large table in the corner. Marco slid into the chair opposite the lawyer. Milton waited another beat and then made his way across the room.

Isobel was shaking Marco's hand as Milton sat down.

"Hello," she said, looking at him. "You came."

"I did," Milton said.

"Sorry we couldn't speak before," she said. "Hopefully it'll be easier today."

She indicated that he should take a seat, and he did. There were a dozen men and women around the table, and Milton recognised them all from the meeting. There was Marco, of course, plus the man who had been in charge—Carlo—and several others who had spoken. A waitress came over to take their orders, and as the barista prepared their drinks, Isobel suggested that Milton should share his own story. He wouldn't have been able to do it yesterday, but now, with the benefit of his research, he felt better able to spin a story that might be credible enough to be believed.

"I'm travelling," he said. "I trained as a chef in London, and I work in kitchens to pay for my room and board while I'm on the road. I go to a city, work there for six months, then go somewhere else. I've been at the Venice Ibis since March. It was one of my colleagues who first mentioned TrueCoin. He'd seen the ads on Facebook. I didn't pay much attention, but then he showed me one of the videos. Valentina was in it—we all know how convincing she is."

Milton glanced around the table, gauging their reactions. They were nodding their recognition. Encouraged, he pressed on.

"I didn't think much of it at first. I'd heard of Bitcoin but never thought it was for me. But the ads kept popping up, and my friend wouldn't stop talking about it. Then there was a seminar, and he convinced me to go along. The place was packed. Valentina was there."

"Go on," Isobel said.

"So... I wasn't sure at first, but the more I listened, the more it sounded like the kind of opportunity that only comes once in a blue moon. So I took a chance. I took what savings I had—ten thousand euros—and I invested." He swallowed hard, feigning a pang of bitterness. "I thought I was being smart. Obviously, I feel like a total fool now." He leaned back, clasping his hands together on the table. "At first it seemed like it was working. The dashboard showed how my investment was growing. Ten thousand became fifteen, then twenty. It looked real. But then the dashboard stopped working. I couldn't log in. I thought it was just a glitch, but the days turned into weeks, and I knew I'd been had."

Isobel nodded. "I hope it should be obvious now that it's not your fault. It's easy to blame yourself for what happened, but they're *so* polished. We've seen people with years of experience in the financial industries giving them money. If they can fool professionals like that, I don't know what chance ordinary people ever had."

Milton nodded. "Thank you. Do you think you might be able to help me?"

"Of course," she said with a reassuring smile.

The waitress came over with their drinks. Milton watched Marco as he sipped his espresso. He looked older than his years. His dark hair was slightly unkempt, as though he hadn't bothered with a comb in days, and there were shadows under his eyes, suggestions of sleepless nights and worry. He had the kind of frame that spoke of someone who'd worked hard once—lean and strong—but there was a sense of weariness now, as though something weighed him down. The cancer, Milton thought. His clothes were simple, a bit worn, though clean. His fingers tapped against the edge of his cup—a nervous, unconscious habit—and Milton caught the flash of a scar on his knuckles.

Isobel sipped her coffee and then set the cup back down in the saucer.

"All right, then," she began. "The purpose of this morning's meeting is to take down all of your details so that we can get back to you about the claim we're going to be bringing in Italy." She gestured to the young man sitting next to her. "This is Alexander. He's a paralegal at my firm, and he's helping with the admin. It'd be really helpful if you could give him your names and addresses and a rough idea of how much you've lost. We'll take that back to London with us, and then someone from our office in Rome will be in touch with the paperwork you'll need to sign so you can be taken on as clients."

"And after that?" a woman at the other end of the table asked.

"We'll do everything we can to bring the claim. But it's like I said yesterday—there are no guarantees with any of this. The people behind TrueCoin are slippery, and it won't be easy. But I can promise you that we're good—*very* good—at what we do, and I'm confident we'll have made progress by the end of the year." She spread her hands. "Shall we get cracking?"

16

Davor Vuković sat at a small desk, the single lamp reflecting against the blade of the butterfly knife. His hands moved with precision as he drew the blade along a whetstone, the metallic whisper punctuating the silence. With each stroke, the edge grew keener, and Vuković's focus sharpened along with it. This had become something of a ritual for him; the repetitive motion calmed him, honing not just the knife but also the detachment he needed for what he was going to do. The blade caught the light as he turned it, testing its sharpness with the pad of his thumb before flipping it shut.

His phone was on the desk beside him. The message had arrived two days ago with the name and address of the man he had been told to kill. Giancarlo Sartori, a lawyer with an office near Campo Santa Margherita in Dorsoduro. Vuković wasn't told what Sartori had done to attract his attention, and didn't care. The names he was sent were all different, with one thing in common: they'd been unlucky enough to draw the attention of the wrong people.

It didn't matter.

Orders were orders, and Vuković just did what he was told.

He was dressed in the brown coveralls that he'd purchased from a cleaning supply store yesterday, the fabric crisp and uncreased, complete with a name patch that read 'Luca.' The uniform wasn't his size—slightly loose around the shoulders and waist—but that didn't matter. It wasn't meant to fit; it was meant to blend in. A cap, matching the coveralls, sat on the desk beside him, its brim worn just enough to appear authentic. Everything about his appearance had been curated for one purpose: to be forgettable. The kind of man you wouldn't look at twice if you passed him in the hall, a nondescript worker busy with a boringly mundane job.

Vuković stood, sliding the butterfly knife into an inside pocket, and then picked up his phone. The dim light caught the edges of his scar, the jagged one that ran from his temple to his jawline, a memento of an earlier life, from the Bosnian war, long before Dragomir Jovanović had recruited him.

He went to the door and pulled out the key card from the slot. The lights went out; Vuković stepped out into the corridor and rode the lift down to the lobby.

17

Isobel asked the others to set out their experiences of the scam, and her paralegal took careful notes. Milton sat back and listened.

"There was... a team," Carlo said, his English as slow as yesterday. "They had software people, customer people, media people—everything. Like a real business. Even an office."

Isobel nodded. "The one in Rome?"

"You know it?"

She nodded. "They had two whole floors. It was closed by the time I was involved."

"I visited," one of the others said. "I wanted to meet the team before investing. It looked real—desks, computers, people working. It felt like a proper company."

"We hear rumours," Carlo said, "they move office to Malta, then Caribbean, somewhere. For tax, they say. To save money, to pass to us." His voice was heavy with sarcasm. "*Stupido*, of course. They were running away."

"They hid everything so well," Marco said. "Do you

remember the updates on the website? And the newsletters? Valentina was always there, in everything."

"What do you know about the people behind it?" Isobel asked. "Other than her?"

Carlo shrugged. "Just a little. The names... they are fake, I think. We only see the faces they put onstage. Valentina was always there. They have crypto experts—so they say—and marketing people. They talk about the technology, what it means, but nothing more. The real bosses stay in the shadows."

"We think the founders might be from Eastern Europe, but it's hard to pin them down."

"Not Italy?"

"Valentina's Italian. We don't think the others are."

"I heard it was Bulgaria," someone at the table said.

"We heard that, too," she said. "And Serbia and Kosovo. One name comes up a lot—Nikolai Petrović—Niko. We think he follows Valentina around." She turned to the paralegal. "Do you have that picture?"

The younger lawyer opened the folder and, after flipping through the pages, took out a sheet with a photograph printed on it. He turned it around so that everyone could see it. Milton looked: it was of a man in his early to mid-thirties, dark hair, expensive suit.

"I see him before," Carlo said. "A seminar I went to in Milan."

She opened a notebook and flipped through it to a list of names. "What about Riccardo Moretti? Do you know him?"

Carlo exchanged a glance with Marco before looking back at her. "We know him."

Marco nodded. "He's the biggest affiliate in Italy."

Milton knew what that meant, but feigned ignorance. "I don't understand."

"It wasn't just about the coin," Marco said. "They offered money for anyone else you could recruit. You had what they called 'investment packages' at different levels. You bought in for a few hundred euros or tens of thousands. Each package came with educational material about cryptocurrency. They encouraged new investors to study up and then use the material to recruit others."

"And then make a commission?"

"Exactly. Recruit five people and you get a cut of their investment. They recruit people under them, and you make a smaller percentage of that commission, and so on."

"Like a pyramid scheme?"

"Exactly," Marco said. "It's classic. They even had ranks—Bronze, Silver, Gold, all the way up. Each rank came with bigger bonuses and access to special events. The higher you climbed, the more you could make. The ones at the top—Platinums like Moretti—they're earning from the level below them, then the level below that, then the level below that. They're making millions."

"And the worst part," Carlo added, "was how it made us... how you say?"

"Complicit," Marco suggested. "Involved."

Carlo nodded. "We ended up recruiting friends and family. Two of my best friends from school, my father-in-law..." His voice trailed off, and he glanced guiltily at Marco.

"I did the same," Marco said.

"But Moretti brings *more* people, more than anyone," Carlo said. "He must know them, the ones at the top—yes? You find him and maybe he can show you a way to find them."

"We've tried," she said. "He's not exactly out in the open. He knows which way the wind's blowing. He's smart enough to keep his head down."

One of the others at the table raised a finger. "I know where he is."

Milton turned. It was a woman, probably in her late thirties, with sharp features and an air of quiet authority. Her dark hair was pulled back into a no-nonsense ponytail, and she wore a tailored blazer over a simple blouse and jeans.

"I used to work with him," she went on. "I was part of his team before I realised what was really going on. He trusted me."

Isobel glanced over at the paralegal to make sure he was getting an accurate note. "That could be very useful. Where is he based?"

"He has an office in Palazzo Cavalli-Franchetti." She paused, glancing at the others at the table. "But if you're going to find him, you'll have to move quickly. You're right—he is smart, and he's paranoid, too. If he thinks someone's looking for him, he'll disappear."

18

Vuković had planned every detail with painstaking care. The car in the street outside was a short-term rental, booked under a false name and paid for in cash. He'd visited an office supplies store in Mestre and bought a roll of heavy-duty black bin liners, nitrile gloves, duct tape, and a small hand torch. He'd also added a selection of cleaning products: industrial-grade disinfectant, a spray bottle of bleach, absorbent rags, and a collapsible mop. They were all in the boot. He probably wouldn't need them if things went the way he planned, but he liked to be prepared. There was a Serbian proverb—*dvaput meri, jednom seci*—that he had tried to live by. *Measure twice, cut once.* It was a useful axiom to keep in mind for a man in his line of work.

Sartori's office was located in a faded palazzo overlooking a quiet canal. He parked the car in a quiet alley near the side entrance and went to the building's service door. He'd checked earlier; there was no CCTV coverage here and none inside. He ought to be able to go up to the office and down again without leaving evidence that he had been here.

The lock was easy to pick; he took out his tools, listened for the faint click of the tumblers falling into place, put the tools back into his pocket and opened the door.

Vuković found the service lift. He got in and rode it to the second floor. The doors slid apart, and he stepped out, following the corridor down to the office. He paused outside the door and listened. He couldn't hear anything. He listened again and thought he could hear the sound of breathing; no, he corrected himself, it was snoring.

He reached for the handle, turned it, and opened the door.

The office was cluttered, papers strewn across the desk and files piled precariously on shelves. A laptop sat in sleep mode, its screen dark. Sartori was slumped in a chair, his head resting on the desk as if he had fallen asleep mid-task.

Vuković stepped inside and closed the door.

He moved to the desk and placed a hand on Sartori's shoulder, shaking him gently.

The lawyer stirred, blinking blearily as he raised his head.

His face immediately dissolved into panic.

Vuković had decided to use English on account of his Italian being more rudimentary. He knew Sartori spoke English since it was noted on his listing on the website of the Consiglio Nazionale Forense. "I need to talk to you."

"What is it?" he started, but the words died in his throat as he guessed why Vuković was here.

"We need to talk."

Sartori's mouth opened, then closed again. He swallowed hard, his eyes darting to the papers on his desk as if they might offer him a way out.

"You were told to pass on everything about the case Mr. Everett's lawyers are building."

"I did," he protested.

"Then why do we find his English lawyer here, in Venice, today? Why didn't you tell us she was coming?"

"I didn't know. She just came. It was last minute. They didn't tell me. They—"

Vuković raised a hand, cutting him off. "There was a meeting."

"I know."

"You didn't go."

"I *couldn't* go."

"Why not?"

"Because they'll know I've sold them out."

"How would they know that?"

"They'll know as soon as they see me. It'll be written all over my face."

"That's a pity. How can you do what you promised to do if you can't be with them?"

Sartori tried to answer, his mouth opening and closing, but no words came. Vuković's gaze swept the room, taking it all in. He smelled stale coffee and sweat. Sartori was unravelling. Vuković wanted the man to think that he had some choice in deciding what came next, but it was an act. He didn't. Vuković's orders were unambiguous; it was just a question of how he carried them out. He preferred it to be neat and tidy, but that wasn't the only way.

"I'm sorry," Sartori said at last. "I just needed to take a break. There's a meeting tomorrow. Turner—the English lawyer—she emailed me to say she met local investors today so they could be added to the case. She wants to see me to speak about it. I'll be able to find out whom she's speaking to. I'll get everything they need."

"You can tell them that," Vuković said.

"Okay—that's fine. I'll call them." He reached for his phone and held it up. "I'll do it now."

Vuković shook his head. "It needs to be face to face."

"What? They're *here*? In Venice?"

"They are. And they want to give you a chance to persuade them that you can still be trusted."

"When?"

"Now."

He bit down on his lip. "It's six. Could I go and see them in the morning?"

"It has to be now. They fly out of the city tonight. I'm here to collect you. I'll take you to the hotel and bring you back."

Sartori looked up at Vuković's face and saw there was no point in arguing. "Okay."

19

The woman at the meeting had said that Riccardo operated out of an office in Palazzo Cavalli-Franchetti. Isobel noted it down and said she'd look into it.

Milton decided there was no time to wait.

He stepped out of the café into the crisp early evening sun. The Grand Canal was a short walk away. He made his way to the water's edge and flagged down a river taxi. The driver, a wiry man with weathered skin and a cigarette dangling from his lips, nodded Milton aboard. Milton stepped down carefully, taking a seat near the gunwale as the driver pushed off, steering the vessel into the busy water.

Milton was well travelled, but the journey was impressive even by his own standards. The canal presented a mesmerising collision of old-world charm and the fizz of modern life; the boat slipped past rows of pastel-coloured buildings with balconies leaning precariously over the water while gondoliers manoeuvred through narrow side channels, passengers snapping photos and gawping at their surroundings. Larger water busses rumbled by, packed with tourists and locals alike, their wakes sending ripples out to both sides.

The office was located in San Marco. They approached the Ponte dell'Accademia, and Milton caught his first glimpse of the Palazzo. Its Gothic arches and stately presence stood out even among the grandeur of the other buildings. The driver guided the taxi toward a private mooring, slowing the boat as it glided to a stop. Milton paid him and stepped off the boat onto the small dock, the polished wood slick under his shoes.

Milton looked up at the building: the frontage was a tapestry of arched windows, stone carvings and decorative balconies, everything painted in warm shades that glowed in the light. It was four storeys high and crowned with battlement-like details that made it look like a fortress. It surely would have been an expensive property to rent. It was evident that Moretti wasn't short of cash.

The woman at the meeting had said that Moretti's office was on the fourth floor. Milton walked to the entrance, which featured a pair of heavy wooden doors framed by marble columns, and stepped into a cool and echoing foyer. The floors were polished terrazzo, reflecting the light from the tall, arched windows and ringing with the echo of footsteps. Lights hung from high ceilings, and the walls were hung with classical artwork and decorated with gilded mouldings. There was an atmosphere of obvious wealth, and Milton could see how Moretti would have wanted to associate himself with it; having an office here spoke of success, and that would allow him to suggest—even if it was implicit—that similar success would be possible for anyone who bought into the scheme he was pitching.

A marble reception desk sat to one side, manned by a sharp-eyed concierge who looked up as Milton approached.

"Riccardo Moretti?" he said.

The man held up four fingers and pointed to the lift at the back of the lobby. Milton thanked him and stepped inside the lift, pressed the button for the fourth floor and waited as it bore him up.

The doors opened, and he stepped into a hushed corridor lined with heavy wooden doors. The name "Moretti Associati" was engraved on a brass plaque beside one of them.

Milton knocked on the door, but there was no answer.

He knocked again: still nothing.

Milton looked left and right and, happy that he wasn't about to be disturbed, assessed the lock. It was old, the metal slightly tarnished, and the frame showed faint signs of wear. He pulled out his wallet and took out his fake driving licence. He slid the card into the gap between the door and the frame and applied gentle pressure, angling it toward the latch. He jiggled it down, coaxing the latch to retract just enough.

The door gave a faint creak as it eased open.

Milton slipped inside and closed the door softly behind him.

Moretti's office would have been impressive were it not for the fact that it had been left in such a muddle. The tall windows offered sweeping views of the canal, and the room was lavishly appointed with leather furniture: a modern desk and gaudy decorations evidently meant to impress. But the room had been left in a state, and it was obvious that Moretti hadn't used it for some time. Dust had settled over everything, dulling the sheen of the leather chairs and coating the polished antique desk. A faint, stale odour hung in the air, as though the room had been closed up for weeks without fresh air. Papers were scattered across the desk, some slipping off the edge as if abandoned mid-task, and a few had been stacked on the floor in untidy piles. A half-empty glass sat forgotten on a side table, the water turned murky and a ring of dust forming around the rim. The computer was dark, its screen layered with fingerprints and grime, and Milton noticed a fine spiderweb stretching from the monitor to the paperweight beside it.

He searched the office, starting with the desk. He sifted through the papers and rifled through the drawers, but they held only generic files: sales reports, promotional materials for TrueCoin, and a few unpaid bills. Nothing personal and certainly nothing that hinted at where Moretti might be found. Milton checked the filing cabinet next, tugging open each drawer to find neatly labelled folders with details of the 'investors' who had been scammed into parting with their money. Another drawer contained the details of those labelled as 'prospects.' The computer offered nothing, either; it wouldn't even power on.

Milton walked over to the bookshelves, running his fingers along the spines, looking for anything out of place; all he found were business books, their pages unturned, arranged more for show than for use. There was a ring binder at the end of one of the shelves that looked as if it had been used, and Milton took it down and opened it on the desk. The binder contained what looked like a printout from a spreadsheet; it was titled 'Elenco degli Affiliati.' Milton ran the phrase through Google Translate; it meant 'List of Affiliates.'

The list was broken down into three distinct sections: Bronzo, Argento and Oro.

Milton didn't need to translate those: Bronze, Silver, Gold.

He turned to the back and ran his finger down the list of

affiliates who had been recruited by Moretti. There were sixty at the Bronze level, tapering to fifteen at Silver and just two at Gold. Milton knew that Moretti himself sat atop the pyramid, the only Platinum affiliate in Italy. He ignored the Bronzes on the basis that the only information they would be able to provide him would likely be the details for the Silvers, and he already had that. He ignored the Silvers for the same reason, with the proviso that they would be his next port of call if he struck out with the two above them.

The two Gold affiliates—Stefano Biagi and Elena Maldini—had pages all to themselves, with detailed notes that Milton photographed and then translated.

Moretti reported that Biagi was a small-time hustler. He was a failed entrepreneur with a string of dead-end ventures behind him. He was based in an office above a bookshop in Piazza San Bartolomeo and recruited local investors through free seminars and presentations provided by True-Coin's marketing team.

Maldini was a finance professional with a background in banking. She had risen through the ranks by targeting young professionals and persuading them to invest significant amounts that were way above the levels that someone like Biagi could manage. She was said to operate out of a shared workspace in Campo Santa Maria Formosa. A note added in pen said that she'd run when one of her investors had sued her, retreating to the homes of sympathetic friends to keep herself out of sight.

Biagi was the more promising of the two. He'd probably be easier to find than Maldini, who seemed likely to be more sophisticated and better at dropping out of sight. Biagi's history of failure also made him a prime candidate for manipulation; someone desperate to save his own skin and perhaps even eager to shift blame onto others if it meant buying himself some protection. Isobel could apply pressure, so could Milton. With that in mind, Biagi seemed the most accessible—and exploitable—option to explore.

Milton took photos of the key pages in the binder and put it back on the shelf. He glanced around the room one last time, but it was clear: Moretti had left nothing behind that could reveal his whereabouts.

Milton would have to get to him another way.

20

There had come a point when Sartori must have realised Vuković wasn't taking him to meet True-Coin's management. He might have known it at the office, but he surely would have guessed when Vuković turned away from the city and into the industrial area on the outskirts. But if Sartori *had* realised, he didn't protest. Vuković had seen this sort of behaviour from the men and women he'd been sent to attend to before. It was resignation. He remembered, before the war when he worked on the farm in the mountains, how cattle would sometimes show the same docility as they were led to the slaughterhouse. They knew, but they didn't struggle. They didn't try to escape. They knew that it would have been pointless.

He'd pulled over near the breaker's yard, stepped out of the car, pulled out the pistol he wore in the shoulder holster beneath his jacket, and shot Sartori through the window three times, hitting him twice in the head and once in the neck. Then Vuković had driven the car into the yard and transferred the dead body into the boot. The owner of the business had been paid well and had agreed to destroy the vehicle. There would be no questions asked.

By morning, there would be no trace at all of Sartori.

It was Vuković's specialty: he made people disappear.

He had a short walk back to the main road, where he would be able to get a taxi to take him back into the city. He stopped to check his surroundings, breathing in the cold air tinged with saltwater and the earthy aroma of algae from the canals, and then set off, taking out his phone and calling Dragomir as he walked.

"Done," he said.

"Any problems?"

"No. It was easy."

"Did he say anything?"

"He said the English lawyer didn't tell him she was coming."

"That seems unlikely."

A truck rumbled along the road, and Vuković waited until the noise had faded before speaking again. "He said she's here to recruit others to their claim."

"Fucking Everett," Dragomir cursed. "And that fucking woman. She's like a thorn in my side."

"Do you want me to deal with her?"

"I think now might be the time," Dragomir said.

"I'll take care of it."

Vuković ended the call, then opened the note where he'd pasted the names he had been given.

Sartori's was first.

Vuković highlighted it and then tapped to delete it.

Isobel Turner's name was next.

He would have reached her in London eventually, one way or another, but now it would be easy.

21

Milton left Moretti's office. The corridor was still empty as he made his way back to the lift. He went back down to the foyer, nodding a brief farewell to the concierge, who barely looked up.

He walked along the canal toward the nearest vaporetto stop. He waited as one of the water busses pulled in, its engines churning the green water as passengers disembarked. Milton stepped aboard, taking a spot near the rail as the boat glided away, picking up speed and slipping into the flow of the canal.

The water bus wound its way along the Rio de Ca' Foscari and headed for the quieter, less opulent side of the city, a sharp contrast to Moretti's address. Stefano Biagi's office was in Santa Croce, a district known more for its modest shops and businesses than for luxury or status.

Milton disembarked near the Ponte Tre Ponti bridge and blended into the crowd, following the route to Rio Terà Sant'Andrea. Milton found the address for Biagi's office on a second floor above a bookshop. There was a faded sign hanging over the door and a worn staircase leading up to the entrance. The building was older, with an unassuming air, nondescript and anonymous.

He approached the narrow doorway between the bookshop and a trattoria, the sign above it bearing Biagi's name and the title 'Consulente Finanziario'; Milton held up his phone and used Google to translate it: it meant 'Financial Consultant.' The paint on the door was chipped, and there was a layer of grime on the handle. Milton rapped his knuckles firmly against the wood, listening for any sounds of movement from inside. He waited a moment, knocked again, then pressed his ear to the door, but—like Moretti's office—there was nothing.

Milton stepped back and scanned the building. The upper windows were dark, with no sign of anyone within. He slipped down the narrow alley alongside the building, passing bins overflowing with the day's rubbish and the faint smell of bread from the trattoria's kitchen. At the end of the alley, he found himself in a cramped courtyard behind the row of shops and offices. The buildings showed their age more clearly here: crumbling bricks, peeling paint, and rusted fire escapes. Someone had scrawled 'Free Palestine' in bright green paint.

Milton looked up, noticing that a first-floor window was ajar, and took stock of his options. The fire escape was to the right, too far to reach directly from the ground, but close enough to the window he was thinking of using. He backed up a few paces and then launched himself at the wall, catching the edge of a drainpipe and using it to pull himself up. It wasn't as easy as it had been twenty years earlier, but Milton was still strong enough to move hand over hand along the windowsill until he was level with the window. He swung to the left once and then twice until he had enough momentum to hook a foot onto the fire escape. With a final pull, he hoisted himself up to the small metal landing outside the window.

The window was stuck, likely from lack of use, but a firm shove loosened it enough for him to slide it open. Milton eased himself over the sill and into the room. The office was dark and still, illuminated only by a line of light that bled in through the gap between the bottom of the door and the floor. The stale air suggested no one had been here in days, maybe even weeks.

Milton sighed. He was going to strike out for a second time.

He looked around. Biagi's office was much smaller than Moretti's and more cluttered. There were stacks of folders and papers on a worn desk in the corner. Posters promoting financial independence and success were stuck to the walls, sun-bleached and curling at the edges. Valentina Rossi beamed down at him from one of them, all ice-white smile and sparkling eyes.

Milton took a moment to listen for any sounds from the hallway, but everything remained quiet. He was satisfied he was alone and set to work, careful to disturb as little as possible. Stacks of papers and folders were piled haphazardly on the desk and floor, along with several empty takeaway containers and a half-finished carton of cheap wine. Milton began at the desk, rifling through papers without much expectation: there were scattered notes on clients, reminders to make calls, spreadsheets filled with meaningless numbers, and remnants of the presentation packs TrueCoin affiliates deployed to lure in more victims. It was a mess of abandoned promises and financial jargon, and none of it was useful.

But as Milton shifted aside a stack of client files, he noticed a worn, leather-bound notebook half-buried beneath loose papers. He flipped it open and found lists of names—likely Biagi's local recruits—and crude notes about each one. He took photographs of everything and put the book back.

He noticed a stack of envelopes dumped in a drawer. Most were junk mail or bills addressed to the office itself, but one envelope caught his eye; it was a letter from a utility company, but this one was addressed to Via Donatello, No. 9, 30175 Marghera, with the name Stefano Biagi printed at the top.

Milton opened the envelope and took out the demand inside, seeing that it was dated from a month ago. It was an electricity bill, something Biagi might have brought to the office to pay but then forgotten.

Milton pocketed the envelope. He took a last look around, ensuring he hadn't missed anything that might prove useful, then left the room through the window. He climbed onto the fire escape, clambered down the ladder and dropped down to the ground.

He made his way back through the alleyway and found a late-opening café where he could sit down with a coffee. He took out his phone and entered the address on the envelope. Marghera was a district in the Venice Metropolitan Area on the mainland, just across the lagoon from Venice itself. It was close—reachable in about twenty minutes by train or car—making it a practical place for those who wanted to commute in and out of the city.

Milton looked at the time: it was seven, and the light was almost all gone. He decided that there was no point in waiting. He wanted to get to Moretti as quickly as he could, and Biagi offered the fastest way to do that.

He set off.

22

The Belgrade office of TrueCoin was functional but uninspiring, very different from the opulence of the building they'd used in Rome. This building was a nondescript, concrete block on the outskirts of the city and had been chosen deliberately for its anonymity.

Dragomir pushed through the double doors, crossed the empty reception area—they had no need for it since they never entertained guests—and went into the rooms at the back. It all felt transient: cardboard boxes were stacked against the walls, along with half-packed files and equipment ready for an abrupt departure. The furniture was cheap and would all be left behind.

The staff—or what remained of them—were sat in front of their monitors. There was an atmosphere of anxiety that was impossible to miss. Everyone knew the end was near; it was no longer a question of if, but when. The once-bustling operations floor now hummed with a subdued chatter as accounts were finalised, complaints were deflected or ignored, and money was moved out of the reach of the authorities.

Dragomir pushed open the door to the small conference room that served as their impromptu legal department. Milan Djoković, the Serbian-born lawyer they'd recruited from a major litigation practice in London, was waiting for him. Djoković was a sharp, wiry man in his forties; Dragomir had been told that he'd been in the office for a week without going back to his hotel, sleeping on the floor of his office and surviving on takeouts. He looked exhausted, and his eyes had the harried look of someone who had been fighting a losing battle for too long.

"Dragomir," he said, "we need to talk."

"So you said." Dragomir sat down with a sigh, rubbing his temples. "I'm busy. Get to it."

Djoković opened a folder and spread several sheets of paper across the table. "We've got pending legal threats across multiple jurisdictions. Italy, of course—that'll be filed first, we think. The financial crimes unit in Rome is moving fast—they've compiled enough evidence to issue arrest warrants."

Dragomir's jaw tightened. "Go on."

"Spain has frozen some of our accounts after a complaint was filed by a group of investors in Barcelona. The French are looking into fraudulent advertising claims, and the Germans are investigating unlicensed financial services. There are also ongoing class action lawsuits in the United Kingdom, the Netherlands, and Switzerland."

"How long do we have before they get here?"

"To Belgrade?" Djoković hesitated. "That's hard to say."

"No bullshit. How long?"

"Weeks, if we're lucky. Days, possibly. Some of the regulators are collaborating with Interpol—I'd expect to see border alerts in place by the end of next week. When are Niko and Valentina leaving Italy?"

"Before then."

"They'll need to be careful."

"I was going to send them to Africa."

"There's nothing happening there, as far as I know."

"Good." Dragomir leaned back in his chair, staring at the ceiling, exhaling slowly. "What about the money?"

"Better news there. We've been routing funds through new channels, and I haven't seen anything that makes me worry that we've been flagged."

"What about the offshore accounts? Are they secure?"

"All fine. I can send you statements—"

"As *soon* as we're done," Dragomir interrupted.

Djoković nodded, making a note.

"Anything else?"

"We've been contacted by RAI in Italy. They're planning a documentary, and they wanted to give us the chance to address victims' concerns. I told them we're not interested, of course, but I thought you should know. We can't contain it anymore. Journalists are sniffing around, and there's a risk that when the first one publishes, the dam will break. They're all waiting to see what happens. If we don't sue—and I strongly suggest we don't—there'll be a flood soon after."

Dragomir slapped his palm onto the table. "*Jobote!*" He took a deep breath. "Fine. Tell Lizzie in London. She's in charge of keeping a lid on things—time for her to earn her salary."

Djoković gathered his documents. "I'll call her now."

"And pick up the pace here. I want us to be out of here by the end of tomorrow."

"By the end of—"

"Don't complain—just do it. You're paid enough. You can relax once it's done."

Djoković left the room, and Dragomir stood alone for a moment, staring out of the window at the bleak Belgrade skyline. He'd always known their empire had been built on unstable foundations, and that it was only a matter of time before it all collapsed, but he had hoped for a little longer. But it was what it was; no sense in crying about it. They'd made their fortunes, and now they would have the chance to enjoy the fruits of their labours.

Dragomir had friends in the government in Belgrade, and they'd promised to warn him when things became too hot for them to ignore. But in the meantime, it would do him no harm to leave the city. His villa in the mountains was remote and easier to defend; he'd fly out there, regroup and put the final touches on his next steps.

And then, like magic, he would disappear.

23

Marco unlocked the door to their apartment and stepped inside. Chiara was in the living room, sitting in the armchair with a blanket draped over her legs. She looked up as he entered, a tired but happy smile on her lips.

"Hey," she said softly, watching him as he hung his coat by the door.

"Hey," Marco replied, crossing the room and leaning down to kiss her forehead. "How are you feeling?"

"A bit tired tonight," she said, attempting to brush off the obvious fatigue with a smile. "But I'll live."

"Kids okay?"

"They're in bed," she said. "They're fine. How did it go in the city?"

Marco sighed and sat down on the couch opposite her. "Better than I expected. The lawyer's really impressive. She's putting together a solid case. There are already dozens of people who've signed on, and she thinks we might be able to get even more if we can get the right kind of publicity."

"And the more people there are, the more pressure on them."

"Exactly." He ran a hand through his hair. "But she said it'll take time. And even then, there's no guarantee we'll ever see our money again."

Chiara reached out and squeezed his hand. "We knew that, didn't we? Before yesterday we didn't think we had *any* chance at all—so if you look at it like that, we're already in a better position than we were."

Marco's phone buzzed in his pocket before he had the chance to answer. He glanced at the screen and saw Isobel's name. "It's her," he said, giving Chiara a look. "Isobel."

"What does she want?"

"I have no idea. I'll put it on speaker."

Marco answered the call, placing the phone on the coffee table between them.

"Marco—it's Isobel Turner. We spoke today. Do you have a minute?"

"Of course," he said. "My wife's here too."

"Hi, Chiara," Isobel said warmly. Marco was impressed that she'd remembered Chiara's name. "I'm glad you're both there—I wanted to talk to you about something important. Look—I'll cut straight to it. I've been working with a team from RAI for the last month, and they've been putting together a feature on TrueCoin. I spoke to them this evening, and they think telling your story would be a powerful way to bring home what they've done."

Marco's stomach clenched. "Our story?"

"Yes," Isobel confirmed. "What happened to you both is incredibly compelling. I saw it straight away when we spoke, and I haven't been able to stop thinking about it. Your cancer, Marco, and then Chiara's diagnosis. The financial strain you've both been put under. It's a human story people will be able to connect with. The problem with something like TrueCoin is that it can just look like numbers on a screen. Add in the fact that it's crypto and it makes it worse—it feels esoteric. The audience won't understand it, and it's difficult to show the real-world effect on those who have been caught up in it. RAI want their story to be about real people whose lives have been impacted. They want something tangible that will resonate with viewers, and I completely agree with them."

Chiara glanced at Marco, concern flickering across her face. "What exactly would it involve?"

"A sit-down interview," Isobel said. "They want to film it tomorrow. They're sending a team to Venice to save you from travelling. It wouldn't be invasive. You'd talk about your experience, how it's affected you both and your family, and why it's so important to hold TrueCoin accountable."

Marco rubbed his chin. "I don't know. I'm not sure we want our faces all over TV. I don't want people judging us—they'll just think I was stupid for falling for it."

Isobel's voice softened. "I understand the hesitation—I really, really do. But think about it. This could put enormous pressure on TrueCoin and their backers. It could help more victims come forward. You'd be making a difference, not just for yourselves, but for hundreds—for *thousands*—of people."

"I'm not sure."

"They're willing to be flexible on certain aspects," she said. "And I can make sure they don't disclose anything you're uncomfortable with."

Marco exhaled slowly. "We'd need to think about it."

"Of course," Isobel said. "Take the night to talk it over. The journalist will be in Venice tomorrow evening, but we'll need to let them know in the morning. If you decide to do it, I'll be there with you the whole time. You won't be alone."

Marco looked at Chiara. She met his gaze and offered him an encouraging smile.

"All right," he said after a moment. "We'll sleep on it."

"I'll call in the morning," Isobel said.

She ended the call, and silence settled over the room for a moment. Chiara reached over and took his hand. "What do you think?"

Marco shook his head. "I don't know. Putting our faces out there..."

"But what if she's right? If it helps even *one* other family, isn't it worth it?"

"I want to be selfish," he said. "I want us to get our money back. Would it help us or make it less likely?"

"Getting our money still isn't likely. You said it yourself—she's not making any guarantees. What do we have to lose?"

"You want to do it?"

"Maybe. Probably."

Marco bit down on his lip, sighed, and then nodded. "Let's sleep on it. We can decide in the morning."

Chiara smiled and squeezed his hand again. "Whatever we do—whatever we decide—we do it together. Right? This isn't just your problem to fix."

24

Milton took an Uber out to the suburbs. The address he'd found in the office led him to a quiet, unassuming neighbourhood. The streets were lined with modest homes, a mix of older stucco buildings and more modern constructions that suggested middle-class stability. Biagi's property was on the edge of the suburb, a two-storey house with pale yellow walls, a terracotta-tiled roof, and green shutters that had seen better days. A small, fenced-in yard surrounded the property, its garden neat but uninspired, with trimmed hedges and a patch of wilting marigolds near the gate.

Milton told the driver to let him out at the corner of the street, far enough away not to draw attention but close enough to keep the house in view. He got out and watched the house. It was nine in the evening and dark. The curtains were drawn on both floors, and no lights were visible from the street. A Mercedes was parked in the driveway.

Milton crossed the street, staying in the pockets of gloom next to the buildings. A glance over his shoulder confirmed that no one was watching him. He approached the house and paused at the gate, letting his eyes sweep over the property one last time. He listened for movement but heard nothing. He pushed open the gate and stepped into the yard. He went to the front door and knocked twice.

He heard the creak of floorboards. The door opened a crack, and a wary face peered out.

"Stefano Biagi?"

The man hesitated, his frown deepening.

"Do you speak English?"

"Who's asking?"

"I'd like to talk to you about TrueCoin."

Biagi tried to close the door.

Milton blocked it with his foot.

"Leave me alone," Biagi said. "I have nothing to say about that."

"You do."

Biagi tried to close the door again, but Milton reached out and held it open with his hand.

"That's very rude," Milton said. "I'm just here for a friendly chat—that's all."

"And I told you—I don't want to talk about it. Get away from the door."

"Or?"

"I'll call the police."

Milton smiled at him. "I doubt it. Because we both know that if you do that, I'm going to tell them why I'm here and how you've defrauded people out of their money."

"I haven't defrauded anyone."

"Bullshit." Milton stared at him, allowing the avuncularity he had opened with to slide away. "I'm coming inside, Stefano, and we're going to have a chat about TrueCoin. I'd rather you invited me to come in—it'd be much more pleasant than me kicking the door down and then persuading you to be polite."

The message still didn't appear to be getting through. Biagi put his shoulder to the door and tried to shove it. Milton absorbed his effort, and as Biagi drew back for another attempt, he shoved it back as hard as he could. The edge of the door cracked into the side of Biagi's head, sending him spinning back into the corridor. Milton stepped inside and quickly looked for threats: he was in a corridor with two doors to the left and a flight of stairs straight ahead. He could hear a television from one of the doors and the sound of someone talking upstairs. Biagi was on his backside, blood running down the side of his face from where the door had caught him just above his hairline.

Milton closed the distance to him in two long steps, then reached down and grabbed his shirt in both fists. He hauled him up, tearing the shirt in the process, and slammed him against the wall.

He nodded in the direction of the stairs. "Who's up there?"

"My wife."

"Probably best if we don't disturb her—yes?"

He nodded.

"Answer my questions, and I'll be gone."

Biagi nodded again, fear shining in his eyes.

Milton loosened his grip slightly but kept Biagi pinned against the wall.

"Riccardo Moretti."

Biagi hesitated, his eyes darting toward the stairs as if willing his wife to stay upstairs. "What about him?"

"Where does he live?"

"I don't know."

Milton slammed Biagi against the wall again. "Try again."

"He has a villa near Florence, but he could've moved by now."

"Why would he do that?"

"Don't you know? Everyone's scrambling—the police are about to go after the company."

Milton tightened his grip. "Think they'll come after you?"

"They'll come after everyone."

"Who runs the show?"

"Valentina."

"Have you met her?"

"Not really."

"Who else?"

Biagi flinched. "I don't know."

"Nikolai Petrović?"

"Niko? I met him once, but it was to say hello and that's it, I swear. I just know Moretti."

Milton studied Biagi's face for any hint of deceit, then released him. He slumped against the wall, clutching the torn remains of his shirt.

"Where's the villa?"

"I have the address in my phone."

"Get it."

Biagi took his phone out of his pocket, and with Milton watching for any suggestion he might be trying to raise the alarm, he did what he promised and found the address. Milton took the phone from him and took a photograph of the screen.

He handed the phone back to him. "Here's how this is going to work. You're going to stay quiet. If you even *think* about warning Moretti or anyone else, I'll know. And if I find out you've been running your mouth, I'll come back. And if I come back, I promise I'll be much more unfriendly. The police will be the least of your problems. Do you understand me?"

Biagi nodded rapidly, his face pale.

"Good boy." He put his finger to his lips. "Remember—shush."

Milton turned and stepped outside, closing the door behind him, and took out his phone.

Florence was just two hours by train, and the first one tomorrow morning would get him in before eight.

He would pay Moretti a visit.

PART II

ROME

25

The hum of the jet engines was soothing, a world away from the rumble of the commercial planes Valentina would have taken before she'd accepted the offer to work for TrueCoin. She remembered her last 'normal' flight: a fifty-euro special offer from Rome to Malaga with her girlfriends, serenaded by half a dozen men on a stag do who were already drunk when they boarded and the screams of the baby in the row ahead of her. This, though, was different. She and Niko had flown commercial when they launched, but the success they'd enjoyed since then meant that they'd quickly upgraded to private jets.

The experience felt more like being in a high-end penthouse than thirty-five thousand feet above the ground. The interior was panelled in cream-coloured leather accentuated with polished walnut trim. Armchairs were arranged around a low glass table with an assortment of fresh fruit, luxury chocolates from Amedei in Tuscany, and a bottle of chilled champagne in an ice bucket. The seating area gave way to a small dining space, where a table was set with fine china and crystal glasses, though neither she nor Niko had touched the meal prepared by the onboard chef. Valentina spent the flight in her seat, reviewing her presentations and stealing anxious glances at Niko.

She looked down at the screen of the tablet balanced on her lap. She'd been watching the footage from the presentation in Venice and was unhappy. Niko had said it'd been okay, but she wasn't happy. Her smile seemed forced, her voice a fraction too high.

She paused the video and leaned back, closing her eyes. She was carrying tension in her neck, and she rubbed it absentmindedly. She hadn't been perfect. The crowd had been harder to win over than usual, and she'd been glad they had the videos to run to give her an excuse to ignore the raised hands that signified questions she knew she wouldn't be able to answer. Niko had warned her that posters in some of the TrueCoin forums were questioning the blockchain they were using. Valentina knew the term but had no idea what it meant, and she would have been monumentally unprepared to discuss the solution that Niko said they had in place.

She looked across the cabin to where Niko reclined in his seat. A tumbler of whisky sat on the table beside him, untouched for the last twenty minutes. He was scrolling through something on his phone, his expression inscrutable.

The flight attendant approached Niko with a smile that was a little too eager, asking if he needed anything. He waved her off with a subtle flick of his hand, his focus still on his phone. Valentina bit her lip and looked back down at her tablet, pretending to study the notes for the seminar, but her thoughts refused to stay focused.

She thought about her conversation with him in the car to the airport. He'd been relaxed on the surface, but the undertone had been clear: Dragomir was watching, and he wasn't happy. She needed to do better. There was no room for missteps, no tolerance for hesitation and no acceptance of second-guessing or doubt. She'd met Dragomir only once, but that had been enough. She could see he wasn't someone it would be wise to disappoint.

The flight attendant returned, this time offering her a cup of green tea. She accepted the drink with a tight smile and took a small sip, her gaze drifting toward the window.

Her nerves were raw by the time Niko finally spoke. "You've been quiet," he said. He set his phone down on the table beside him and turned his piercing gaze toward her. "Not like you."

Valentina forced a smile, though it felt brittle. "Just going over the material," she said, gesturing at the tablet. "I want to make sure everything's perfect."

"Go on."

She set the tablet down and folded her hands in her lap to keep them from trembling. "I know what went wrong in Venice."

"I said it was fine."

"It can be better. *I* can be better. It's like you said—people have been influenced by the negative press. I need to think about my approach—make it less about the technical aspects and more about the vision."

Niko nodded. "Play to your strengths. Make them believe in you. That makes sense. *You* are TrueCoin. If they believe you, they'll believe in what we're offering."

"I'll be better next time."

Niko leaned back in his seat, picked up his tumbler and took a slow sip of whisky.

She looked out of the window again.

"Are you sure you're okay?" he asked her.

She forced a smile. "Absolutely."

"Tired?"

She nodded.

"Because we haven't stopped for weeks."

"I know."

He laughed. "We said a month when we started, didn't we? Six weeks if things went well. But it's been much longer than that."

"Eighteen months," she said. "I'm not ungrateful. You've looked after me well, and I always wanted to travel."

"You've certainly been able to do that," he said with a smile. "And the money's not bad, either."

"I know."

"Half a million. You never would've made that doing what you were doing before, would you?"

"Not a chance."

"How much did you make in your last year?"

"In the restaurant?"

"It was twelve thousand, wasn't it?"

He said it with a smile, but Valentina knew he was very subtly threatening her: if he knew about how much money she made then, what else did he know?

"A little less, actually."

"I'll tell you what," he said. "How about I pay you that as a bonus after we've finished in Rome?"

"You don't have to—"

"No," he cut across her. "I do. I *want* to. I haven't shown you how grateful we are for the work you've done. You should be rewarded for it."

"I have been rewarded," she said. "I don't need—"

He put up his hand to silence her. "The job has been bigger than we expected, and I don't think it's unreasonable that you get a bonus. I'll make it another fifteen, as soon as we've finished in Italy."

"Thank you," she said, aware that by accepting the money, she would be sinking deeper into the quicksand that had already sucked her deeper than she should ever have allowed.

The plane began its descent, the cabin lights dimming slightly in preparation for landing. Valentina took a deep breath, trying to steady herself. She was scared, but she couldn't afford to let fear control her. Not now. Too much at stake.

The wheels touched down, the rubber squealing and then the reverse thrusters roaring to slow them down. The flight attendant reappeared, all smiles as she prepared the cabin for disembarkation. Valentina rose from her seat, smoothing the wrinkles from her blouse, and forced her face into the confident mask of the *other* Valentina.

The door to the jet opened. She squared her shoulders and stepped out.

But deep down, a tiny voice whispered: You're walking a tightrope, and a fall is coming.

PART III

VENICE

26

Marco woke early, lying in bed and staring at the ceiling, turning over the conversation with Isobel from last night. His sleep had been fitful, and every time he woke, his thoughts buzzed so relentlessly with what they'd been asked to do that he knew he'd been dreaming about it, too.

The early morning light seeped through the curtains, casting soft shadows across the room. He glanced over at Chiara; she was still curled up under the duvet, her breathing slow and steady. She'd always had no trouble sleeping. He'd been the same, once, but with everything—his cancer, her MND, the money they'd lost—he hadn't had a solid night's sleep for months. He wanted to rouse her so he'd have someone to talk to, but he knew he couldn't. Her sleep was too precious. He lay in bed feeling vulnerable and alone, but that was a small price to pay if it meant she felt better in the morning.

He shifted now, careful not to wake her, but she stirred anyway.

"Morning," she murmured, her voice thick with sleep.

"Morning."

"Sleep okay?"

"Not really."

Chiara pushed herself up onto her elbow. "You're thinking about the call?"

He nodded.

"What do you think about it now?"

"Part of me wants to do it."

"But you're scared?"

Marco sighed and sat up, resting his elbows on his knees. "I am, but it's not just that. What'll people say when they find out?"

"Who?"

"Our friends. What if they think I was stupid to fall for it? Or that I was greedy and got what I deserved?"

"They wouldn't think that," she interrupted gently, reaching for his hand. "We needed money, and you saw something that looked good. They took advantage of the fact we were desperate. And it's not like we're the only ones, is it?"

"What if we do it and they come after us? What if—"

She squeezed his hand. "Do you *really* think they'd want the extra attention?"

He shook his head. "I suppose not."

"Once the story is out, it's out. What are they going to do to us then?"

"But what about the kids? What if they get dragged into this? The media, the neighbours… People talk, don't they? I don't want them to feel ashamed because their father got scammed."

Chiara leaned in. "Look at it another way—what do we tell the kids if we do nothing? That it's okay to let people get away with stealing? That we should stay quiet and let them ruin more lives? Marco... no. We've lost so much already."

Her voice wavered, and he saw the pain in her eyes.

He swallowed hard. "I know," he said. "I don't want to lose any more."

"Neither do I. But we *have* to fight back. How many people were at the meeting yesterday?"

"Twenty."

"And they've all suffered like we have—some of them will've lost *more*. Think about them. And then think about everyone else who doesn't know that there are ways to fight back. Think about everyone who thinks TrueCoin is legitimate. We've had awful luck with everything, but maybe we can use it to our advantage. How can people feel anything other than sympathy? Maybe it will give hope to those at the meeting. Maybe it will show others how to find help, and maybe it will warn everyone else never to go anywhere near scams like that."

"I know—you're right." Marco rubbed his temples. "It's just... it's humiliating."

She cupped his face gently, making him look at her. "You were trying to help us. You did it for our future—for the kids. There's no shame in that. And we did it together, didn't we? You told me, and I agreed we should go for it."

"I know."

She smiled softly. "Show them you're not going to take what happened to us lying down. You've—*we've*—been handed a chance to do something about what they did. We've got to take it."

Marco looked down. She was right. He'd been wallowing in his own shame and guilt and fear for too long; it was time to do something about it.

He exhaled and nodded. "Okay. I'll call her. I'll do it."

"You're not listening," she said. "It's not you—it's *us*. *We'll* do it. Both of us."

"You don't have to."

"I do, Marco. And I want to."

"What if it makes you ill?"

"I had a good night's sleep," she said. "I'll be fine today."

He looked at her and doubted that. The diagnosis was still fresh, but the symptoms had become more obvious now he knew something was wrong and what to look for. She looked tired all the time despite what she said. It was more than just looking as if she was physically exhausted; it was that she looked drained in a way that went deeper, like a weight pressing down on her spirit. There were dark circles under her eyes, and her once-vibrant energy had been dulled. She struggled with the simplest of tasks, things that used to come easily to her: the walk to the kitchen left her out of breath; holding a coffee cup too long made her fingers tremble; even the effort of smiling at the children felt like it took something from her.

Marco tried not to let it show, but watching her and cataloguing her decline chipped away at the denial he'd clung to for so long. He knew she was putting on a brave face for him and the children, but he also knew it wouldn't last forever. He was well enough to help her for now, but he was going to sicken, too, and then he would die. He needed to get their affairs in order so that she had the support she needed when he could no longer provide it.

Marco pulled her into a hug, holding her tightly. "I don't know what I'd do without you."

Chiara hugged him back. "Luckily, you don't have to find out."

They stayed like that for a moment before she pulled

away and glanced at the clock. "Call her. I need to get the kids ready before my mum gets here."

PART IV

FLORENCE

27

Milton arrived at Venice's Santa Lucia station just as the first hints of dawn were breaking over the Grand Canal. The terminal was quiet, the sound of muffled announcements and the rattle of wheeled luggage echoing faintly under the steeply arched ceiling. He walked briskly, passing the ticket kiosks and making his way toward the red-and-silver Frecciarossa train waiting at platform eight.

The train was impressive, with an aerodynamic nose gleaming under the fluorescent station lights. He boarded, stowed his backpack in the overhead compartment and settled into a wide, leather seat by the window. A crisp linen headrest bore the Trenitalia logo, and a small fold-out table in front of him offered space for food and drink.

The train slid out of the station with a lurch, and within minutes, Venice's waterways gave way to the open expanse of the mainland. Milton watched as the causeway stretched behind them, the lagoon fading into the distance. The scenery shifted rapidly to the flat, marshy plains of Veneto, dotted with clusters of red-roofed farmhouses and church spires. In the distance, the snow-capped peaks of the Dolomites stood stark against the duck-egg-coloured sky.

Milton went to the buffet car and ordered an espresso, then turned his attention to Moretti. He was a Platinum affiliate, responsible for the cryptocurrency's northern Italian network, a man of considerable charm—if the reports were to be believed—and very wealthy. It was possible that Moretti would be the end of Milton's involvement with the business. He could choose to limit his aims: insist that Marco and the others be reimbursed for the money they'd invested, that Moretti would promise not to recruit any others, and then pass on everything he'd learned to Isobel and leave her to fix the rest.

Milton knew, though, that there was a chance—a *good* chance, knowing himself as he did—that that *wouldn't* be enough.

Moretti was senior, and Milton might be able to pressure him to reveal the person or persons on the rungs of the ladder above him. Isobel had made it plain that the misery TrueCoin had brought to the men and women Milton had met in Venice was not limited to that city, nor even to Italy. And Milton had nowhere to be and nothing else to do; he knew he'd be tempted to tug on the string and follow wherever it took him.

He knew, too, that it might not be as easy as finding Moretti and frightening him. The photos he'd found online suggested he was soft—pampered and insulated by his success—but a man with his kind of resources and plenty to lose might decide to invest some of his ill-gotten gains in security so he could hold onto them for longer. Men like Moretti rarely climbed to their rarefied heights without knowing how to protect themselves. Milton had no illusions about that and wasn't about to make assumptions about what he might encounter when he arrived. He'd be careful: hope for the best while expecting the worst.

The train sliced through the countryside. Milton took a sip of his espresso and watched as, outside, the landscape began to shift. Rolling vineyards stretched out in neat rows, their vines still bare in the winter chill. There were stone farmhouses and rust-coloured barns before the terrain became more varied as they entered Emilia-Romagna. Low hills rose in the distance, the slopes dotted with olive groves and cypress trees. The train passed through small towns built around medieval bell towers. He caught glimpses of daily life as the train sped past: an old man tending to his garden, a mother herding her children toward a school bus, a cyclist pedalling hard along a country road.

Milton planned the questions he wanted to ask Moretti: how TrueCoin was structured; who pulled the strings; where the money had gone; and, most importantly, how their victims could get it back.

28

The train began its descent into Tuscany, and Florence came into view, its skyline dominated by the Duomo and the medieval towers that stood around it. They pulled into Santa Maria Novella station on time, their arrival announced with a polite chime. Milton gathered his belongings and hopped down onto the platform. He walked toward the exit, merging with the stream of travellers heading into the city.

The street outside the station buzzed with life. Vespas weaved through the traffic, their riders bundled up against the cold; tourists consulted maps on their phones; church bells tolled.

Milton hailed a taxi and climbed into the back seat, giving the driver the address of Moretti's villa. The driver nodded, and they set off, winding through Florence's narrow streets and across the Arno River.

MORETTI'S ADDRESS was in Parigi, five kilometres outside the centre of the city. The road—Via della Luigiana—was narrow, and there were several moments during the drive where the taxi was forced to reverse in order to slide into a passing place so oncoming traffic could squeeze through.

Milton paid the driver, waited until he had driven away and then walked by the property. The villa was surrounded by orderly rows of olive trees and cypress-lined pathways. The estate was dominated by the residence: a large building constructed of local stone with a roof of red tile. Ivy crept up the walls, and weathered shutters framed arched windows overlooking the grounds. A smaller outbuilding had been built to the right of the villa; it was less polished than the main house and might have been used by staff or perhaps employed as a guesthouse. The grounds were well maintained: manicured hedges, flower beds bursting with colour, gravel paths. Milton saw the sparkling blue square of a swimming pool with the surrounding gardens sloping gently downward, leading to an orchard that stretched out toward the horizon.

There was money here.

Lots of money.

He looked for strengths and weaknesses. The gate at the entrance to the estate was equipped with an intercom and a small, discreet camera mounted above it. On the other hand, once he was inside the perimeter, the gravel path leading to the villa was flanked by tall cypresses that would offer natural cover to anyone approaching on foot. The high stone wall encircling the estate was topped with spikes, and Milton noted the faint network of wires strung along the top: most likely a motion-sensitive alarm system. Near the main building, concealed among the ivy, were additional cameras that panned slowly, covering the entrance and the surrounding grounds; there would be others he hadn't seen.

Moretti's caution was evident, but even the most carefully protected building had a weakness. It was just a matter of finding it. Milton had an idea how he might go about that: an estate agent's board had been attached to the wall, together with a website and a phone number. He took a picture of the board and then turned back the way he came, heading for the café he'd noticed as the taxi had brought him to the property.

29

Milton ordered an espresso and sipped it as he waited for the floorplan of Moretti's property to download to his phone. He'd visited the estate agent's website as soon as he was connected to the café's Wi-Fi, and the listing had provided him with as much as he had hoped.

The plan loaded, and he opened it. Milton imagined himself at the front door, picturing how it would open onto the spacious foyer. Two doors flanked the entrance, with a wide central hallway bisecting the main floor. To the left of the hallway was the 'Gathering Room,' a forty-by-thirty-foot area that likely served as the villa's main living space. It was connected to the terrace, which ran along the back of the house. Adjacent to that was the master suite. The dining room was on the opposite side of the gallery, connected to the kitchen and family room via a smaller corridor. The kitchen itself was tucked neatly into the corner of the house, with an adjoining breakfast room. There were other rooms —a gym, office, library and six bedrooms—but Milton doubted he'd have any need to visit them. The practical rooms—utility spaces and a large garage—sat to the far right, near the guest quarters.

Milton leaned back, taking another sip of his coffee.

Why was Moretti selling up? Biagi had said that the police were closing in on TrueCoin, and Milton knew from his own experience that civil claims were being prepared. The people behind the scam must've seen which way the wind was blowing and were getting ready to cut and run.

Milton reviewed the floorplan again and committed it to memory. He'd find somewhere to stay until it was dark, and then go out. The best way to get into the grounds was to go over the wall where it cut through the woody copse he'd seen on the satellite map, the trees offering both a way to scale the wall and cover from anyone who might be watching.

He put his phone in his pocket and had just taken out his wallet to order a second coffee when he saw movement from outside. A flash of neon green caught his eye as a cyclist dismounted just beyond the café's glass doors.

Milton recognised him immediately.

Riccardo Moretti.

He could barely believe it.

Moretti was wearing the aerodynamic Lycra of a serious cyclist, the fabric clinging tightly to his lean frame. His helmet dangled from the handlebars of a high-end road bike, the polished carbon-fibre frame gleaming in the light.

Milton reassessed his plan, deciding whether he ought to take his chance now.

Moretti stepped inside the café, his cleated shoes clacking against the tiles, and walked toward the counter. There was a sheen of sweat on his brow; his face was flushed from exertion. He ordered a bottle of water, a coffee and a pastry.

Milton kept his posture relaxed, his gaze only briefly flicking toward Moretti before turning back to his coffee. He was careful not to draw attention to himself, though his mind raced: this was an unusual stroke of luck and an opportunity.

Moretti waited for his order, paid for it and then took it out to the terrace.

Milton gave him a moment and then followed.

30

Milton had spent the last twenty minutes nursing his second espresso, ignoring Moretti as he lingered on the terrace of the café. Milton had picked a table in the corner, shaded by a striped awning that rippled in the cool afternoon breeze. The terrace was empty save for the table where Moretti was seated. Milton watched him with casual interest: Moretti was relaxed and at ease, drinking from the bottle of water and then taking out his phone to make a call.

Milton was close enough to eavesdrop; he opened Google Translate and activated the microphone, watching the screen as the device translated from Italian to English on the fly. Moretti was speaking to his estate agent and chiding him for the lack of progress on the sale of the villa.

"Didn't I make myself clear?" he said. "I *have* to sell. I'm leaving the country at the end of the month, and I need to have everything sorted out before then—and that most definitely includes getting rid of the house."

Milton waited until Moretti was off the phone and had leaned back in his chair, seemingly lost in thought. Milton stood, picked up his cup and saucer, crossed the terrace, and approached Moretti's table.

"Hello," Milton said in English. He pointed to the chair on the other side of the table. "Do you mind?"

Moretti frowned, his irritation immediate and unfiltered. "I'm sorry?"

Milton pointed again. "Is anyone sitting there?"

Moretti's English was good. "Are you serious? The terrace is empty. Sit somewhere else."

"I like this one," Milton said, pulling out the chair and lowering himself into it before Moretti could protest further.

"Che cazzo fai? Eh? Ma vaffanculo!"

Milton understood instinctively what the man was telling him to do but stayed where he was. He nodded his head in the direction of Moretti's parked road bike. "That yours?"

Moretti didn't answer, thrown by the question and Milton's insouciance.

Milton gestured again. "The bike. Is it yours?"

Moretti's irritation now carried a tinge of confusion. "Yes. Why?"

"What brand is it? Specialized?"

"No," Moretti said. "It's a Pinarello."

"Carbon fibre?" Milton asked, as if they were having a normal conversation, two old friends shooting the breeze.

"Yes."

"How much? Got to be ten thousand, at least."

"More than that," Moretti said, pride slipping through despite himself. He shook his head. "I'm not interested in a conversation. Either you go somewhere else, or I go and get the owner."

"And tell him what?" Milton asked, leaning back. "That I'm sitting next to you? What's wrong with that?"

Moretti leaned forward, his voice low and tight. "I don't know who you are, and I don't like your attitude. Please—I'm asking nicely—go away."

Milton didn't move. "No."

"Fine," Moretti said, standing. "If you won't leave, I will."

Milton stared at him. "Sit *down*, Riccardo."

Moretti's face froze. "How do you know my name?"

"I know more than that. Sit down."

"Who are you?"

Milton didn't answer. He'd roleplayed the line he would take with Moretti on the train, but had imagined he would have had a little longer to refine it. Never mind; if he did a good job now, he could avoid the risk of having to break into the villa altogether.

He leaned forward. "You've made millions from True-Coin, but you've been a sloppy boy. You've left a trail. Bank transfers, shell companies, offshore accounts. I didn't have to try hard to find it. How long do you think it'll take the Guardia di Finanza to build a case that puts you in prison for the next twenty years? Or worse, extradite you somewhere that doesn't have Florence's charm? You know they're coming for you. That's why you're selling your house."

"I haven't done anything wrong," he protested. "True-Coin isn't—"

"—isn't a scam?" Milton spoke over him. "Come on. Don't insult my intelligence. That'll irritate me, and I wouldn't recommend that."

"You can't say it's a scam. It isn't. It's legitimate."

Milton stared him out. "I was in Venice before I came here. I met some people who invested in TrueCoin, and they were telling me they weren't able to cash out. Is that right?"

"The exchange," Moretti said, falling back onto an obviously pre-prepared excuse. "It's not quite ready to go live, but when it does, there'll be a market where they can sell. If they got in early enough, they'll make a fortune."

"No, Riccardo. That's just TrueCoin trying to buy time. The people I met saw through that a long time ago."

Moretti's eyes darted toward the café's entrance, as if calculating how quickly he could get up and leave. Milton followed his gaze but remained unbothered. "Don't be silly," Milton said. "You're wearing cleats."

He found a little chutzpah. "And what would happen if I got up anyway?"

"Are you asking would I hurt you? I might."

"The police—"

"Are miles away, and I'll have broken both your legs and wrapped that carbon frame around your neck before the owner picks up the phone." Milton kept his stare on him. "But it's not really me you want to be worried about, is it? It's obvious there's a lot of money involved here. Millions. Right?"

Moretti didn't answer.

"I know," Milton said. "It's not millions. It's more than that."

Moretti stared at him, his jaw clenching and unclenching.

"I've been to your house. I've seen the listing. Five million. That's a lot of coins."

Moretti's jaw clenched. He looked around the terrace and saw that it was still empty except for them. "What do you want?"

"A few things. We can start with Valentina Rossi."

"Don't know her."

"Never met her?"

"I've met her," he said. "Obviously I've met her."

"Did you see her this week?"

"After the seminar—very briefly. I had a drink with her at the hotel. But I don't know her. I couldn't introduce you to her, if that's what you want."

"How do you contact her?"

"I don't," he said.

"You should probably start being more helpful. I'm trying to be patient, but it's not one of my strengths."

"I don't—"

"Who do you contact if you need something?"

"The office."

"And where's that?"

"Rome."

"They closed the Rome office down. Try again."

"There's another office."

"Where's that?"

"Belgrade."

"Go on."

"No." Moretti pushed his chair back and made to stand. "That's it. Are we done?"

Milton glared at him, hard, and, just as he expected, Moretti froze. "'Are we *done*?' We haven't even started. Sit your arse down *now*."

Moretti did as he was told.

"How do I find the office?"

"I have no idea. I've never been there. I just have a number to call. And, no, I don't have it with me."

"Where is it? The villa?"

"Yes."

"You can give it to me later, then."

"What?"

"When I come to see you tonight."

He closed his eyes. "I can't do that. I—"

"The other thing I want," Milton interrupted, "the main

thing, the thing that'll get me off your back, is for you to contact the people you've recruited and offer them a full refund."

"Don't be—"

Milton quietened him with an upraised palm. "I just want you to offer it to them. They might not want to take you up on it, but at least it'll be their choice."

"Do you know how many people I've brought in? How many invested? And how much they've put in?"

"Like I said—I've seen your house. I'm sure it's a lot."

"It'll bankrupt me."

"Would it? Never mind. At least you won't be in prison, and your legs won't be broken."

"This is crazy. You're crazy."

Milton smiled. "You wouldn't be the first person to say that about me."

"Is that it, then? That's *all* you want?"

"One more thing and then I'll let you get back to enjoying your ride. There's one investor I spoke to who I know wants his money back. His name is Marco Caruso. He gave you thirty thousand euros that he couldn't afford, and he hasn't been able to sell his coins and get out. He has cancer, Riccardo, and his wife is ill. You're going to buy his coins back off him. I'll make it easy for you, too—you can give me the money, and I'll deliver it."

"How do I know he's given you permission to act on his behalf?"

"You're going to have to trust me on that."

"I don't have that kind of money on me," he protested.

"But I'm sure you've got the money at home. Like I said —I'll be coming around tonight anyway. I'll pick it up then."

Moretti muttered a curse. "This is ridiculous."

Milton eyed him. "Thirty thousand in cash. Nine o'clock. Is that going to be okay?"

Moretti looked as though he saw a way out and decided not to make things any more difficult than they already were. "Fine. Whatever."

"Good," Milton said with another smile. "You can go now. I'll see you later—nine o'clock."

31

Moretti hurried back to his bike, slid back into the saddle and clipped one of his shoes to the pedal. He pushed off, clipped the other shoe into place, and accelerated away. He had planned to continue the ride for another fifty kilometres, going out as far as Ponticelli before heading back, but the encounter with the man in the café meant that was impossible. He'd run into aggrieved investors before, but this guy wasn't like them. There'd been something about him that gave Moretti reason to believe that he meant what he said and that he wasn't making empty threats. There was something about him that would have him lose sleep.

Moretti was not as brash as some of the other affiliates. He was more successful than all of them, but that was more down to the ease with which he was able to persuade people to trust him than any force of personality. He thought of Luigi and Stefano, two of the Silvers he'd recruited way back at the start, and how flashy they were, making ostentatious shows of their success and suggesting—as explicitly as they possibly could—that similar success awaited investors brave enough to get into TrueCoin now. Moretti had the office in Venice, but that was a subtle tool that quietly suggested success rather than the in-your-face bling that the others flaunted.

That attracted attention, and Moretti wanted attention like a hole in the head.

He was a worrier, too, and whereas the others gave the impression that they were bulletproof, Moretti had always feared that something like this would happen. He'd long expected a knock on the door from the police; that would have been bad, but he had the best lawyer in Florence on retainer in anticipation of needing her to come to his defence.

This man, though, offered a different kind of danger. Angelina and her team could do nothing to insulate him against someone who looked like he was capable of following through on his violent threats, and now Moretti was going to have to do something that he'd always been loath to do: he was going to have to call Niko and ask for help.

He headed home, pushing hard and unable to stop the occasional backward glance in the fear that the man might be following behind. He wasn't—or at least Moretti didn't think he was—but when he arrived back at the house, he was covered in sweat and his heart was hammering, and not all because of exertion. He wrenched his feet out of the pedals, swung his leg over the saddle and coasted up to the gate. He tapped in the code and pushed the bike up the drive. He would have preferred to have showered to get the sweat off him, but his mind wouldn't stop racing, and he knew he'd only be able to relax once he had spoken with Niko and been told what to do.

He went into his study, picked up the Perspex social

media counter that displayed how many Instagram followers he had—sixty thousand—and peeled away the tape that fixed the scrap of paper to the bottom. Niko's number was written on it; he'd decided not to put it into his phone for fear that there would eventually be some sort of investigation into TrueCoin and needing to keep open the possibility of denying that he'd ever been in contact with him or any of the senior team.

He opened his desk drawer and took out a new burner SIM. He removed the SIM from his phone, replaced it with the new one, and dialled the number.

"Hello?"

"Niko? It's Riccardo."

"Riccardo?"

"Moretti," he said, ignoring the quick flash of disappointment that Niko didn't recognise him. "I saw you and Valentina in Venice."

"Riccardo," Niko said with a warmth that was obviously manufactured. "How are you?"

"Not great."

"What is it?"

"Something's wrong," Moretti said, running a hand through his damp hair. He glanced toward the window, his paranoia spiking as he scanned the empty driveway. "Someone threatened me this morning."

"Really?" Niko's voice remained calm, but the faint edge in his tone betrayed his concern. "Who?"

"A man. I don't know his name, but he was at a café near my villa. He wasn't Italian, probably English or American. He said he knows about TrueCoin."

There was a long silence on the other end of the line, broken only by the faint hum of static. When Niko spoke again, his voice was colder. "Knows what?"

"He mentioned Valentina—I think he wants to meet her."

"And you told him that was impossible."

"Of course I did." Moretti's words spilled out in a rush. "He has some kind of connection to the investors in Venice."

"Police?"

"No—at least I don't think so."

"Why not?"

"Because he threatened to break my legs."

"Did he hurt you?"

"No, but he made it clear that he could. He wants me to refund everyone from Venice. Everyone. He wants me to contact them and make the offer."

"You can't do that."

"I know I can't. It's millions, Niko. *Millions!*"

"No, Riccardo. That's not why you can't—you can't because you'd be setting a precedent, and we can't have that."

"I'm not going to do it."

"Good."

"There's one investor, though—one of the ones from Venice. The man said he wants me to buy his coins back."

"Who?"

"Marco something. I can't remember his name."

"It's the same principle," Niko said. "Someone cashes out and everyone thinks they can cash out. They can't. *He* can't. You're not doing that. How did you leave it?"

"He says he's coming to my house tonight." There was a pause, and Moretti looked out of the window again. "Niko? Are you there?"

Niko's silence stretched out for longer, and Moretti could feel his pulse pounding in his ears as he waited for a response.

When it came, it was measured and almost clinical. "You were right to call me. This man, whoever he is—I'll sort it out. You did the right thing."

Moretti swallowed. "I'm not cut out to handle someone like this."

"You won't have to. We will."

"What does that mean?"

"I'll send someone," Niko said. "He'll deal with him. What time is he coming?"

"Nine."

"Stick to your routine. Let him come. When he does, the man I'm going to send will handle the rest."

Moretti's hand trembled as he gripped the edge of his desk. "I don't know. I can't be involved with anything like that."

"Like what?" Niko said, his voice clipped. "He'll be taken somewhere for a conversation, we'll find out what we need to know, show him it's not a good idea to make threats, and that'll be that. He might get a slap around the face, but nothing more. This is a business, Riccardo. We're businessmen. We're not *barbarians*."

Moretti nodded. "Okay. I know. All right."

"Good." Niko's tone softened. "You've done well to bring this to me. Do whatever it was you were going to do this afternoon. Relax. Enjoy your money. Pretend this never happened."

The line went dead before Moretti could respond. He set the phone down on the desk, his hands shaking so badly he nearly dropped it. The room felt colder, the shadows deeper. The Instagram counter clicked over as another person followed him. He stared at the white numbers on the red background, a hollow reminder of the persona he'd built for himself, the reach he'd built, the money he'd made.

His success had been a source of pride, but now it just made him feel vulnerable.

He thought of the man at the café, his calm demeanour doing nothing to mask the threat of violence. And now Niko's words echoed: Moretti had heard what he'd said about what they would do—and what they wouldn't do—but he didn't believe it. Niko was suave and professional and polished, and the idea of him indulging in violence was difficult to credit, but Moretti had seen some of the men who came with him to the events: big men who looked out of place in the suits they wore with their shaven heads and dead-eyed stares. He'd always wondered why they needed muscle like that on the payroll, why a cryptocurrency firm would need employees who would have looked at home at one of Giorgia Meloni's rallies, and now he had an answer.

And it terrified him.

He rose from his chair and walked to the window. Outside, the cypress trees swayed gently in the breeze. He'd always known there would be a price to pay for the riches his involvement with TrueCoin had granted him, but he'd never imagined the bill would come due so suddenly, or with the promise of violence.

32

Dragomir was out for a hike in the mountains near the villa. It had been bitterly cold when he woke that morning—ten below—but the sun was bright now, and the frost glittered on the ground like glass. The air was bracing and fresh, cutting through the thick wool of his scarf as he stepped outside. He'd eaten a quick breakfast of strong coffee and a warm pita stuffed with *kajmak*, a rich Serbian cream cheese, before rounding up his dogs—two mastiffs, Miloš and Vuk—and setting off.

He had no firm destination in mind, only the need to clear his head and stretch his legs. The dogs bounded ahead of him, their breath steaming in the cold morning air. The climb was steep, the rocky path slick with frost, but Dragomir relished the challenge. The mountains had always been a place of solace, a contrast to the chaos that had defined much of his life. He eventually reached the tor, a jagged outcrop of rock that offered a panoramic view of the plateau below. He stood there, hands on hips, and looked down at everything he had built.

The villa looked almost serene from up high, nestled

into the rugged landscape as if it had always been there. The property had been completed only six months earlier, a project that had cost him twenty million euros and an endless series of logistical headaches. Getting the materials and heavy equipment up the mountain had been a monumental task, even in the milder weather of spring and summer. Now, with the snow and ice, it would have been impossible.

But the effort had been worth it. The place was everything he'd ever wanted: a fortress of luxury and security, perched on a plateau so remote that it felt like the edge of the world. The main villa was all clean lines and glass, blending seamlessly with the natural surroundings. Inside was a haven: Italian marble, bespoke furniture, and technology that meant it could run entirely off-grid if needed. There were guest houses, a gym, a swimming pool that was heated year-round, and a helipad for when he needed to make a quick exit or host visitors who demanded discretion.

Beyond its aesthetic and practical appeal, the villa was a statement: a declaration of his success and his rejoinder to anyone who'd ever doubted him. It was a reminder that he had clawed his way to the top.

Miloš barked; he was hungry.

Dragomir lingered a little longer, letting the cold seep into his bones, before finally turning back.

∼

HE'D COVERED ten kilometres by the time he returned, and he was as hungry as his dogs. He'd called the kitchen when he was a mile away and told them to prepare filet mignon: one for him and one each for the hounds. He took a quick shower and changed and went down to the dining room; his steak was waiting for him.

"Mr. Jovanović," said Vasko, his assistant, "Mr. Petrović called—he says he needs to talk to you."

"I can speak to him now," he said.

Dragomir couldn't remember where Niko was; somewhere in Italy, he thought. He was probably calling about how things were going.

Vasko returned with a phone. "He's on the line."

Dragomir took the phone and put it to his ear. "Niko, where are you?"

"Rome. Just arrived from Venice."

"And?"

"Three hundred new investors—mostly mid-tier."

"How much?"

"Just over twelve million."

"Twelve?" Dragomir was disappointed. "Less than I expected."

"It's Venice," Niko said, trying not to sound defensive. "The northern Italian market isn't what it used to be, but they're still biting."

"What about Valentina?"

"I think she's starting to struggle."

"Fuck, Niko. She needs to be on her game. We have limited time left—we need to squeeze as much out of it as we can."

"We've handled it before," Niko replied. "We know what she's like. She has ups and downs. Her presentation is changing—she actually made the suggestions. I've got the team refining the language for tonight."

"I want more than twelve. It's been months since we were in Rome."

"Three months," Niko corrected defensively.

"Are you trying to set my expectations?"

"Not at all. It'll be good. I'm confident. Ticket sales have been strong. They'll be throwing money at us."

"They'd better."

Dragomir knew Niko would hear that as an unspoken threat, and didn't mind that at all. Fear was healthy. Fear kept people on their toes.

"Don't worry," he said. "I'm on it."

The two of them had known each other for years, their connection forged in the underworld of Balkan conflicts during the nineties. Dragomir had been a warlord, thriving in the never-ending vortex of bloodshed, building his influence through violence and a network of lucrative smuggling operations. Niko, a former law student from Belgrade with an eye for opportunity, had crossed Dragomir's path while looking for a way out of the crumbling economy and into something more profitable. Dragomir started him on small things—running messages and handling logistics—but he quickly proved his value. His charm and sharp mind made him a natural for more sophisticated operations, and it wasn't long before he became Dragomir's right hand.

Niko had suggested the scheme that had become True-Coin, but it was Dragomir's investment—of time and money and, where it was needed, muscle—that had turned it into what it was. While Niko handled the day-to-day—the events and the recruitment that kept the money flowing—Dragomir loomed above it all. Their relationship was a delicate balance of mutual need. Niko knew his value: he was the one who kept the machine running. But Dragomir pulled the strings.

"I was calling about something else," Niko went on, choosing his words with evident care. "*Someone* else, actually. Riccardo Moretti."

"Why do I know the name?"

"He's a Platinum."

"And?"

"And he called me this afternoon in a panic. Says there's someone threatening him—a man who's with the investors in Venice who want their money back."

"That can't happen."

"I know. I told him."

"So?"

"It brought some things into focus. Moretti's been a problem for a while. He's been skimming. Underreporting contributions from investors."

"How much?"

"Enough. He recruits investors—the bigger fish. He convinces them to put in a hundred thousand, records part of it—maybe tells us it was fifty—and pockets the difference."

Dragomir laughed. "And he thought we wouldn't realise?"

"I know—it's stupid. One of the Golds got nosy, noticed his commission payouts didn't match what he expected based on the contributions he'd brought in and started asking questions. I audited Moretti's records. It didn't take much to see he was playing us. He probably thought we wouldn't bother checking the numbers as long as he kept the money flowing, and for a while, he was right. But it's been going on for months. I let it slide on account of the fact that he recruits so many people."

"That was a mistake."

"Do you know how much money he's made us? There are only half a dozen affiliates worldwide who've made more. Letting it slide was pragmatic, but it wasn't as if I took my eye off him. He's just been on borrowed time—"

"—which has now run out. It also makes me wonder about his loyalty. If this man who saw him puts the pressure on..." Dragomir tutted. "I'm not sure I'd trust Moretti to keep his mouth shut."

"I agree," Niko said.

"Vuković is still in Venice." He refilled his glass. "I'll call him. What do we know about the other man?"

"Moretti didn't have much to say about him. Not Italian—thinks he was British or American. Asked questions about Valentina, the affiliates, the investors. Moretti said he thought he was dangerous."

"I'll speak to Davor." He sipped his wine.

"Is everything ready for when we pull the plug?"

"It's all good," he said. "You keep the money coming in. I'll make sure we get to spend it without looking over our shoulders."

33

Vuković's eyes were fixed on the road ahead. It was quiet in the car. He'd listened to his Duolingo lesson for the first hour, but that had finished, and he hadn't really got the appetite for another. His English was getting better, he thought. He wasn't ready to sit the exam yet, but it wouldn't be long. He already spoke several languages, and improving his English would be sensible in the event that Dragomir sent him to take care of business in America again. Learning languages was a useful distraction, and given that his life was spent in hotel rooms and on the road, like this, it was an excellent way to fill the time.

He'd left Venice an hour ago, the city's lights receding in the rear-view mirror as he sped toward Florence. The GPS said it was another two hours; plenty of time to get there before the meeting at nine.

Dragomir had called him earlier and told him that Isobel Turner would have to wait. An issue had arisen in Florence, and it was important that he attend to it quickly.

Two new targets had taken her place.

Riccardo Moretti and the man who was going to visit him at his villa.

Vuković would deal with Moretti first. He'd speak to him, find out what he needed to know, then do what needed to be done.

And then he'd turn his attention to the other man, whoever he was.

His lip curled at the thought of Moretti. He'd never met him, but he'd met men like him. Dragomir had told him what he'd done. Thieving, from them? That was stupid. He was weak and desperate, with no spine, and Vuković despised him for it.

Dragomir didn't tolerate disloyalty.

Neither did Vuković.

Vuković glanced at the GPS again. He would arrive at Moretti's villa after dark. It ought to be a simple enough thing to slip inside and handle Moretti quickly. He would do that and then wait for the other man, the one Moretti had told Niko was dangerous.

That might well be, but the man wouldn't know Vuković was there.

And Vuković was dangerous, too.

He raced by a road sign that announced five kilometres to Bologna. There was a little additional traffic on the road, but it was still quiet. He'd been able to cruise at the speed limit without needing to use the fast lane. He wasn't rushing —there was no need—and he was quite happy not to do anything that might attract the attention of a bored traffic cop.

Vuković and Dragomir had a long history together. Vuković owed him everything. Dragomir had plucked him from obscurity and given him a purpose. Vuković respected him and even feared him a little, though he'd never admit it.

Dragomir had an uncanny ability to see through people, to understand their motivations and weaknesses, and to detect lies. It was what made him so dangerous and so successful. And it was why Vuković had pledged his loyalty to him, years ago, without hesitation.

He had grown up in a small village in Bosnia, the son of a factory worker and a schoolteacher. Life had been hard but honest until the war came, and everything went to shit. He was only a boy when the soldiers arrived, burning houses and dragging families into the streets. They shot his father because he wouldn't cooperate. His mother was taken away, and he never saw her again. Vuković had been fifteen and would have been shot, too, so he fled into the hills and lived on his wits for six months until he was sixteen and able to join one of the paramilitary groups.

The war shaped him, hardened him, stripped away whatever innocence he might have had, but, when it ended, Vuković was left adrift. He was a soldier without a war, and he had no future until Dragomir found him. He'd been working as a mercenary in the Balkans when they met, taking jobs from anyone who could pay. Dragomir had approached him with an offer: a way out of the chaos into something bigger and more permanent. It wasn't just the money that appealed to Vuković, though there was plenty of that. It was the sense of purpose, the structure, the clarity of knowing exactly where he fitted into things.

Dragomir had seen his potential and shaped it, honing him into what he needed.

And Vuković had never looked back.

He glanced at the GPS again: another hour.

The anticipation settled in his chest, a familiar weight that he'd learned to channel into focus.

He thought about the future. He had no illusions about

his life or his role. Men like him didn't retire. They didn't get a pension and a house by the sea. His work would end the way it always did: with violence.

Fun while it lasted.

Vuković glanced at the clock on the dashboard. Almost there. He looked over to the passenger seat and the satchel that held his weapons and tools: a silenced pistol, a knife, a small lock-picking kit.

A sign for Florence flashed by: ten kilometres.

Vuković shifted in his seat.

Nearly time.

34

Moretti lay on his back in the gloom of his bedroom and stared up at the ceiling. He got up, went to the French door and opened it, stepping out onto the balcony and looking out over the dusky countryside. The faint chirp of crickets, the occasional rustle of wind through the olive trees in the grove... it should've been soothing, but it wasn't. He'd been unable to still his mind, and his thoughts raced, chasing around and around and around in endless circles. He looked at his watch: coming up to eight. Niko had said he was going to send someone to help with his problem, and he ought to be here soon. Moretti hoped he'd know what to do.

The meeting with the man in the café had worried him; Niko's reaction had worried him even more. He'd replayed both conversations, every word dissected and analysed, but it didn't help. The man in the café was unknown to him. He'd been so calm, as if the conversation they were having was entirely routine. He hadn't raised his voice, but the threat was unmistakeable. There was something about him that said he'd do exactly what he promised. And those eyes... Moretti had never seen eyes so cold. The man's stare had terrified him more than anything he'd said.

It wasn't just him, though. He'd known Niko would be irritated, but had hoped that he would have said something to ease his fears. He hadn't. He'd been as urbane as ever, but Moretti wouldn't allow his tone to distract him from what was very obviously a warning.

It didn't take long for his thoughts to go from Niko to Dragomir.

Moretti had never spoken to him directly—as far as he knew, almost no one had—but his reputation went before him. If Dragomir thought for a second that Moretti's actions might jeopardise TrueCoin, there'd be no conversation and no negotiation. He'd heard the rumours of what happened to people who stepped out of line; he'd be lucky to get away with just a broken bone or two.

And what if they knew about the money he'd been skimming?

Bringing unnecessary attention to himself was excruciating.

The thought of what they'd do to him if they found out about *that*...

The first time he'd kept more money than he'd been entitled to had been a complete accident. He'd been sick to his stomach when he realised he'd paid himself more than he was due, and had spent the next week terrified that his mistake would cause him serious trouble. He'd almost decided to come clean and tell Niko what had happened when he saw that they hadn't noticed. He could guess why: there was so much money flooding into the business that it would be almost impossible to notice that he'd kept the odd percentage point more than he was entitled to.

The next month's accounting had come around, and

he'd caught himself thinking that there was no harm in taking a little more. They hadn't noticed the first time, he told himself, and nothing had changed. They wouldn't notice a second time or a third. He'd persuaded himself that it would be fine, and even though his sleep was disturbed by the prospect of what would happen if he was found out, he'd even started to justify it to himself: look at how much value he brought to the business, he told himself. Would they really argue over a few additional thousands?

And so the pattern had been set.

Moretti had been inflating his commission for six months and, with every passing month, had grown a little braver. Ten thousand had become twenty and then fifty and then a hundred. His accumulated earnings had swollen by half a million, and he was feeling more confident about the future than might've been the case given the turbulence the business was experiencing. He'd insulated himself, the money had been salted away in hidden accounts all across the world, and he'd formulated an escape plan that would spirit him away from Italy if the heat became too much.

He went downstairs to the kitchen and switched on the coffee machine. He looked at it and realised, with a bitter smile, that the device had been the last thing he'd treated himself to before getting involved with crypto. His career had been comfortable once; it had been boring. He'd worked in finance in Milan, managing portfolios for clients who wanted steady returns with minimal risk. It wasn't glamorous, but it had been safe and predictable. He probably would have stayed in the job, repeating the same day over and over again, but then Mario had called him with a proposition. He was an old friend from university, one of those acquaintances with whom he'd kept in touch and with whom he might meet for a beer once or twice a year and send a card to at Christmas. He'd just returned from a conference in Rome where he'd seen Valentina Rossi present TrueCoin to a capacity crowd of enthusiastic early adopters. The pitch had been flawless, Mario said; it'd be a revolutionary cryptocurrency, backed by a proprietary blockchain, with unlimited growth potential. The returns promised were astronomical. Mario had gotten in early, and he wanted Moretti to join him.

He'd been sceptical. Moretti understood enough about finance to know that anything offering guaranteed returns was almost always too good to be true. But Mario had been insistent, and the numbers he showed Moretti were compelling. The first wave of affiliates was raking in money, and the potential seemed limitless. Moretti had hesitated, but the allure of wealth—and the fear of being left behind—had ultimately been too strong. He'd joined as an affiliate and quickly rose through the ranks, deploying his polish and financial acumen to recruit investors by the dozens. His existing client list was perfect; he'd filleted it to pick those with an appetite for risk and pitched to them; they'd all said yes, so he'd worked his way down to those who were a little more cautious. He could remember the slide in his presentation that determined whether they'd take the bait or not; it was a graph, showing a vertiginous diagonal climb that was almost vertical, followed by a gentle tapering out. The slide showed the anticipated growth for investors who laid down a thousand euros now: five thousand in six months, twenty thousand in a year, fifty thousand in eighteen months. He was receiving average investments of fifty thousand, but some of his whales were laying out ten times that.

He'd made millions, more money than he'd ever dreamed of, but the cost was becoming unbearable. The constant pressure to recruit, the whispers about investigations from the Guardia di Finanza, the gnawing fear that the whole edifice could collapse at any moment... it was beginning to be a little too much.

Yes, he thought. Maybe the morning's unpleasantness was confirmation that his plan was well-timed; now was the time to go.

He took his coffee and went out onto the terrace, looking out at the wide expanse of his property. The olive grove stretched out for acres, the waning sunlight catching the leaves. He loved his villa, but he'd have to leave it behind. He couldn't risk staying in one place, not with the kind of people he was dealing with. He'd been thinking about the Caymans. Somewhere with lots of sun and the kind of financial regime that wouldn't ask questions.

The intercom buzzed.

Shit.

He'd forgotten the time.

He went back inside to the panel and looked at the screen. There was a man standing by the gate, his face lit faintly by the dim security light overhead. The glow cast sharp shadows across his angular face, accentuating high cheekbones and a square jaw dusted with stubble. His dark hair was slicked back, and he wore a black jacket zipped high against the cool night air. He glanced toward the camera, not directly but close enough that Moretti felt his stomach tighten.

He hesitated, his finger hovering over the button that would allow him to speak. He considered ignoring it but knew better. Niko had promised to send someone to help; this must be him.

He pressed the button. "Hello?"

"Signor Moretti," the man said, "can you let me in?"

"Who are you?"

"A friend."

Moretti swallowed hard. "Give me a moment."

His hand trembled as he disabled the motion sensors and opened the gate. The sound of a car engine filled the night, growing louder until headlights cut through the gloom. The car rolled up the drive and stopped just outside the front door.

A man stepped out. His expression was unreadable.

Moretti opened the door, forcing a smile that he hoped didn't look as strained as it felt. "Thank you for coming."

"Not a problem."

"What's your name?"

"You can call me Vuković."

"I'm Riccardo."

"I know."

"Please—come in."

The man stepped inside. "You called Nikolai with a problem."

Moretti closed the door behind him. The man wasn't Italian and spoke with an Eastern European accent.

"I didn't mean to cause alarm," Moretti said. "I just thought it was important to report the situation."

"Of course."

"The man who spoke to me... he's serious."

Vuković nodded. "What exactly do you think he knows?"

"I told Niko."

"Tell me."

Moretti hesitated, choosing his words carefully. "Enough to make trouble. He asked about Valentina, about the affiliates, about the investors in Venice."

"He was fishing?"

"I don't think so—he knew things."

Vuković's expression didn't change, but Moretti could

feel the weight of his scrutiny. "And he says he will be visiting here?"

Moretti nodded his head. "Tonight. Nine."

Vuković took a step closer. "I'll deal with him. But first, we need to make sure your security is good. No surprises later."

Moretti felt a burst of relief. "Of course. Anything you need."

"Is anyone else here?"

"No. Just me."

"Good." Vuković glanced around the room. "Show me around the house."

Moretti led him down the hall, aware of Vuković's gaze on his back. As they entered his office, he remembered he had left out the paperwork from the latest transfer of funds to his offshore account. It was on the desk. He tried to ignore it, hoping that Vuković wouldn't see it or, if he did, wouldn't understand what it meant.

"Your office?"

"That's right."

Moretti's palms were damp as Vuković flipped on the light switch. Moretti walked to the desk, leaning forward slightly as if adjusting something, his movement blocking the papers from view. The transaction logs, neatly organised, were stacked next to the keyboard.

Vuković followed him into the room. His eyes swept over the space. Moretti had that feeling of guilt he had whenever he spoke to a police officer or someone else in authority; even if he hadn't done anything wrong, it still felt like he had. This time, though, he *had* done something. He'd stolen from them, and now he was getting ready to run. He was sure it must have been written all over his face, yet Vuković said nothing.

"Thank you—let's keep going."

Moretti's throat was dry. "The living room is this way."

Vuković went back outside and stepped aside so Moretti could lead the way.

Moretti stopped to switch off the light.

Vuković's hand moved to his jacket.

Moretti saw a glint of steel as Vuković drew a blade.

Moretti raised his hands in a feeble attempt to protect himself, but it was pointless. The first thrust found its mark, the blade sliding between his ribs.

He gasped, the pain sharp, his hands clutching at the wound as he staggered back.

Blood seeped between his fingers, warm and sticky.

He tried to speak—to beg—but no words came.

Vuković grabbed him by the collar to hold him in place and then thrust again. It was swift and final, the blade plunging into Moretti's heart. His body went limp, his knees buckling as he was carefully lowered to the floor.

Vuković knelt beside him, wiping the blade clean on Moretti's shirt. He rose to his feet, his expression unreadable.

The room blurred, the edges fading into darkness.

35

Milton spent the rest of the day killing time in Florence. He'd taken the first taxi he could find back into the city, and the driver had dropped him near the Ponte Vecchio, the ancient bridge always bustling with tourists. He stopped briefly at the Uffizi courtyard, glancing at the long line of visitors waiting to get in, then continued toward the Duomo. Its massive dome loomed overhead, but he didn't go in. He walked on, letting the rhythm of the city distract him while he mused on what he was going to do when he returned to the villa.

He stopped at a small trattoria for a simple lunch—ribollita and a glass of sparkling water—and then lingered over an espresso at the counter. His thoughts returned to Moretti. The man was weak, a braggart who'd made himself important—and rich—by preying on others.

Milton doubted he'd hold up under real pressure.

Dusk began to fall. Milton caught another taxi and gave the driver the villa's address. The trip out of the city felt different this time. The light was softer, the hills bathed in gold, but Milton felt a more definite sense of purpose. Resolution seemed possible, and once he'd achieved that—returned the money to Marco and the others and provided Isobel with the list of the affiliates and the other evidence he'd found—he'd make his way to wherever might be next. He might head south. He hadn't been to Sicily since Control had sent him to investigate the assassination of an agent, and that had been years ago. Somewhere warm. He wanted to feel the sun on his face.

The taxi wound through the narrow roads, and when they were close, Milton instructed the driver to stop and paid him before stepping out. He walked the rest of the way, his boots crunching on the gravel shoulder of the road.

The villa loomed ahead, even more picturesque in the dying light. The gate came into view, its ornamental lanterns making faint shadows across the gravel driveway.

Milton stepped forward, his boots crunching softly on the gravel path leading up to the gate. He pressed the button on the intercom and stood back slightly, his gaze flicking to the camera above him. He knew he was being watched.

The lock disengaged with a clunk, the motors buzzed, and the gates swung open.

36

Milton stepped through the gate and climbed the steps to the front door. Something felt off. The house was quiet. There was no movement, no sound of footsteps, nothing to suggest anyone was inside.

He reached for the doorbell but stopped short as the door swung open before he could press it.

The man who greeted him was not Moretti.

He was tall and broad-shouldered and filled the doorway. Milton had seen more than his fair share of tough guys, and this man—whoever he was—was definitely tough. A palpable sense of threat radiated from him.

"You're early," the man said. He spoke English, but his voice was accented: Eastern European, Milton thought.

Milton's eyes flicked to the man's hands: steady, relaxed, held down by his sides. No immediate sign of a weapon, but that meant nothing.

"I'm here to see Moretti."

"He's busy. He asked me to meet you instead."

Milton felt the welcome buzz of adrenaline. Whoever

this man was, he certainly wasn't an errand boy. There was a quiet menace to him, a predator's calm that Milton recognised. He was going to have to step carefully.

"I'm sorry," Milton said. "I don't think we've met. Who are you?"

"My name is Davor," he said. "I work for TrueCoin. Signor Moretti says you have some concerns about what he's been doing."

"That's right."

"I'd like to have the chance to address them. Please—come in."

He stepped aside and gestured for Milton to enter.

Milton hesitated, weighing his options. If this was a trap, his best chance of getting away in one piece was to turn back now. Going inside would make it much more difficult to withdraw. But his lack of familiarity with the man waiting just inside cut both ways. There was no way he could know anything about Milton, either.

And Milton *really* wanted to know who he was.

He smiled and stepped inside. The man—Davor—closed the door behind him.

Milton looked around, quickly taking in as much of the interior as he could. The villa was as opulent as he'd imagined: vaulted ceilings, elaborate light fixtures, polished stone that gleamed underfoot. But there was no warmth to it. It felt more like a stage set than a home.

The man leaned casually against the doorway. "What do you want with Moretti?"

"That's between me and him."

"But he isn't here. Maybe I can help. Your problem with TrueCoin—please, tell me about it."

Milton eyed him, making sure to keep a pace or two between them. "What do you do for them?"

"I help our members deal with difficult situations. Moretti called and said that you'd been threatening him. Is that true?"

"'Threatening' might be overegging it."

"Sorry?"

"Apologies—turn of phrase," Milton said. "I think he might have exaggerated what I said during our conversation."

"Really? He told me that you said he was going to have to repay one of our investors."

"That's right."

"It doesn't work like that. The man or woman—whoever it is you are representing—made their investment. They can't just cancel it."

"No," Milton said. "That's exactly what's going to happen."

"This investor—who is it?"

"Doesn't matter."

"And what are you? Husband? Brother? Father?"

"Someone who doesn't like seeing people ripped off—especially vulnerable people." Milton eyed him. "I get the feeling you're here to waste my time, Davor. Where's Moretti? When he's given me the money, I'll be gone."

"You need to tell me who this investor is."

"I don't think so."

Milton felt the old familiar prickle run up and down his back. He felt the adrenaline in his blood and the beating of his heart, faster and faster. He glanced left and right. The man didn't appear to be fazed by Milton's attitude. Most people would have found his manner disconcerting and been aware of the threat that he gave off; if this man had noticed, it didn't seem to have concerned him. Violence increasingly felt as if it might be unavoidable.

"Last chance," Milton said. "Tell me where he is."

Milton watched as Davor's posture changed: his eyes narrowed, his body shifted ever so slightly, his fists clenched.

The man shook his hand, and a flick knife that he must've kept hidden in his sleeve dropped into his palm.

37

Davor opened it with a flourish, the blade gleaming from the light overhead. Milton shifted his stance, fists clenched, already calculating. He'd fought men with blades many times before, but there was something about Davor's calm—almost casual—demeanour that was disconcerting.

He obviously wasn't a thug; more likely he was a professional.

He sent a quick slash toward Milton's ribs.

Milton stepped back, narrowly avoiding the blade, but Davor was already adjusting, pivoting and slashing upward.

Milton deflected the uppercut with his forearm, the blade grazing his sleeve, and countered with a jab to the man's face.

The punch landed, but Davor barely flinched.

Milton pressed forward, throwing a combination of rights and lefts, but Davor blocked each one easily.

He swivelled, catching Milton's wrist mid-swing and twisting it sharply. Pain shot up Milton's arm as the man used the momentum to drive him backward into a sideboard. The edge of the furniture dug into Milton's lower back, but he ignored it and lashed out with a knee into the man's midsection.

Davor blocked the knee with a downward slap of his free hand and shoved Milton away like he was nothing.

Milton stumbled but recovered quickly, grabbing a brass candlestick from the sideboard and swinging it in a wide arc.

Davor ducked, stepping inside Milton's guard and driving his shoulder into his chest.

The impact sent Milton sprawling to the floor, the candlestick clattering away. He tried to get up, but the man was on him too fast, his movements fluid and precise. He delivered a kick to Milton's ribs, the force of it rolled him onto his side, and he gasped for air.

Milton scrambled to his feet, his vision swimming, and threw a desperate punch.

Davor caught it again, yanking Milton's arm and pulling him into a headbutt.

Stars exploded behind Milton's eyes as he staggered back, barely keeping his balance.

Davor advanced, his knife flashing as he feinted left and lunged right. Milton managed to block the thrust with both hands, but the force of it drove him back into the wall.

He tried to retaliate, throwing his weight into the man in an attempt to knock him off balance, but it—like everything else he'd tried—had no effect. Davor gave a sharp twist and broke free, driving his knee into Milton's stomach. The air rushed out of his lungs, and he doubled over, vulnerable and exposed.

The man grabbed Milton by the back of his jacket and

hurled him across the room. Milton crashed into the edge of a desk, papers scattering to the floor and a lamp toppling off and smashing. He rolled just in time to avoid the knife plunging into the wood where his head had been moments before.

Milton clawed at the desk, pulling himself upright, but Davor was already there. He delivered a backhanded slap with the flat of the blade that sent Milton reeling, blood trickling from a shallow cut on his cheek.

Milton was outmatched and knew it.

Another slash.

Milton ducked, the blade slicing through the air inches above his head.

He looked left and right, searching for an escape, anything that could give him a chance.

The window.

Milton feinted a move to the left, drawing the man forward, then twisted sharply, driving his shoulder into his chest. It didn't knock him down, but it gave Milton just enough space to run.

Milton drove forward, arms raised to shield his face as he crashed through the glass.

He hit the sloped roof of the lower level with a bone-jarring thud, his momentum carrying him in a tumbling slide toward the edge. He scrabbled fruitlessly for purchase on the tiles and pitched over the side.

The fall to the ground was shorter than he'd feared, but the impact was still enough to drive the wind from his lungs and leave him sprawled in the gravel driveway, dazed and gasping.

He forced himself to his feet, his ribs aching, blood dripping from a dozen small cuts.

He staggered toward the cover of the olive trees.

The crack of gunfire shattered the still air, and a bullet whipped past Milton's ear, striking a trunk with a dull thud.

Milton ducked, zigzagging to make himself a harder target. Another shot rang out, this one closer, the snap of it slicing through the leaves beside him.

38

Milton glanced over his shoulder just long enough to see Davor stepping down from the front porch with a pistol steady in his hand.

He'd had a gun the whole time?

The man had been toying with him.

Jesus... what had he got himself into this time?

The gate was ahead, but it was shut. Milton cursed. It would take too long to climb, and Davor would shoot him down before he reached the top.

He veered to the left, toward the perimeter wall where the trees offered some cover.

Another shot rang out, the bullet kicking up gravel near Milton's feet.

He pushed harder, the urge to get clear overriding the pain from his ribs. He reached the wall and sprang up, his fingers scrabbling for a hold on the rough stone. He found a lip and then one of the spikes, using it as an anchor to pull himself up, his muscles screaming as he swung a leg over the top.

The next shot struck the stone near Milton's hand,

sending a shower of dust and chips into his face. Milton gritted his teeth, negotiated the spikes and dropped down on the other side, landing awkwardly in the dirt. The impact jolted his already bruised ribs, but he forced himself to move, scrambling to his feet.

He heard the hum of an engine before he saw the car. A red hatchback pulled up on the narrow road. The passenger door opened, and a man leaned out, his face obscured by the shadows.

"Get in."

Milton hesitated for half a second.

A quick glance over his shoulder sealed the decision: Davor had opened the gate and was running toward him.

Milton threw himself into the passenger seat just as the driver hammered down on the accelerator. The door swung shut behind him, the tyres screeching as the car surged forward. Milton barely had time to catch his breath before the man beside him turned his head, revealing a face hardened by experience.

"I'll be honest, Number One," the man said, his eyes flicking between Milton and the rear-view mirror. "You're about the last person I expected to see here."

Milton stopped. He recognised him but couldn't place him.

Davor had reached the road, his pistol raised, but the car was already too far away for a clean shot.

They sped through the winding countryside, the olive groves and stone walls blurring past. Milton slumped back in the seat, his chest heaving as the adrenaline began to ebb, leaving behind a sharp ache in his ribs and a burning in his lungs.

The driver turned to him again. "You don't remember me?"

Milton looked at him. He was of medium build and average height. Brown hair, a soft jawline and thick-rimmed glasses. He was unobtrusive and nondescript. Milton had worked with him once in Cairo, when he was in the Group; Milton had bailed him out of a mess he'd found himself in during an assignment. Milton remembered: his file noted his nickname—the Chameleon—on account of his knack for blending into the environment.

"Number..." he began, unable to remember.

"Eleven," he said.

"That's right. You were Ambrose when we met."

The man put his hand out across the cabin, and Milton shook it.

"Neither of us are in the Group now," he said. "I think we can dispense with the cloak and dagger. You're Milton."

He nodded.

"Charlie Cooper. Nice to meet you again. Looks like I was just in time."

39

The car sped away from the villa. Milton glanced in the side mirror, watching the distant glow of the house shrink behind them, then disappear altogether as they rounded a bend. Cooper drove with a focused intensity, his hands gripping the wheel tightly, his knuckles pale under the dim light of the dashboard. Milton was still buzzing with the adrenaline from the fight, and Cooper was concentrating on putting some distance between them and the man with the knife and the gun; for a moment, it was quiet save for the throb of the engine and the rush of the tyres on the road.

Milton adjusted the seatbelt across his chest.

Cooper broke the silence. "Are you going to tell me what you're doing here?"

His eyes flicked from the road to Milton, searching for an answer.

"I could ask you the same thing."

"You go first—I just saved your neck."

"The man who lives there—"

"Riccardo Moretti," Cooper said over him.

"Moretti," Milton said, nodding. "He scammed a lot of money out of some people I met in Venice."

"He's scammed a lot of money out of a *lot* of people."

"I'd gathered that."

"So what does that have to do with you?"

That was a good question. "I'm helping them."

"You're doing what?"

"How long were you in the Group for?"

"Long enough," Cooper said.

"But not as long as me."

"Not many people lasted as long as you."

"No." Milton gazed out of the window and tried to find the words to explain why he did what he did. "I was in for years. And I did... I did a lot I'm not proud of."

"You killed a lot of people," Cooper said. "There's no need for euphemisms. I'm just the same."

"Thing is... it messed me up. The guilt. I don't know how you deal with what they had us do, but I've been trying to make amends by helping those who can't help themselves."

"That's very noble."

"It's very self-serving, given that I do it to make myself feel less shitty, but I suppose putting right things that need to be put right is a useful side effect."

"I heard you had a crisis of conscience," Cooper said. "I heard it didn't go down well, either."

"If you mean did they try to kill me after I quit—yes, they did."

"And now?"

"And now we've reached an understanding. I keep a low profile; they leave me alone."

"Very nice."

"For now," he said. "How about you?"

"I didn't last much longer than you did. I took my eye off

the ball and nearly bought the farm. I was chasing a very bad man in Moscow, and the GRU decided it was time for me to go. Sprayed Novichok on my Starbucks coffee cup. I was lucky it didn't kill me outright—most people don't survive. I nearly didn't. A tiny dose, they said, but it was enough to put me in a coma for three weeks and wreck half my nervous system. I couldn't walk, couldn't hold a fork, couldn't even keep my eyes open for longer than a few minutes at a time." He paused, his expression hardening.

"By the time I woke up, Control had already decided I was done. Grounded me, obviously, offered me the chance to fly a desk, and I said no thanks." He shrugged. "It took months of rehab to get back to anything close to normal. I'm still not the man I was, but I'm alive, and I made use of that time. I had six weeks in hospital, and I used it setting myself up for what I was going to do next."

"Which is?"

"Corporate intelligence," he said. "I know—no shit, very original, but it fits my experience. People tend not to shoot at me quite as often as they used to, I can get a coffee without worrying if it'll kill me, and it pays well."

"With your own set-up?"

Cooper nodded. "I've got an office on Fleet Street. I work for other professionals, mostly—accountants, lawyers—looking for an edge they can use in whatever they're doing."

"And now?"

"What am I doing in Italy saving your arse, you mean? I'm working for a law firm. They've been hired by a very, very high-net-worth individual in London who was scammed for millions—literally *millions*—by these shysters." Cooper glanced over at Milton. "TrueCoin—how much do you know about it?"

"I know it's a big deal."

"That's underselling it. They've made billions, and I'm not kidding. They're saying this is the biggest fraud in history. It's one of those cases where the professionals are happy to wait to get paid and then charge a little extra."

"No win, no fee."

"Exactly—with a big uplift if they win. There'll be a lot to go around." He glanced over again. "Plus, who turns down the chance to come to Florence? The guy hired the lawyers, and the lawyers hired me. He's trying to bring them down—he's funding claims when they're slam-dunk winners. He uses the law to keep the pressure on while he collects the information that comes out of discovery and passes that over to the media. It's a crusade, and he's going to win. The end game is to hand a file over to the authorities to bring them down, but I wouldn't know about that—my job's to pull on the strings and unravel as much of it as I can."

Cooper pulled out to overtake a slower-moving car.

"Why were you watching Moretti?" Milton said.

"I've been looking at ways to get into the network, and Moretti's been teetering on the edge for a while. We're pretty sure he's been getting ready to make a run for it. I've been tracking very large deposits from his Italian accounts into accounts in the Caymans, and we think it's just a matter of time before he bolts. What about you?"

"Similar," Milton said. "I lucked out at his office in Venice, found a list of affiliates and decided I'd go through them, top to bottom, until I found out where he was. The first guy I saw gave me Moretti's address—I got the train and bumped into him this morning."

"He went out on his bike."

"That's when I saw him."

Cooper grinned. "He came back looking like he'd seen a ghost."

"That would've been me."

"Was that your first time at the villa?"

"No," Milton said. "I was there this morning."

"I only got here just before lunch. Must've missed you. Did you see anything inside the house when you went in just now?"

Milton shook his head. "Too busy trying not to get killed. The man—do you know who he is?"

"Actually, I do. His name is Davor Vuković. And I know you're good, Milton, but you were lucky. He's about the scariest man I've ever met."

They reached the outskirts of Florence.

"I've got a place in the city," Cooper said. "You want a beer? I'll tell you what I know."

40

Cooper had taken a room in a cheap hotel on the outskirts. When they arrived, he told Milton he had to make a call and that he'd meet him in the bar. Milton took his order and had a cool beer waiting for him when he eventually came down from his room.

Cooper gestured to Milton's glass. "What is *that*?"

"It's an orange juice and lemonade."

"You don't drink?"

"Not for years."

"Hangover from the Group?" He winced. "Sorry—pardon the pun."

"Yes," Milton said. "That and other things. The only thing that helped with the guilt was getting drunk."

"Until it didn't help anymore," Cooper said.

Milton eyed him. "How'd you deal with it?"

"Told myself the people they sent me after were bad people who had it coming."

"And when they weren't?"

"Tried not to think about that too much," Cooper said. "'That way madness lies.'"

"Thank you, Shakespeare."

Cooper raised his glass, Milton raised his, and they touched.

Milton watched as Cooper took a long sip of his beer. The men and women in the Group didn't really fit a profile, but most of them were drawn from the military. He remembered, from his reading of his file, that Cooper had been recruited directly from MI6. He didn't have the martial bearing that Milton had grown used to—the athletic builds, the squared shoulders—and, instead, had the understated demeanour of someone who preferred to remain in the background. His slightly dishevelled appearance and unassuming posture suggested someone who relied on his wits and adaptability rather than physical prowess, although Milton knew it would have been a fool who underestimated him.

He had mentioned being poisoned, and there were signs of how it had affected him: his skin had a pallid, almost sickly tone beneath the bar's dim lighting, and there was a slight tremor in his hand as he set the glass back down on the table. His movements had a subtle hesitation, as though his muscles were stiff or weakened. The sharp intelligence in his eyes remained, but it was dulled by something else: an underlying fatigue that came from more than just lack of sleep. Cooper might have survived the poison, but his body was still fighting its effects.

"So," Milton said, "what can you tell me?"

"I have someone on my team who used to be in Group Two. Very good at digging up stuff online for me."

"I have someone like that, too," Milton said, thinking of Ziggy.

Cooper cocked an eyebrow. "Is he as annoying as mine?"

"It'd be hard to be more annoying."

"But you put up with him because he's good."

"He's *very* good."

"Same. I asked my guy to keep an eye on Moretti's place. The police just sent a car. Davor wasn't there—surprise, surprise—but Moretti was. He'd been stabbed to death."

"Moretti had cameras," Milton said. "I'll be on them."

"No, you won't. The footage of you has been wiped from the drives—my little gift to you."

"Much obliged."

"Can't do anything much about prints and DNA, though. Are yours on file anywhere?"

"They were," Milton said, "but I was promised they'd be wiped after I finished up the last thing I did with the Group." He shrugged. "If they did that, and did a decent job, I might be okay. If not, I'll be moving on soon anyway."

"Things might get a little warmer for Vuković, though."

"He doesn't strike me as the sort who'd be particularly worried about that."

"No," Cooper said. "He isn't."

"You said you had something on him?"

"We were making progress with a programmer in Dubrovnik who'd been hired to build a fake exchange for TrueCoin—somewhere investors could buy and sell their coins, although it wouldn't work like they said it would. He decided he'd had enough and started posting on one of the forums. We tracked him down and persuaded him the right thing to do was to help us build our case. He agreed, said he'd hand over everything he had—code, emails, you name it. But two days later—the day before we were supposed to meet—he disappears. Vanishes. No calls, no emails, nothing."

"Inconvenient."

"Very. We pulled the camera footage from his doorbell

and found this." Cooper took out his phone, opened the gallery, and slid it across the table so Milton could look.

He glanced down. It was a still from a security camera, branded with the manufacturer's logo in the top right-hand corner. Two figures were visible. The first, a man dressed in a UPS uniform, stood at the front door, looking directly into the camera. The second figure lingered in the background, partially obscured by the edge of the frame, but caught in profile.

"Vuković got unlucky. Just happened to be in shot when the driver rang the bell."

Milton studied the second figure, trying to pick out any details, but the angle and lighting made it impossible. "Not much to go on."

"Swipe right."

Milton swiped and saw a different image: an official photo, sharp and clear, with the telltale blue background of an ID card. The man in the picture had harsh features, with a prominent nose and narrow, deep-set eyes. He wore a faint sneer, like he'd been irritated even during the few seconds it took to capture the photo.

"There he is—Vuković. We pulled all the details we could on him. Comes from Sijekovac, near Bosanski Brod in northern Bosnia, and he has quite the history."

Milton leaned back. "Go on."

"Vuković was a member of the White Wolves militia during the war in the Balkans. They weren't exactly subtle. Ethnic cleansing, scorched earth, executions. Vuković was *particularly* enthusiastic. So much so that the locals gave him a nickname. *Vukodlak*—the Serbian take on a werewolf—and if even half the stories about him are true, he's earned it."

Cooper took the phone. "He was picked up by the UN

toward the end of the war. There's a record of his capture, along with statements from witnesses who claim he led massacres in several villages. He was detained at The Hague for war crimes but released after a few years when the case against him fell apart. Witnesses mysteriously disappeared or changed their testimony, and the records from his unit went missing. After that, he went underground."

"Until now."

"Looks like he's TrueCoin's enforcer. They send him in when they want to scare someone or make a problem disappear. He enjoys it. There's a psychological profile from his time in custody. Textbook sadist. No remorse, no hesitation."

Milton studied the photo again, committing Vuković's face to memory. "Good to know."

Cooper put down his glass. "Tell me what you know about TrueCoin."

"I know it's a cryptocurrency scam. A pyramid scheme. I know a lot of people have lost a lot of money. Beyond that?" He shrugged. "I'm too old and set in my ways to be able to pretend to understand how it works."

"Want me to explain it?"

"It's fine," Milton said. "I got the basic introduction in Venice, and it didn't really do me any good. It doesn't matter if I know how it's all supposed to work. All I need to know is that it's run by thieves, and they've stolen money from people who can't afford it."

"Do you know where it came from?"

Milton shook his head.

"It's been going for a couple of years," he said. "As far as we can make out, it started in Rome."

"With Valentina?"

Cooper nodded. "She's always fronted it. You ever seen her speak?"

"Just the YouTube videos."

"She's impressive."

"Credible."

Cooper nodded. "Charismatic, smart, photogenic—exactly what they needed to sell the dream. We've been able to dig up quite a bit about her, but it's mostly surface, and there's a lot we haven't been able to corroborate. On paper, she's got the perfect backstory. Born and raised in Naples. Supposedly from a working-class family. Nothing unusual."

"Supposedly?"

"That's the thing—we've checked the official records: birth certificates, school enrolments, things like that. It all checks out, but it feels too... convenient. It's textbook—graduated from the University of Rome with a degree in economics, started working at a consultancy, and then suddenly, boom, she's the face of TrueCoin."

"Too good to be true?"

"There's nothing in her history to suggest she'd have the kind of expertise or resources to launch something this big. No big-name firms, no flashy jobs, no obvious experience in crypto. And yet here she is, rubbing shoulders with millionaires and running a company that claims it's going to revolutionise finance. And you know what else is strange? Some of the details about her early life don't add up. A researcher on my team found a school alumni list from Naples where she supposedly graduated—it's missing her name for the years she claims to have attended. And then there's her degree. The university records list her as having graduated with honours in economics, but we dug a little deeper and found that her student ID number doesn't match the programme she said she was in. It's small stuff, easy to overlook, but when you start putting it all together, it feels like she built her background from scratch. Like she wanted to look perfect but didn't quite get the finer details right."

"There must be others involved."

"For sure. There's no way she's running this show by herself. The structure is too sophisticated—shell companies, offshore accounts, weapons-grade smoke and mirrors. It's not the kind of operation a solo player could manage. They've got the affiliates, but they're just generating the cash."

"And senior management?"

"As far as we can make out, it's Valentina plus two other names. One is Niko Petrović. He usually travels with her. Here—check him out."

He opened the gallery on his phone again and showed Milton a picture of a young man in a very expensive suit stepping out of a car. He was handsome, with neatly styled dark hair and sharp cheekbones. His expression was smug, the type of confidence that came from someone used to getting his way.

"I took that three days ago," Cooper said. "He and Valentina had just got into Venice. They were staying at the Cipriani. Fairly standard for them—they always stay at the best hotels in the cities they're visiting. Unlimited budget for the better things in life. Helps cement the image of success they're selling."

"What's his background?"

"Serbian. Early thirties. Used to work as a fixer in Belgrade—smuggling, bribery, whatever needed doing. He's clever, ambitious, and knows how to cover his tracks."

"Who else?"

"The man Petrović works for—Dragomir Jovanović. We've got next to nothing on him, though. No pictures. No last known address. No friends or acquaintances. We think he's Serbian, like Niko, rumoured to have ties to organised crime in the Balkans. People trafficking, weapons, drugs. But that's it. He's slippery. Doesn't leave a trail, doesn't show his face. He's the shadow—most of the money trails lead back to him or entities we believe he controls."

"Where is he now?"

"Like I said—no idea. He keeps a low profile, rarely travels, lets Valentina handle the spotlight."

Milton stared at the image of Petrović again, memorising the man's features before handing the phone back to Cooper. "Professionals."

"Exactly," Cooper said. "And that's what makes this operation so hard to crack. They've built it carefully—every layer is designed to protect the people at the top. We've got a decent dossier on Valentina, but Niko and Dragomir are harder to work out."

"Valentina, then," Milton said. "She's who we go after first."

Cooper cocked his head. "Define 'go after.'"

"Put the pressure on," Milton said. "And it's better if it was me. You have a legitimate business. And a reputation you probably want to keep."

"What does that mean? I'm too corporate now? I might not push the boundaries as much as I used to?"

"I'm just saying I might have a little more freedom of action than you. Less to lose."

"Maybe," Cooper said. "And you want to be involved?"

"I *am* involved. I want to help the people I met in Venice. I'd like them to get their money out. If I can help your client find out more about TrueCoin while I do that?" He shrugged. "Win-win."

Cooper sucked on his teeth as he mulled over Milton's proposal. "That might have some legs."

"What do we know about Valentina that we could use?"

"Pressure points? We don't really have any. She's careful. Keeps her personal life private, doesn't leave a lot of breadcrumbs. No kids that we can find. No husband. Don't know her parents. We wondered whether she and Niko might be a thing but can't prove it."

"So we might have to use the more direct approach," Milton said. "Do you know where she is?"

"That I *do* know," he said. "She and Niko flew to Rome yesterday. There's another event there."

"Do you know where they're staying?"

"No, but it'd be easy enough to follow her back to their hotel afterwards."

Milton sipped his drink, eyeing Cooper over the top of the glass. "What do you think?" he said. "Worth a try?"

"Time to up the ante?" Cooper shrugged. "Maybe. They're definitely rattled."

"What time is the event?"

"Ten in the morning."

"How long to drive to Rome? Three hours?"

"Nearer four." Cooper drained his pint and put the glass back on the table. "If we leave now, we'll get there with time to spare."

PART V

VENICE

41

Marco and Chiara stepped off the water bus and onto the path. Chiara looped her arm through Marco's and gave it a reassuring squeeze.

"It's going to be fine," she said.

Marco nodded, though the anxiety twisting in his gut told him otherwise.

Isobel was waiting for them outside the small studio.

"Evening," she said. "How are you feeling?"

Marco forced a smile. "Like I'd rather be anywhere else."

Isobel chuckled. "That's understandable. But I'm glad you're here. You're doing something important. Telling your story will make a difference."

Chiara nodded. "We know. We're just a little overwhelmed."

Isobel smiled reassuringly. "The journalist's name is Alessia Romano, and she's great. Very professional. She's done work with victims of financial fraud before, so she understands how sensitive this is."

Marco swallowed. "How will it go? We just answer her questions?"

"Exactly. You don't have to go into any details you're not comfortable with, and remember, we're keeping things general—no specifics about your home or work. Alessia will guide you through it."

Chiara looked toward the entrance of the studio, her expression tight. "What if we say something that makes things worse?"

"You won't. Just speak from the heart."

Isobel led them inside. The reception area was modern, with soft lighting and a few plush chairs arranged neatly along the walls. Marco and Chiara took a seat while Isobel checked them in with the receptionist.

Alessia Romano stepped inside a moment later. She was petite but carried herself with an air of quiet authority, her dark hair was pulled back into a neat bun, and she wore a stylishly understated black dress. She greeted them with a warm smile.

"It's lovely to meet you both," Alessia said, shaking their hands firmly. "I appreciate you taking the time to come here today."

Marco managed a tight smile. "Thanks. I hope we can help."

"I'm sure you will," Alessia assured him. "Come with me—let's get you settled in."

She led them down a quiet hallway into the studio itself. The room was smaller than Marco had imagined, with a backdrop displaying the station's logo and two chairs positioned in front of a row of cameras. A sound technician bustled around, adjusting wires and setting up microphones.

Chiara gave Marco a nervous glance. He could see the worry etched into her features and took her hand in his, squeezing it gently. She nodded, her grip tightening around his.

Alessia gestured to the chairs. "Take a seat, and we'll get you mic'd up."

Marco sat down, his fingers twitching in his lap as a technician clipped a microphone to his collar. He was acutely aware of the lenses of the cameras pointed at him. Speaking to Isobel in a quiet café had been difficult enough, but this was on a whole different level; this felt real. It felt permanent, that anything they said here would be written in ink and not pencil.

Alessia crouched in front of them. "Just remember," she said, "you're here to tell your story. There's no right or wrong way to do it—just tell the truth and speak from your own experience."

Marco nodded.

"Do you want to go through the questions, or do you just want to get started?"

"I'd like to know what you want to talk about," Marco said.

"We'll start with the two of you—about your health, if that's okay? And then we'll move on to how you found out about TrueCoin, how you got involved, and what made you trust them."

Marco shifted in his seat, exchanging a glance with Chiara. Isobel caught the hesitation. "Alessia won't push you on anything you're not comfortable with."

"Absolutely not," Alessia said. "Just share what feels right."

"Okay," Marco said. "And after that?"

"After that," Alessia continued, "I'll ask you to explain how things started to unravel—the promises they made against the reality. What happened when you realised something was wrong and how it affected your family. The focus is on your story and what needs to change to prevent this from happening to others."

Marco nodded, his jaw tightening. "Okay. We're good. Let's get started."

Alessia stood and smoothed out her dress. "We'll go slow, and if you need a break at any time, just signal me. We can stop and start whenever you like."

Chiara squeezed Marco's hand.

Alessia smiled, stepping back as the production assistant signalled they were about to begin.

The producer called out from behind the cameras, "We're going to start rolling now."

A red light on the first camera blinked on, and the interview started.

PART VI

ROME

42

Milton shifted in his seat, his ribs still sore from the encounter at Moretti's villa. He would have backed himself in a fistfight with almost anyone, but the man who had attacked him had been something else, and Milton was left with little doubt that he'd had little chance of beating him. The last time Milton had been so badly outmatched had been with Claude Boon in New Orleans, and he'd only been able to best *him* on account of the fact that Boon couldn't swim.

Milton and Cooper had discussed what might have happened and agreed that Moretti must have called for help after Milton had accosted him, and Vuković had been dispatched. It was impossible to say why Moretti had been murdered, but Cooper wondered whether it might have been because the people behind the scam had grown concerned that Moretti was vulnerable to being flipped. Cooper had detected evidence that he was getting ready to run, and it was at least possible that others had come to the same conclusion.

Milton was sure he would cross paths with Vuković again, and when that happened, he'd ensure he was better prepared.

He rolled his shoulder, testing the tenderness of the muscles, and winced. He hadn't broken anything, at least not that he could tell, but the bruising started at his hip and went all the way up to just beneath his arm. It had been a chastening experience, but he didn't let it divert him from what he had promised to do. Marco and the others were counting on him, to recover what had been stolen from them, and he didn't mean to let them down. But his time in Florence had taught him one thing: he had walked into something larger than he'd expected.

They continued their discussion during the drive. Cooper explained that the event in Rome was a large-scale TrueCoin seminar, the kind Valentina Rossi had become famous for hosting. A thousand attendees, all eager to hear her speak and give her their money. Milton had seen how effective she was onstage—charismatic and commanding, weaving a spell over her audience—and knew that people would gladly hand over savings they couldn't afford to lose, never to see it again. Valentina was the face of a scam that had ruined thousands of lives, and, if Moretti could no longer help Milton, maybe she would.

She'd either decide to help, or he'd make her.

They hadn't worked out how to get to her yet. Milton had seen what the event in Venice had been like: tightly controlled, with plenty of security. Getting inside would be easy—he'd bought a ticket for two hundred euros from the TrueCoin website—but what then? He couldn't just walk up to her and demand answers. It was going to require subtlety and a careful plan.

THEY WERE APPROACHING Orvieto when Cooper's phone rang. Milton had taken over the driving and glanced over to see Cooper look down at the screen.

"It's Isobel," he said. "Better take it."

Milton concentrated on the road ahead while Cooper spoke to the lawyer. Cooper spent a moment listening and then muttered a curse under his breath. He told Isobel he was ninety minutes away from Rome and that he would call her to arrange a meeting when he arrived; he ended the call and stared down at the screen until it buzzed with several incoming messages. He tapped the screen and looked at whatever it was that had been sent; Milton glanced across and saw what looked like stills from a low-quality video.

"What's going on?" Milton asked.

"We had a lawyer working with us in Venice," he said. "Giancarlo Sartori. He went missing yesterday. My online guy's been looking for him and managed to pull footage from the security cameras outside his office. He got this—look."

Milton glanced over again at the phone as Cooper turned it so the screen was facing him. He saw a man, a cap obscuring his face for the first few stills. Cooper continue to swipe across the screen until the camera caught the man looking up directly into the lens. Milton recognised him at once.

Vuković.

"Shit," Milton said.

Cooper put the phone into his pocket. "They're desperate. They know we're getting close, and they've killed him and Moretti because of it."

"We might not have long. If they think the game's up, they'll bolt. And if they've got as much money as you say they do, they'll disappear."

"Rome still looks like it's going ahead. Isobel checked and confirmed it."

"A thousand easy marks in one place, ready to open their wallets?"

"Hard to turn it down."

"One more payday and then they'll call it quits?"

"Maybe," Cooper said.

Milton turned his attention back to the road, drumming his fingers against the wheel as he ran through his options. Vuković's appearance made it obvious: they were cleaning house.

He had to get to Valentina.

Milton could feel the tension radiating from Cooper. He knew—just as Milton knew—that they were running out of time.

"How close are the lawyers to having something they can file?" Milton asked.

"Very close. Why?"

"It might be an idea if they drag their feet for a day or two."

Cooper stared out of the window, his jaw tight. "Easier said than done. There's pressure from the client. He won't want to wait. We've been priming stories in the press, too. Several big newspapers are running joint exposés and putting them out at the same time. What's the name of your friend in Venice?"

"Marco."

"That's right—Marco. Isobel arranged for him to be interviewed. The Italian story's going to hang off what happened to him. The idea is that it'll run in the next couple of days. The timing on that is out of our hands."

Milton didn't respond right away.

"All right," he said finally. "That probably gives us a deadline. We won't be able to stop them from running. We just have to make sure they can't hide."

43

It was two in the morning when they checked into a modest hotel in the centre of Rome. The TrueCoin event was due to begin in eight hours, and they agreed to reconvene in reception at seven, so they had time to sleep and then scout the venue to iron out the kinks in their plan.

Milton's room was simple and functional and more than adequate for his needs. He undressed and took a shower, standing in the hot water for long enough to wash off the dried sweat and grime of the last couple of days. He looked down at his body and saw that a series of impressive bruises were already purpling the skin in several places: his torso, his left shoulder, his right thigh.

He thought again of Vuković and the beating that he had administered. There was a decent chance that the man would have followed them south to Rome and that he might attend the event. Milton wasn't concerned about that; he'd never been one to shy away from a fight and was looking forward to seeing Vuković again to renew their acquaintance. In many ways, their encounter at Moretti's villa had been useful: it confirmed that the men and women behind

TrueCoin were prepared to murder if it meant protecting themselves, and it reminded Milton that it would do him no good to underestimate the challenges that he faced if he wanted to bring them down.

He would be prepared the next time they met, and he would make sure the outcome was different.

He got into bed and was asleep in moments.

∽

MILTON WOKE BEFORE HIS ALARM, took another shower and then dressed and went down to reception. Cooper was waiting for him at a table with two coffees in polystyrene cups.

Cooper handed one of the coffees to Milton. "Everything okay?"

"Got some sleep," Milton said.

"Me too."

Cooper lifted the lid from his coffee and took a sip. "I've been thinking about how we can handle this. One of us needs to be inside to watch while the other waits outside to follow when Valentina is finished."

"I'll go inside," Milton said. "I haven't seen her speak in the flesh. I'd like to see what the fuss is all about."

"She won't hang around for long afterwards. The usual pattern is for her to go on, speak for half an hour or so, then leave. I'll watch from outside. Tell me when she's left the stage, and I'll fall in behind her when she comes out."

They agreed that Milton would need a hire car and arranged one through the concierge desk. Milton checked his watch and saw that they had two and a half hours before the event was due to start. He said he'd go and pick up the car and call Cooper once he was inside the venue.

They parted, and as Cooper made his way to the car park where he'd left his own vehicle, Milton thought, for the first time, that Cooper looked fatigued. He leaned slightly to one side, as if conserving energy, and every now and then his jaw clenched involuntarily, a telltale sign of residual pain. The poisoning that had cashiered him out of the Group had left a lasting mark. Neither of them were young men, and Milton could see they were going to have to rely upon their wits rather than just their brawn if they were going to do what they had come here to do.

44

The Convention Centre was in the Europa district of Rome. The streets bore little relation to the architecture of the historic centre: it was a hub of sleek offices and wide boulevards. The area was a mix of corporate headquarters, embassies, and government departments. He passed the Palazzo della Civiltà Italiana—nicknamed the Square Colosseum—a stark, minimalist building that felt both futuristic and out of time. Cafés and restaurants dotted the streets. He parked the hire car in a nearby car park and headed over to the Convention Centre.

The Convention Centre itself was an imposing, modern structure of glass and steel with angular lines and reflective surfaces. A wide plaza stretched in front of the main entrance, its geometric paving dotted with planters and sculptures. The event was due to start in half an hour, and there was still a long queue of attendees waiting to get inside. Milton joined the end of the line; there was a tangible buzz of electricity as the attendees shuffled toward the entrance. A digital marquee above the entrance read

TrueCoin Global Seminar – Unlock Your Financial Freedom!

The queue moved quickly, and Milton was soon up at the registration desks. The atrium was enormous, with booths on either side, each one manned by TrueCoin representatives who handed out brochures and answered questions with practiced enthusiasm. Banners hung from the high ceilings. Milton looked up and saw 'TrueCoin: The Future of Finance' and 'Be Your Own Bank!'

He collected his attendee badge—registered under the fake name he'd used when he bought his ticket—and entered the main hall. The size of the crowd struck him immediately. Rows upon rows of chairs stretched from the front to the back of the cavernous room. The stage at the front was lit by an array of lights, flanked by enormous screens displaying the TrueCoin logo in gold.

Milton found a seat near the back, positioning himself for both a clear view of the stage and an easy exit if he had to leave quickly. He scanned the room and noted the demographic spread: young professionals in sharp suits, middle-aged couples with notepads, retirees who looked as though they were ready to empty their savings for one last chance at financial security. The sense of hope in the room was palpable; it made Milton angry.

He took out his phone and texted Cooper to tell him he was inside and then settled down to wait. The lights dipped down, a DJ started a warm-up track of high-energy dance music, and then an MC—a slick-haired man in a tuxedo and bow tie—bounded onto the stage with the energy of a game-show host. Several cameras provided feeds of the event for those at the back of the room. Milton took out his phone and opened Google Translate, hoping it would be able to pick up the presentation and translate it in time for him to follow.

The MC welcomed everyone, his voice booming over the sound system as he hyped the crowd up for what he promised would be 'an unforgettable day.'

"Are you excited?" he said, pacing the stage with a wireless microphone in hand. "Are you pumped up?" The crowd cheered. "You're not just here to learn about TrueCoin—you're here to change your lives. To take control of your financial future and join a financial revolution that's sweeping the globe."

The crowd erupted into applause, some at the front even standing to cheer. Milton remained seated, watching the feed on the screens as it switched to show the front rows. Some of the audience seemed particularly excited, and Milton wondered how many of them were plants and how many had just been swept up in the atmosphere. The MC split the hall into two separate sections and began a crude call and response to see which was the louder and more enthusiastic. It was obvious what he was trying to do, but Milton could see that his neighbours were either oblivious to the ruse or didn't care. "TrueCoin, TrueCoin, TrueCoin," they chanted, louder and louder. It was the kind of fervour that one might expect to see at the Olympico for the Rome derby.

The MC handed over to two lesser-known names. The first was a young man who claimed to have turned an initial investment of €5,000 into €500,000 in just a year. He was earnest and wide-eyed, his story punctuated by slides of luxury vacations, a new sports car, and a sprawling villa. The crowd ate it up.

Next was a middle-aged woman who described herself as a single mother who'd been drowning in debt before discovering TrueCoin. Her testimony brought some in the audience to tears—the director cut to close-ups several times—as she recounted how her investment, described as a last throw of the dice, had given her a second chance at life.

There was a formula to the presentations: each one was a rags-to-riches story, peppered with just enough technical jargon to lend credibility without alienating the audience. Milton was jaded by his experience in Venice, but he could see how it might work. The speakers were slick, and their pitches were designed to inspire trust and aspiration. It was all very believable, and the sheer scale of the event lent it credibility: *Look at all these other people, just like me. How could we all be tricked? There must be something in it.*

The MC returned to the stage, his tone shifting to one approaching reverence. "And now, ladies and gentlemen, the moment you've all been waiting for. I'm honoured to be able to introduce the visionary leader of TrueCoin, the woman who's inspired millions around the world: Valentina Rossi!"

Another high-energy dance track boomed out, strobes fired, and the crowd rose, a thunderous ovation filling the hall as Valentina stepped onto the stage.

Milton leaned forward and watched.

She was much more impressive in the flesh than she had been in the YouTube video he'd watched before. She was radiant, dressed in a white trouser suit that contrasted sharply with the deep blue backdrop of the stage. Her hair was styled in loose waves, and her makeup was immaculate; she looked more like a model than a financial guru. She smiled warmly, raising her hands to quiet the crowd as she approached the microphone that had been set up for her at the centre of the stage.

Her charisma was obvious. Every word and gesture was designed to draw the audience in. But there was something else, too, something subtle and just below the polish: a slight hesitation as she glanced down at her notes, a quick inhale before her next sentence. Nerves seemed unlikely given how many of these presentations she must have given, but she was definitely nervous.

The investigation, he wondered. She must have known what was coming.

Or was it something else?

45

Milton joined the queue to leave the auditorium. The atmosphere had reached a crescendo, and, encouraged by Rossi, plenty of the attendees had formed queues leading to the TrueCoin booths. Rossi had told them that they were offering a special deal to anyone who signed up today, including the chance to get two TrueCoins for the price of one. The men and women staffing the booths all had card readers, and they were taking details and ringing up purchases at a steady rate. Everyone seemed glassy-eyed: the customers, beguiled by the fortunes they envisaged in their near futures, and those taking the money, incentivised—Milton had no doubt—by the commissions they were making. He thought of the pyramid that Rossi and the others had built, with cash flowing up from bottom to top, and wondered how many millions would be added today to the accounts of the affiliates in the tiers above the sellers.

Milton weaved through the crowd until he was outside. He reached a quieter corner of the piazza and pulled out his phone, dialling Cooper's number. The line rang twice before Cooper picked up.

"Anything?" Milton asked.

"Not yet."

Milton jogged down to the car park. He looked up as a black car with tinted windows rolled by a row of taxis. It was waved through the security cordon so it could get close to the road that led down the side of the conference centre.

"Black Mercedes, side entrance," Milton said.

"I have it," Cooper said. "She's coming out."

Milton left the call open but slipped the phone into his pocket. He hurried to his car, opened the door and got inside. He edged to the front of the queue of traffic waiting to join the main road; he was lucky, getting outside quickly meant he'd avoided the longer wait that was in store for those still emerging.

The black Mercedes pulled away, its taillights gleaming red.

Milton took out his phone and left it on the dash. "She's on the move."

"Got her. Are you in the car?"

"Affirmative."

"Keep the line open," Cooper said. "We can switch after ten minutes."

46

The streets of Rome spooled by the window as Milton drove through the city. There had been no need for them to switch; Cooper had just reported that Valentina's car had just pulled into the back entrance of the Hotel de Russie on Via del Babuino.

"Where are you?" Cooper asked.

"Five minutes out."

"No rush. I doubt they'll go anywhere now."

"Where are you?"

"Outside," Cooper said. "Watching the entrance."

"Can you call your guy to find the room she's in?"

"Just sent him a message. Won't take him long."

"Call me when you've got it," Milton said, and rang off.

~

MILTON PARKED the car in a lot on Via del Vantaggio and walked the four minutes to the hotel on Via del Babuino. He'd just crossed Via del Corso when his phone buzzed.

"Tell me you've got something."

"I do," Cooper said. "She checked in under an alias. Marina Delacroix. Room 603—one of the suites on the top floor. We've got footage from the cameras in the lobby, too. She went in through a private entrance with her entourage."

"How many?" Milton asked, weaving through the thinning crowd of tourists and locals enjoying the noon sun.

"Three. Security's tight. They avoided the main lobby, went straight up. Looks like they don't want her seen by anyone who doesn't need to see her."

"She feels exposed. She wouldn't do that if she was comfortable."

"Agreed."

"Anyone else on the floor with her?"

"They've booked all of the rooms—none of the names are familiar. They'll all be pseudonyms, same as her."

"What about the hotel? Anything useful?"

"The suites have their own elevator access. The penthouse levels are locked off unless you've got a key card. It won't be easy."

"I'll work it out. What's your location?"

"Across the street. I'll keep an eye on the exits."

Milton ended the call, tucking the phone back into his pocket.

He found a spot where he could lean against the wall of the building at the mouth of Via del Babuino. The road was narrow—just wide enough for one car—and a clutch of electric scooters had been abandoned on one side. The hotel itself was marked out by flags above the entrance: Italy, the United Kingdom, Germany, France. The hotel had a narrow margin off the street where taxis and limousines could pull in when dropping off their passengers. It wasn't the kind of place where someone could slip in unnoticed, especially not if they were aiming for the penthouse. He was going to have to move with a light touch.

He approached the entrance and nodded to the bellhop. The man opened the door for him, welcoming him to the hotel; Milton thanked him and went inside.

The interior was every bit as opulent as he'd expected: soaring ceilings with intricate frescoes, chandeliers, plush carpets that muffled the sound of his boots. The front desk was to his left, manned by a trio of impeccably dressed staff. Milton bypassed them, doing his best to look like a returning guest. He went to the lounge area near the back of the lobby and ordered a coffee from the bar, sitting at a corner table that afforded him a clear view of the lifts. He nursed his drink and scanned the room. The lobby was busy: guests coming and going, bellhops ferrying luggage, concierge staff attending to requests.

Milton drained the last of his coffee, set the cup down, and rose to his feet. A bellhop had just stepped away from the front desk, heading toward a side door marked 'Solo per il personale.'

Milton trailed him as if he were heading to the bathroom.

The bellhop paused at the door, pulling a key card from his pocket to unlock it. Milton slowed his pace, letting the man disappear through the door. Milton paused, glad that the self-closing mechanism on the door was slow, and then followed.

The staff area was starkly different from the opulence of the guest spaces. The polished marble floors gave way to scuffed linoleum, and the air carried the faint scent of cleaning supplies and industrial kitchens. Milton moved quickly but deliberately, keeping his steps soft as he scanned the signs on the walls: 'Lavanderia,' 'Manutenzione,' 'Sala del Personale.'

He followed the sound of muted voices and laughter, stopping just short of the open door ahead of him. He saw three staff members: the bellhop, a housekeeper, and a maintenance worker. They were chatting over cups of coffee.

Milton continued down the corridor until he found the changing room for male members of staff. He went inside and looked around: banks of lockers on two walls and, opposite, the entrance to another room with several showers. He could hear the sound of running water from one of them. There were several seats in the middle of the room, and on the back of one of them, someone had hung a jacket. It was a crisp navy blue with gold trim, complete with the hotel's emblem stitched over the breast pocket. He found the matching trousers folded neatly on the chair. A cord led from one of the belt loops into the trouser pocket; Milton pulled out a key card that was clipped to the cord.

He took it.

The staff lift was at the end of the hall and was utilitarian compared to the grand glass lifts in the lobby. Milton swiped the key card at the reader, and the doors slid open with a soft chime. He stepped inside, pressing the button for the top floor. The lift hummed to life, carrying him upward.

The numbers climbed.

Milton prepared himself.

The lift dinged, and the doors slid open to reveal a quiet corridor. The top floor was a world unto itself, the carpet plush underfoot and the lighting soft. Milton stepped out and looked left and right. He spotted a security camera mounted in the corner and kept his face angled down.

The corridor led to a set of double doors at the far end.

He walked toward them.

47

Milton made his way around the floor until he found what he was looking for: a room service trolley, complete with a plate covered by a silver cloche, left outside one of the rooms by the guest who had finished his or her meal. Milton pushed it back around to the door to Valentina's suite, making sure to position it so that it would be visible if she put her eye to the peephole and looked out. He knew that he wouldn't pass for a member of staff—he wasn't wearing the uniform, for a start—but he only needed her to open the door.

He took a breath and pressed the doorbell, the soft chime barely audible in the hallway. He tilted his head, listening for movement inside. After a few moments, he heard footsteps.

Milton had memorised the Italian for 'room service.'

"Servizio in camera."

The door opened.

Milton moved without hesitation, putting his boot in the gap and then pushing with his shoulder.

Valentina, clad in a silk robe, stepped back in shock.

She said something in Italian, Milton didn't understand it, but her face spoke volumes: confusion turning to alarm.

Milton moved quickly. He closed the door with a backward prod of his foot and put a finger to his lips.

"I know you speak English," he said.

She backed away.

"No noise," Milton said, his voice low and firm but not aggressive. He raised his hands, palms open, showing her that he wasn't holding a weapon. "I'm not here to hurt you." Her eyes widened, and she glanced toward the suite's phone on the desk, but Milton shook his head. "Don't make it difficult. I only want to talk."

Valentina took another step back.

Milton quickly scanned the suite: luxurious but impersonal, accommodation designed to impress. The living area was dominated by a glass-topped coffee table surrounded by a low-slung leather sofa and matching armchairs. A flat-screen TV was mounted on the wall opposite, silently cycling through a muted news channel. The curtains were half-drawn, letting in just enough light to cast soft shadows across the room's neutral tones. To his left, an open doorway revealed the bedroom, where a king-sized bed sat against the far wall. To his right, a small dining table sat under a modern light fitting, and next to it, a minibar gleamed with bottles of premium spirits and an untouched bowl of fresh fruit. Milton looked for threats: the corners where someone could be hiding and the objects that could be turned into weapons.

"Who are you?" Valentina said in English. "What do you want?"

"I need you to sit down. We're going to have a talk."

Valentina hesitated, her chest rising and falling as she weighed her options.

Milton took a step closer, deliberately filling the space between them.

"The hotel security won't get here fast enough if you call for them," he said bluntly. "Sit down. I'm not asking again."

Her flimsy defiance faltered, and she backed toward the sitting area, lowering herself onto the edge of an armchair. Milton followed, pulling a chair from the dining table and positioning it a few feet away from her. He sat.

"Ground rules," he said. "Number one: I'm going to ask you some questions, and you're going to answer them. Okay?"

"Who—"

"Number two," he cut across her. "No noise. No shouting or screaming. That wouldn't be a good idea. Okay?"

She stared at him, eyes blinking rapidly.

"Number three," he said, leaning forward. "Sit still and take it easy. Don't reach for a phone, don't try to run, don't even think about doing something stupid. Do that and this will get more unpleasant for both of us. Understand?"

Valentina's eyes flickered to the door, then back to him. She nodded. "I understand."

"Number four. Be honest. I'll know if you're lying. Got it?"

She nodded.

"Good," Milton said, sitting back slightly but keeping his eyes on her. "This doesn't have to take long. The sooner you tell me what I want to know, the sooner I'm gone. You're going to cooperate—right?"

"Yes," she said, her voice a little steadier now, but her hands remained tightly clenched on the armrests.

"Excellent," Milton said. "Let's get started."

48

Milton took a moment to examine Valentina a little more carefully. It looked like she had showered—her hair was wet and clung to her shoulders in strands—and she had removed her makeup. She was still striking without it: her symmetrical features gave her a natural elegance, and her skin was clear. There was a softness to her now, a vulnerability in her face that contrasted with the polished confidence that shone out when she was onstage. Her deep-set green eyes, though tired, still carried a quiet intensity, and her lips, free of lipstick, revealed the natural fullness that made her smile so captivating when she chose to use it.

She glared at him. "What do you want?"

"I want to talk to you about TrueCoin."

"What about it?"

Milton leaned forward, and Valentina responded by leaning back as far as she could, her back up against the chair.

"You know," Milton said, "I've met a lot of people like you."

"What does that mean?"

"Grifters," he said.

"I don't know what that means."

"Con artists."

"I don't know what *that* means, either."

"People who put on a good show, make promises they can't keep. Trick people. Steal from them. You've got the act down, I'll give you that. You play the part well. But here's the thing about pretending to be something you're not: sooner or later, someone like me comes along and sees through it."

Valentina stiffened, her jaw tightening. "I don't know what you're talking about."

"Cryptocurrency."

"What about it?"

"Explain it to me."

Valentina hesitated for a fraction of a second, but she recovered quickly. "I don't understand what you want me to say."

"Assume I don't know anything about crypto—tell me how it works."

"You push your way into my suite, threaten me—"

"You're deflecting." Milton leaned back. "Come on. Humour me. Give me the sales pitch. Explain how TrueCoin works. Pretend I'm thinking about investing. Convince me."

She lifted her chin, her lips pressing into a thin line. "I'm not here to educate people like you."

"'People like me'?" Milton allowed a wry smile to play at his lips. "I was there today. I watched you onstage. You're good. Charismatic. But you know what stood out to me the most?" He paused, but she didn't answer. "I don't speak Italian, but I've seen your English presentations, and it looked just the same. You never actually explain anything. It's all buzzwords and promises. Big numbers on the screen and fancy charts. But no substance." His voice hardened. "That's because you don't understand it yourself, do you?"

"Look," she said, her tone shifting to one of annoyance, "I don't have to justify myself to you. TrueCoin is a legitimate operation—"

Milton interrupted, his voice cutting across her: "Bullshit."

Her eyes flashed with defiance, but he saw the flicker of doubt.

"You know what *I* think? *I* think you're in over your head. I think someone put you in this role, gave you a script, and told you how to play it. They were casting for someone to sell a dream, and they found you. But they didn't tell you the whole story, did they? They didn't tell you what you'd be getting yourself into."

"That's ridiculous," she snapped, but there was a tremor in her voice that told him he was on the right track.

"Fine. Prove me wrong. Tell me how TrueCoin works. Explain the blockchain."

Her mouth opened, then closed. Her eyes darted away from his, her façade cracking ever so slightly.

"You can't, can you?" Milton's voice was almost gentle now. "Because you don't know. And that's okay. I'm not here to judge you. I don't know the background. But I need you to be honest with me. Because if you're not, things are going to get a lot worse, and they're going to get worse very quickly."

Her knuckles became even whiter. "I don't understand what you're asking me to do."

"I'm asking you to tell me the truth. Stop pretending. You think the people behind this care about you? You think they'll protect you when things fall apart? They don't, and they won't. You're expendable to them. You're a face. A name. Nothing more. You *must* know the authorities are closing in. Investors who've lost millions don't tend to let that go—they sue. And governments can't have you stealing money like you've been doing. Do you know what will happen when they start to investigate properly? You'll be the fall guy. The people who tell you what to do will throw you under the bus without a second thought, and then all of this"—he spread his arms to take in the suite—"will be a distant memory. It'll be swapped for a ten-by-ten concrete box for the next ten years."

She looked at him, her eyes wide with fear. "You don't know what they're like. What they'll do if I—"

"They're not here," Milton interrupted. "I am. And right now, I'm your best shot at getting out of this mess in one piece."

Valentina's front crumbled completely. She looked down at her lap and began to sob. "I *didn't* know. Not at first. They said it was just a job. They said I wouldn't have to…"

She stopped herself, her hands going to her mouth. Milton didn't move, didn't press her. He waited, letting the silence do the work.

"I'm an actress," she said finally, her voice barely above a whisper. "That's all I am. You're right. They hired me to play a role. They gave me the name and the backstory. They gave me the wardrobe. They told me what to say and how to say it. They told me it was just marketing, just a way to get people interested."

"And you believed them?"

"At first," she said, tears coursing down her cheeks. "Why wouldn't I? I didn't ask questions. It was weird, what they wanted me to do, but I didn't see the harm in it. I met people who said they were making money. Lots of money, in some cases, in the early days. But then I started to see other things. People who couldn't get their money back. People who said they lost their savings. There was pressure to keep performing. They made threats about what would happen if I didn't. And now I'm trapped. If I try to leave, they'll come after me. If I tell the truth, they'll—" She stopped, shaking her head. "I don't know what to do."

Milton made sure his voice was steady and reassuring. "I'll tell you exactly what to do. You tell me everything you know. Names, locations—"

"Of whom?" she cut over him.

"The people running it."

"You're mad."

"Tell me how to find them, and I'll take care of the rest."

Valentina looked at him and then laughed. "You?"

"That's right."

"You don't understand what you're getting into."

"So tell me."

49

Valentina shifted uncomfortably, her gaze darting to the door again before settling on Milton. Her fingers knotted together in her lap. For a moment, she didn't speak, and Milton let the silence stretch, doubting she'd be able to bear it for very long. He also had the impression that she'd welcome the chance to unburden herself; it was just a question of finding the place to start. The words would flow easily once she'd worked that out.

"I'm an actress," she said again, her voice subdued. "I *say* that—*trying* to be an actress."

"You're not Valentina Rossi?"

"My first name is Valentina, but my surname is Giordano. I've been to drama school, and I've done some theatre. I've done ads and things like that. I've been trying to get onto TV, but it's... it's hard. Lot of competition. Drama school was expensive, and I was in debt. I told my agent I'd take anything if it paid the bills. That's how he found me—through her."

"Who?"

"Niko. I didn't know anything about him or TrueCoin—not then. My agent said it was a corporate gig. Confidential. He wanted someone who could present well and who could sell. He'd seen some of my work—there was a commercial I did for a bank after I got out of school and a training video for a tech firm." She laughed at herself. "He saw my reel and said I had the right 'presence.'" She hesitated, her eyes flitting toward Milton's face, then away again. "I wasn't in a position to say no. The money was substantial. More than I'd ever made in a year, all for a few appearances. That's all it was supposed to be. Just appearances."

"Events like today?"

Valentina nodded. "The first one was here, in Rome—in a little venue, nothing like this morning. It was small—maybe a hundred people, mostly investors and business types. They gave me a script. It didn't make any sense to me, so I just said it and hoped it sounded right. It was a mess—full of buzzwords I didn't understand—but it was easy to sell. The numbers looked good, the audience was enthusiastic, and I didn't have to answer any real questions. I was just the face." She laughed bitterly. "And you were right. I didn't even know what cryptocurrency was. Still don't, not really. I memorised the lines, smiled when they told me to smile, posed for photos with the investors. It felt harmless. Like acting."

"But it didn't stay that way?"

"No." Her voice dropped. "It got big really fast. They were surprised by how quickly it changed. The events got bigger. Flashier. We went all around Italy—Rome again, Milan, Naples, Venice. Then they took me to London, Paris, Dubai. We had hundreds of people, then thousands. I started seeing the same faces at different events—people who'd already invested coming back for more. They were so desperate to believe in it. And the money they were making... God, the *money*."

"How much?"

"I don't know exactly," Valentina admitted. "They never told me the full numbers, but I heard things. Hundreds of millions, definitely. Someone said billions, but I can't even imagine what that would look like."

"When did you realise what was really happening?"

"After one of the events in Paris. A man came up to me afterward, a little older than my father, with tears in his eyes—he thanked me, said I'd given him hope again. He'd put everything into TrueCoin—his life savings, his pension, even borrowed money from his children. He told me he'd been so close to losing his home, but now, because of what I'd said, he believed things were going to turn around. I smiled and thanked him, but... something about the way he spoke stayed with me." She paused, her voice growing quieter. "Later that night, Niko laughed about how gullible people like him were. That's when I knew. These were people's lives. Their futures. And we were destroying them."

"And you didn't think to walk away?"

"I tried," she said, her voice rising before she caught herself. "After the first few months, when I realised. People started asking questions I couldn't answer. I asked Niko about it, and he brushed me off, told me to stick to the script. But I couldn't unsee it—the way they manipulated people. The way they lied." She paused, swallowing hard. "When I told Niko I wanted out, he just laughed. Said I was too valuable. Said they'd invested too much in me to let me go. And then he made it clear—leaving wasn't an option."

"Threatened you?"

Her eyes filled with tears again, but she blinked them away. "They showed me what happens to people who cross them. There was a man—one of the affiliates—who tried to take some of the money and disappear. Niko had him brought to one of their events, backstage, and they made me watch while one of their thugs dealt with him."

Milton's jaw tightened. "How?"

"He beat him up. But I heard rumours afterwards. Maybe that wasn't all he did."

She looked away, and Milton let her recover her composure.

"They threatened my parents," she continued, her voice trembling. "My parents don't even know where I am. They think I'm working for a startup. But Niko knows where they are. And every time I've even hinted at quitting, Niko reminds me how easily accidents happen." She looked at Milton, her expression a mix of desperation and anger. "You think I wanted this? You think I signed up for this? I didn't know. I didn't know what they were doing, how far they'd go. By the time I realised, it was too late. They had me. What choice do I have now? I can't just walk away. They'd kill me."

"Then help me," Milton said. "Help *me* help *you*."

"How?"

"Give me something I can use."

"And what could you possibly do?"

"You leave that to me. You said there was someone called Niko?"

She nodded. "He runs the day-to-day."

"Who else?"

"Dragomir."

"You need to tell me about them both."

Valentina shook her head, a fresh wave of tears spilling down her cheeks. "You don't understand. They'll come for me. For you. For anyone who tries to stop them. You can't fight them. They've got so much money. They're too powerful."

Milton leaned forward. "I've seen worse, and I'm still here. Tell me about them."

50

Niko went back to his suite, switched on the Do Not Disturb light, and took a bottle of beer from the minibar. He cracked it open and took a long swig. He could still feel the adrenaline from the morning's event, and his mind was buzzing as he recalled the enthusiasm with which the attendees had made their investments. The queues had been fifteen and twenty people deep, and he had seen one team member ringing up an investment of €100,000 and had heard reports of others taking even more.

He dropped into the leather armchair by the window, prised off his shoes, and stared out at the Roman skyline. He had been optimistic, but today had gone better than even he had anticipated.

His phone buzzed. He reached into his jacket pocket, took it out and woke the screen. A message from his financial controller, a terse, efficient man back in Belgrade, appeared.

>> Was a very good night. Total take circa €17.5m.

Niko let out a low whistle. He was surprised; it was more than even his most optimistic estimate. Nearly eighteen million in a single evening. He typed a quick acknowledgement, then leaned back, putting the bottle to his lips for a second time. The mark of a successful operation wasn't *just* in the money, although that certainly mattered. It was in the execution, the momentum they built for the next event, the enthusiasm that kept people buying in and believing the dream they'd been sold.

And that had gone well, too.

He swiped to his contact list and tapped Dragomir's name. The call connected after a single ring.

"Hey."

"Well?"

"Seventeen-point-five."

There was a pause, then a low chuckle on the other end. "Better."

"More than I thought we'd do."

"And Valentina?"

"Good. The crowd ate it up."

"Not nervous?"

Niko swirled the beer bottle absently. "Scared, but you know her—she knows how to put on a show."

"Keep her scared. She's only useful because she's afraid of us. The moment she thinks she has leverage, we have a problem."

"She's very, very far from thinking that. She'll do whatever we tell her to do for however long we tell her to do it."

"Good."

"And, anyway, it's not *for* much longer, is it?"

"About that," Dragomir said. "I think we finish up when the Italian leg is done, then that'll be that for Europe."

"Wind it all up?"

"Just Europe," Dragomir said firmly. "We move to Africa. I've been looking into it—there's scope for expansion. Nigeria, South Africa, Kenya... maybe even Ghana and Uganda. The infrastructure is developing, and people are desperate for opportunities. They'll jump at the chance to make their money work for them."

"I don't know—it's risky. We're already pushing our luck."

"Everett's lawsuit?"

"That's just for starters."

"I spoke to Davor. He took care of the lawyer."

"That's not the end of it, is it?" Niko said. "He wasn't the only one. You think Everett is going to stop?"

"I'm not worried about him, Niko. And I've been thinking—maybe we offer to pay him back."

"We said we'd never do that," Niko protested. "We said it'd set a bad precedent."

"It's just one time. He's made enough of a nuisance of himself to justify it. And, anyway, he wouldn't be stupid enough to say anything if we settled, would he?"

"What if he says no?"

"Then maybe it's time to send Davor to see him."

Niko held up his beer and stared at the label. This felt like an escalation, and he wasn't sure he was comfortable with it. "What about the police?"

"We have the best lawyers in Italy ready to delay them for as long as we need. Anyway—you'll be out of the country by the time they're ready to do anything." He paused, and when he spoke again, his tone was more conciliatory. "Look," he said, "I'm not worried about the police, but, if I was, it's another reason why Africa's perfect. It's under-regulated compared to Europe and the US, and the appetite for investment is massive. It's the same greed everywhere, Niko—people want to believe they can get rich quick. They'll buy into it. I don't care what happens in Europe. By the time they have anything on us, we'll have extracted everything we need and disappeared."

Niko ran his finger around the top of the bottle. "How much more do we need?"

"As much as we can get," Dragomir snapped. "Don't start with this again. You're too cautious. Africa is ripe for the picking. We already have contacts in Lagos and Johannesburg. All we need to do is put Valentina in front of a camera with the right messaging. A pretty white woman like her? Come on—they'll lap it up."

Niko didn't reply immediately. He turned his gaze to the window, with Rome stretching out before him. Africa was enticing, but it was also a gamble. They had an established network in Europe, and even though it was nearly time to abandon it, it gave them protection. Africa was virgin territory in comparison. But Dragomir's confidence was as infectious as it had always been, and the potential payoff was hard to ignore.

He drained the bottle. "All right. Fine. You win. Africa it is."

"Good," Dragomir said. "Call the office and get them to make the arrangements."

Niko ended the call and set the phone down. He allowed his thoughts to drift to the whirlwind of the past year. It was hard to believe how far they'd come. When he had gone to Dragomir and proposed the plan, it had seemed audacious, almost ludicrous. But they'd pulled off scams like that before—not at this scale, perhaps—and Niko knew he had the operational expertise and Dragomir had the cash to execute it. They were an excellent team, and, working together, they'd taken the idea and turned it into a phenomenon.

He went to the minibar and took out a second bottle. He popped the top and went back to the window.

TrueCoin's early days had been slow. Smaller events and fewer investors. Back then, the operation had been low risk, a trial run to see if the concept could gain traction. They'd hosted modest seminars in rented conference rooms and relied on cheap promotional material, focusing on a handful of early adopters who believed they were getting in on the ground floor of something big. The initial investors had been able to cash out their coins with little resistance, the payouts smooth and efficient, bolstered by the funds from new investors pouring in. It was a classic pyramid scheme at its most effective, the illusion of legitimacy maintained by fulfilling just enough promises to avoid suspicion.

As the word spread and the promises grew bolder, the money began to pour in like a flood. People weren't just investing their savings; they were mortgaging their homes, borrowing from friends and family, and selling assets to buy into the dream. The events grew bigger and glitzier. The crowds swelled, drawn by testimonials from the earliest investors who had cashed out with handsome returns. These success stories were carefully curated and amplified, a living advertisement for what seemed like an unstoppable financial phenomenon.

Niko remembered one of those early adopters, a man named Cohen, who'd become a poster child for TrueCoin's success. Cohen had invested a modest sum, cashed out at the right moment, and used his profits to pay off debts and buy a flashy new car. His story was showcased at every event, an embodiment of the promises Valentina made from the stage. What Cohen—and everyone else—didn't realise was that his payout had only been possible because dozens of new investors had poured their money into the system. It was a house of cards, but it worked as long as the base kept expanding.

The illusion of transparency was critical. Dragomir went to great lengths to make TrueCoin appear legitimate. They hired professional web developers to create dashboards where investors could track their 'earnings' in real time, complete with graphs and statistics that meant nothing but looked convincing. They circulated white papers filled with esoteric jargon about blockchain technology, promising innovations that didn't exist and never would. And all the while, every penny they made was laundered through a labyrinth of offshore companies and real cryptocurrencies, out of reach of governments or victims.

The cracks began to show only when the payouts became unsustainable. By the time Cohen's story was no longer useful—when his success became an anomaly rather than the norm—the questions had started. Investors who tried to cash out were met with delays and excuses. The payouts slowed, then stopped altogether. And that was when people began to suspect what was going on. But by then, it was too late. The machine Niko and Dragomir had built—a carefully engineered lie supported by showy events, credible promises, the relentless illusion of growth and Valentina's star quality—had already devoured their money.

And guilt? Niko had long since stopped feeling anything like that. The people they targeted weren't innocent; they were greedy fools.

If it hadn't been TrueCoin, it would have been something else.

He was halfway through the second beer when there was a knock at the door. He frowned, checking to confirm that he had switched on the Do Not Disturb light, and set the bottle down. He walked to the door and opened it a crack, his gaze narrowing at the man on the other side. It was Peskov, one of his security team.

"What?"

"Someone's in Valentina's suite."

Niko's stomach tightened. "Who?"

"A man. Older, medium build. Didn't see much else."

"Is he there now?"

"Yes."

Niko's mind raced. A random visit from law enforcement? That seemed unlikely, given that the lawyers had said the authorities were weeks away from making their first move. An investor? No, they wouldn't have the means to sneak in. Someone to do with Everett? A romantic connection? When would she have had the opportunity for that?

"Do you want me to—?"

"Shut up," Niko interrupted.

He needed to think. He'd been in a good mood half an hour earlier, but his nagging fear that Dragomir was pushing too hard had soured it, and now this. It was a complication, and Niko didn't like complications.

"Niko?"

"Keep an eye on her room. Follow him when he comes out."

"And?"

"Just follow him. I'll tell you what to do next."

51

Milton crossed his arms as Valentina drew a shaky breath. She seemed smaller than she'd appeared onstage, diminished, her confidence crumbling under the weight of Milton's scrutiny. He said nothing, letting the silence stretch, waiting for her to continue.

"Niko's the one you'll see most often. He's in charge of everything day-to-day. If there's an event, he's there. If there's a problem, he fixes it. He's efficient. I've never seen anyone run a show like he does." She nodded to herself. "Because that's what all this is, really. The events, the speeches, the promises—it's a circus, and he's the ringmaster. He travels with me to every city. He arranges the venues, the marketing, the teams. Every detail is planned down to the second. He makes sure the investors see exactly what they're supposed to see and hear what they're supposed to hear."

"And Dragomir?"

Valentina hesitated and bit down on her lip. "I don't know much about him. He doesn't travel. At least, not that I've ever seen. He stays in Serbia."

"What's the connection between them?"

Valentina's fingers twisted together in her lap. "They've known each other for years. Dragomir is older."

"How old?"

"Late fifties. Niko's his protégé. He does what Dragomir tells him to do. But it's more than that. Dragomir trusts Niko to make decisions on the ground. They don't need to speak often because Niko knows exactly what Dragomir would want him to do. And they'll do anything to protect what they've built. Dragomir doesn't leave loose ends. If someone becomes a liability, they're dealt with."

Milton thought of the lawyer in Venice and Moretti in Florence. "What does that mean?"

"I've heard rumours," she said. "People disappearing. Affiliates who asked too many questions or got greedy. Niko doesn't talk about it, but he doesn't have to. It's just... understood."

Milton leaned forward. "It can't just be the two of them? There must be others?"

Valentina looked away. "Dragomir has ties to organised crime."

"And he's Serbian?"

"They both are."

"Mafia, then?"

"I wouldn't know anything about that. But I've seen enough to know they're powerful. They keep me on a short leash. Every city we go to, they control everything—where I stay, who I talk to, where I go to eat—even *what* I eat sometimes. Niko says it's for my protection, but it's not. They're making sure I don't do anything stupid."

"Like talk to people like me?"

"Talk to anyone."

"Or leave?"

Valentina nodded. "Exactly. I've thought about it. But where would I go? They'd find me. And if they didn't, they'd go after my parents. They've made that clear."

Milton stood and paced the room. He glanced back at her. "You said Niko's in charge of the day-to-day. That means he's here?"

She nodded. "He's staying on this floor."

Milton's mind worked quickly, connecting the dots. Valentina watched him, and Milton fancied he saw a flicker of hope in her eyes.

"What are you going to do?" she asked.

He didn't answer. Instead, he crossed to the window and stared out at the city. Finally, he turned back to her. "If you want to get out of this, you're going to have to help me."

"I'd need to know who you are."

"I'm probably the nearest thing to a friend you've got."

"And if I do help?"

"I'll get you out."

"But you heard what I said about my parents."

"I'll do everything I can to keep you safe."

"How? I'm not exaggerating. They're dangerous. They've got a lot to lose."

"I'm dangerous, too," Milton said. "And I've got nothing to lose."

52

Niko strode down the corridor with a practiced calm that belied the way he felt. He was angry; not a fiery anger, but a simmering rage that churned in his gut. Whatever had happened with Valentina needed to be handled carefully, but decisively.

Niko paused in front of her door and exhaled. He knocked twice.

There was no response.

He knocked again, more insistently, and waited. The seconds dragged, his patience fraying with each one.

Finally, the door opened. Valentina peered out, her face pale and uncertain.

"We need to talk," Niko said, pushing the door open wider and stepping inside without waiting for an invitation.

Valentina took a step back. Niko scanned the suite as he entered, looking for anything that might give him an idea as to who had been here earlier. The room was immaculate.

He turned to Valentina. "Close the door."

She did as she was told, her fingers fumbling with the

handle. Niko walked to the centre of the room and stopped. He fixed her with a look that made her wilt.

"Want to tell me anything?"

"Like?"

"*Like*? Like who was here."

Her eyes darted to the floor.

"We saw him. A man came here, and you let him in. Who was he?"

Her mouth opened, but no words came out. She hesitated too long, and Niko's patience snapped.

"Who?" he barked.

"He said he was interested in TrueCoin," she blurted. "He wanted to know about the company. He wanted to know about you and Dragomir."

Niko's jaw tightened. He turned and went to the window, then turned back to her, his hands clenched into fists.

"And you told him?"

"I didn't want to," she said quickly. "But he already knew so much. He'd figured it out."

"Figured out what?" Niko stepped closer.

She shrank back. "He knows I'm not who we say I am."

Niko froze. "You confirmed it?"

"He already knew! I just—he wouldn't let it go. He kept pressing, and I—"

"And you told him he was right."

Valentina's eyes filled with tears, but Niko didn't care.

He took another step closer. "What else?"

Her voice was barely above a whisper. "He asked about how the company is run. I told him I didn't know."

Niko's nostrils flared as he exhaled sharply. "And the money? The events? Did you tell him about that?"

"No," she said. "What could I have told him? I don't know anything."

Niko turned away again to keep from losing his cool completely.

"Niko? I'm sorry. I didn't know what else—"

"You've put us *all* in danger." He spoke over her. "Do you understand that?"

"I didn't mean to," she said, tears streaming down her face. "He was different. He knew things. And he looked like he might be dangerous."

"And now he knows more than he did," Niko shot back. "Because of you."

Valentina sank onto the sofa. Niko stared at her, and, for a moment, the room was silent except for her quiet sobs.

He took a breath and tried to find his equilibrium. He needed to maintain his balance if he was going to bring this situation back under control again. He knew he'd have to speak to Dragomir—and had no illusions that that was going to be anything other than a very difficult conversation—but, he thought, if he could keep his composure and make Valentina realise she needed to help him fix her mess, then perhaps there was a way out.

"Listen very carefully," he said. "If he contacts you again, you call me immediately. Do you understand?"

Valentina nodded.

Niko turned and headed for the door, but he stopped before opening it. He looked back at her, his expression hard. "You've let us down. I'm going to have to tell Dragomir. I have no idea what he'll say."

He left without another word, slamming the door behind him.

53

Milton stepped out of the lobby and into the warm afternoon. He walked south along the Via del Babuino and called Cooper.

"It's me," he said when Cooper picked up.

"You okay?"

"All good."

"Did you get in?"

"I did."

"And?"

Milton glanced over his shoulder, his eyes scanning the street behind him. "She admitted it," he said. "She's not who she's pretending to be. Valentina Rossi is an actress. They hired her to front it. Her real name is Valentina Giordano."

"Did she say anything about who's running the show?"

"It's like you said—Niko and Dragomir. Niko handles the day-to-day, but Dragomir owns it. The money, the connections, all of it leads back to him in Serbia."

"Lines up with what we've heard."

"She's terrified, but I think she'll cooperate if I push her the right way. I just need to work out how much of this I can use without getting her killed."

Milton paused, stepping into the shadow of a nearby building to check his surroundings again.

Something felt off.

"What do you want her to do?"

"Dragomir's in Serbia. I'd like to meet him."

"And?"

Milton set off again. "And show him the good sense of handing himself over to the police."

"That's not going to happen."

"Only fair I give him the opportunity to do the right thing. He doesn't have to take it."

"And if—no, *when*—he doesn't?"

"You don't really need to ask me that, do you?"

"No," he said. "I suppose not. How have you left it with her?"

"I gave her my number and told her to call me when she's had a chance to think about it."

"You think she will?"

Milton's gaze lingered on a man standing at the corner, pretending to do something with his phone. The man looked up briefly, meeting Milton's eyes before looking away too quickly.

"Shit," Milton said. "I think I'm being followed."

"Sure?"

"Not yet. But someone's definitely interested in me."

Milton turned onto a side street lined with shopfronts. He slowed his pace, forcing the man behind him to adjust. It was a subtle tell, but enough to confirm his suspicion.

"Yeah," he muttered. "I've got a tail."

"Can you lose him?"

"I could, but I'm not sure I want to. I'd like to know who he is and why he's following me."

"If they know you were at the hotel..."

"Yes," Milton finished. "They probably know I was with Valentina."

"That might not be good for her."

Cooper was right. Milton's instinct was to lead his pursuer into a quieter area where he could wait for him and then, with the benefit of surprise, subdue him. But if he did that, Niko would know that Milton was more than just someone who might've been investigating on behalf of the legal consortium looking into TrueCoin's affairs. An investigator wouldn't likely have the tradecraft to make a tail and would be even less likely to have the easy facility to violence that Milton did. The alternative would be to question the man and then kill him, but Milton didn't want his blood on his conscience—at least, not yet—and Niko would still know what had happened and that Milton was more than Valentina might have said he was.

"Where are you?" Milton said into the phone.

"Outside the Europa."

"Can you book me a room in another hotel? Somewhere you might choose for yourself."

"I could. Why?"

"I don't want them to know who I am or what I might be prepared to do. I want them to think I'm working for your client."

"Somewhere nice, but not too nice?"

"Exactly. I'm a lawyer or an investigator, speaking to Valentina, not particularly threatening. I'm at the junction of Via Vittoria and Via del Corso, heading south. It'll need to be in that direction—it'll look weird if I double back now."

"Hold on—I'll call you back."

Milton kept walking, his pace deliberate but unhurried, as though he hadn't noticed the man tailing him. He reached a crossroads and turned onto a busier street. The man behind him was competent but not a professional; Milton made him easily.

The phone vibrated in Milton's pocket. He pulled it out, keeping his other hand free, and saw Cooper's number flashing on the screen. He pressed the phone to his ear.

"Got you a room. The Grand Hotel Plaza, south of the junction between Via del Corso and Via delle Carrozze. You're Greg Maddox."

"Perfect," Milton replied, scanning his surroundings again. "I'll head there now."

"You sure you're good?"

"I'm fine. Call me tomorrow to debrief."

Milton ended the call just as an incoming text arrived with the details of the hotel Cooper had booked for him. The hotel was close, just a few streets away; it was not a diversion from the route that he'd followed so far, and Milton's walking there would not suggest anything odd to the man behind him.

Milton continued on his way, blending into the flow of late-afternoon pedestrians. The man behind him, shadowing him with the kind of caution that suggested basic training but not mastery, kept his distance. Milton's instinct to draw him out was tempered by the need to avoid suspicion. For now, maintaining the idea that he was oblivious was important.

Milton didn't look back again but used the reflection in the window of a high-end shoe store to see that his pursuer had slowed, pausing near a tobacconist, pretending to browse the shelves of postcards.

Milton approached the hotel. He pushed through the revolving door and entered the lobby. The receptionist, a woman in her twenties with black hair and a warm smile, glanced up from her desk.

"Good evening," Milton said. "Greg Maddox. I believe there's a reservation."

"One moment, sir." She typed quickly on her keyboard. "Yes, Mr. Maddox. Room 203." She handed him a key card. "Enjoy your stay."

Milton smiled and made his way toward the lifts. He pressed the button for the second floor, stepping out into a quiet hallway. Room 203 was near the end, overlooking Via del Corso. He drew the curtain back just enough to see if his pursuer had followed him further. A figure loitered near a lamppost, his phone pressed to his ear.

Milton let the curtain fall and stepped back into the room.

54

Peskov leaned against the wall of the building opposite the hotel, his hands shoved deep into the pockets of his jacket. He kept his head down and watched the hotel's entrance.

The man had entered the hotel twenty minutes ago. Peskov hadn't followed him inside, knowing better than to risk being seen. He'd waited here, close enough to the entrance to spot him if he came back out but far enough to avoid drawing attention to himself.

The man was unremarkable. There was nothing noticeable about him.

Following him had been easy enough. Peskov had kept a steady distance, pausing now and then to check his phone or duck into the shadow of a doorway. Peskov had been careful, making sure his movements were natural. If the man had noticed him, he hadn't shown it. Peskov was confident that he hadn't been seen.

He glanced at his phone and called Niko.

"I'm outside his hotel," Peskov said, his voice low. "He went in about twenty minutes ago. Hasn't come out."

"Which hotel?" Niko asked.

"Grand Hotel Plaza."

"What else?"

"Not much. He walked here. Took his time, didn't look back once. If he spotted me, he didn't show it."

"Good."

"You want me to stay here? Wait for him to come out?"

"Yes," Niko said. "If he leaves, follow him. I want to know everything he's doing."

"And if he doesn't leave?"

Niko paused, the silence stretching just long enough to make Peskov uneasy. "Then wait. I'll send someone to take over in a couple of hours. We'll decide what to do in the morning."

Peskov nodded. "Understood."

"Don't screw this up. Dragomir won't be happy. And neither will I."

The line went dead. Peskov slipped the phone back into his pocket. Niko had been tense since they'd left Venice. He knew there had been a problem with lawyers looking into the company and had heard that Davor had been sent to make a point to one of them. Peskov didn't scare easily, but Davor put the fear of God into him. Peskov had seen what happened to men who disappointed Niko and Dragomir, and he had no intention of joining them.

He shifted his position, his eyes returning to the hotel's entrance. The sun was slowly dipping down beneath the tops of the buildings, throwing long shadows across the pavement. Peskov settled in. He would wait as long as it took.

55

Valentina woke to a knock at the door to the suite. She looked at the clock—eight—and pulled on her robe and made her way across the room. She'd tried to take a nap, but sleep had been fitful, and now she was awake she felt worse than she had before. Her thoughts had swirled around the stranger's visit and then what Niko had said. It was all incredibly unsettling.

She opened the door and saw Niko. He didn't wait for her to invite him in and brushed past her.

"Close the door."

Valentina did as he said. Niko paced the room.

"Sit," he said, pointing to the armchair by the window.

Valentina obeyed, clutching her robe tightly around herself. Niko leaned against the edge of the desk, crossing his arms as he fixed her with a cold stare.

"I'm going to ask you again," he said. "Who was he?"

"I told you—he didn't say. He just wanted to ask me questions."

"What do you think?"

"A lawyer, maybe?"

Niko snorted with disdain. "Lawyers don't break into hotel rooms."

"Not a lawyer himself—maybe working for them."

"Like an investigator?"

"Like that."

Niko leaned forward. "I'm not sure I believe you."

"Please, Niko. I swear—it's the truth."

"I'm going to give you one chance—one—to fix this."

She swallowed hard, her palms damp with sweat. "What do you want me to do?"

"You're going to tell him something for me. He wanted to meet Dragomir—right?"

"That's what he said."

"Then we'll let him think you're going to arrange that. Tell him that you're going to Serbia. Tell him if he's so interested in TrueCoin, this is his chance to get the answers he's looking for."

Valentina's eyes widened. "You're taking me to Serbia?"

Niko nodded. "Dragomir wants to see you anyway. Europe's finished—we're going to plan what's next. And if this man—whoever he is—wants to follow, he can. We'll find out who he is, who he's working for, and what he thinks he's going to do with the information he's digging up. Then..." He shrugged. "Then we'll let Davor deal with him."

Valentina felt her chest tighten. "You want me to lie?"

"That's right."

"What if he doesn't believe me?"

Niko's expression darkened. "We pay you to lie. You're good at it. Make sure he believes you."

She looked up at him. "And what if I don't want to go?"

"Seriously?" Niko straightened. "You don't have a choice. Do you think this is negotiable?" He stepped closer, looming over her. "Do you have any idea how much money is at stake? How many people are watching us right now? One slip—just one—and it all comes crashing down. And if that happens..."

He let the sentence hang in the air.

"All right," she said. "I'll tell him."

"Do it now," he said. "It'll be easier."

56

Milton had dinner in the restaurant of the hotel and ran back through what he had learned from Valentina. Her confession was troubling, but it was the larger implications that gnawed at him: the reach of TrueCoin, the ruthlessness of the men behind it, and how she was caught between her fear of them and the consequences of her complicity.

His phone vibrated. He picked it up and saw an unfamiliar number.

"Hello?"

"It's me." Valentina's voice was low, hushed, as though she didn't want anyone to overhear.

Milton sat up straight. "Good evening."

"I wanted to thank you for earlier," she said.

"For what?"

"For... listening. I haven't been able to talk to anyone about this, not like that."

Milton didn't respond, letting her fill the silence.

"I've been thinking about what you said—about how this needs to stop."

"It does," Milton said.

She hesitated. "I agree. I want it to happen. But I can't do it alone."

"You're not alone."

"That's why I'm calling. Niko and I are leaving Rome tonight. We're flying to Serbia. I'm supposed to meet Dragomir."

Milton's grip tightened on the phone. "Why?"

"Something to do with the business. We were supposed to have a couple more events in Italy, but Niko says they've been cancelled, and we're going to move on to somewhere else. That's all I know."

Milton could hear the edge in her voice. He wasn't convinced. She was trying too hard to sell the story.

She paused for a beat. "This is your chance if you want to meet Dragomir. He never leaves Serbia. I was thinking—if you followed me, you'd probably end up with him."

Milton looked out onto the quiet street outside. This felt much too abrupt. He suspected there was more to this, that Valentina wasn't telling him everything. But she was also right: Dragomir probably was the key to unravelling everything, but the timing—the sudden shift—felt orchestrated.

"Where are you flying from?"

"Ciampino."

"And where in Serbia are you going?"

"I don't know. Niko likes to keep things vague until the last minute."

Milton paused, then decided to chance the idea he'd considered earlier. "Would you carry a tracker?"

"What's that?"

"A small device—it'd fit in your purse. It'll tell me where you are."

She paused. "What if they find it?"

"That wouldn't be good," he admitted, "but it's easy to hide."

She was quiet again; that was hardly surprising.

"Okay," she said.

Milton's jaw tightened, he'd seen how frightened she was yesterday, and she'd accepted something he'd told her was dangerous much more readily than he would have expected. His doubts became a little bit more pronounced. The conversation felt contrived.

Niko must have got to her.

"Are you sure?"

"I don't have a choice, do I?"

"Not really."

There was a pause on the other end of the line, and when Valentina spoke again, her voice was softer, almost relieved. "How are you going to get it to me?"

"I'll find a way to give it to you in the airport."

"How will I know where it is?"

"I'll figure that out. Answer the phone when I call."

Milton ended the call and stared at the phone. He didn't trust her, but he believed her fear was real. Whether she was acting on Niko's orders or her own instincts, he couldn't ignore the opportunity to find Dragomir. He doubted that either man would listen to him when he said they needed to fold TrueCoin, but there were other means to achieve the same end: he could find intelligence that Cooper's legal friends could use, or, if that didn't work, he'd fall back on his old ways.

He finished his lemonade, taking the moment to think about what he was going to do. If he was walking into a trap, he'd do so on his own terms.

Dragomir probably thought he controlled the game.

He didn't.

Milton would change the rules.

57

Valentina ended the call and lowered the phone to her lap, her fingers trembling. It had been on the speaker, and Niko had listened in. She dared not look at him, standing a few steps behind her, his presence as oppressive as the silence that now filled the room. She had felt his eyes on her, waiting for her to slip up.

"You think he bought it?" Niko said.

"I think so."

Niko stepped closer. "You 'think'?"

"I don't know him, Niko. But I think so."

"You'd better hope so." He leaned in. "Dragomir doesn't tolerate mistakes, and neither do I."

"You heard him," she said, forcing more certainty into her tone. "I told him what you wanted me to say. He'll be there."

Niko eyed her, his face unreadable. Valentina felt her pulse pounding in her temples, and fear tightened around her throat. She hated it: she was a pawn in their game, caught between her terror of them and what the man she'd just spoken to would do once he realised he'd been betrayed.

"Good," Niko said finally. "Just do what he wants you to do when you get to the airport."

"And you're sure? You *want* me to lead him to you?"

"That's exactly what I want. He wants a meeting? Fine. He can have one. But it'll be on our terms, not his. Behave normally at the airport and do whatever it is he wants. We'll be watching. And then we'll speak again on the jet."

Valentina nodded, her stomach twisting as he strode to the door. She slumped as soon as he was outside. She stared at the phone in her hands, her chest tightening with dread. But somewhere beneath it all, buried beneath the fear, was something else. She didn't know anything about the man—not his name, not his background, nothing—but there was an obvious competence to him that was impossible to miss.

For the first time, she wondered if he could offer her a way out.

58

Cooper called Milton and then listened as he replayed the call he had just had with Valentina.

"What do you think?" Cooper asked when the playback was finished.

"I think Valentina had that on the speaker, and I think we had an audience."

"Me too," Cooper said. "That bother you?"

"No," Milton said. "Not at all."

"Me neither," Cooper said. "Might be useful. How do you want to play it?"

"We give her the tracker at the airport," Milton said.

"They'll be watching."

"Definitely. But I don't want them to see either of us. I want what happens when we get to where she's going to be a surprise."

"Dead drop?"

"That was what I was thinking," Milton said.

They hashed out the details for a moment until they were both happy with their plan.

"What about the tracker?" Milton asked.

"I've got one in my kit. It's not Group Two quality, but it'll do well enough for what we need."

"Battery?"

"A week," Cooper said. "It's plenty."

"Meet at the airport at eight?"

"Perfect."

~

Cooper went out to his hire car, pulled up the map on his phone and began searching. Rome had everything: boutiques, back-alley shops, and hole-in-the-wall places where no one asked questions. After scrolling through a few options, Cooper found what he was looking for: a theatrical costume shop called Maschera. It was tucked away on a side street not far from the Campo de' Fiori. The reviews mentioned an eclectic selection of wigs, costumes, and makeup.

It sounded ideal.

He drove to the shop and saw that it was exactly what he'd hoped for. From the outside, it was nothing special: a weathered wooden sign above the door and a faded display window showcasing a mishmash of masks and vintage hats. Inside, though, was a different story. The walls were lined with shelves crammed with everything from wigs to prosthetics, fake beards to theatrical makeup. A faint smell of glue and fabric dye lingered in the air.

"Hello?"

A small, wiry man appeared from behind the counter. He wore thick glasses and had the sharp, appraising look of someone who had seen it all.

"Buongiorno," he said.

"English?"

"A little," the man said. "How can I help?"

"I need a disguise," Cooper said.

The man raised an eyebrow. "For a party?"

"No," Cooper replied. "I have a..." He added a deliberate pause to suggest he was embarrassed and looking for the right word. "I have a domestic issue, and I need to be able to watch someone without them knowing it's me."

The man studied him for a moment, then nodded, gesturing for Cooper to follow him. "You come to the right place. I make you invisible."

Cooper followed him to the back of the shop where a large mirror stood flanked by racks of wigs and shelves filled with an eclectic mix of items that would help to change someone's appearance. The man began pulling items from the shelves: a short brown wig, a pair of thin wire-rimmed glasses, and a prosthetic nose.

"You soften your face," the man said, holding up the prosthetic nose. "Add the wig, glasses, and some light makeup, and no one look twice."

Cooper paid up and left the shop, then checked his phone, searching for the nearest workwear supplier. A few minutes later, he found himself outside a small hardware store with a sign in the window advertising uniforms and safety gear.

He went inside. The store smelled of rubber and sawdust. Shelves were lined with overalls, gloves, and high-visibility vests. Cooper made his way to the back, scanning the racks until he found what he was looking for: navy-blue janitor's overalls with deep pockets and reinforced seams. He added a plain grey T-shirt, then moved to a shelf where sturdy black work shoes were stacked in boxes. He found a pair that fit snugly and added a matching navy-blue cap to complete the look.

The cashier barely glanced at him as he rang up the items. Cooper paid in cash, collected the bag, and stepped back onto the street.

~

Cooper returned to his hotel room and prepared his disguise. He changed into the overalls and then turned his attention to the disguise itself. He applied the prosthetic nose first, carefully blending the edges with a small pot of adhesive. It wasn't perfect, but under the right light, it would pass. Next came the wig, which he adjusted until the short brown hair fell naturally across his forehead. He added the glasses, then practiced small changes in his mannerisms: lowering his voice, adding a slight shuffle to his step. He knew from experience that a good disguise wasn't just about appearance; it was about the way you carried yourself, the way you spoke and moved. The more forgettable you could make yourself, the better.

He looked in the mirror. The man staring back was unremarkable in every way: a middle-aged, slightly rumpled janitor. The kind of man who could slip into a crowd and disappear without a second glance.

He took his bag out of the wardrobe and removed the small plastic case inside. He flipped the clasps and opened it and looked down on his collection of tools, each item stowed in custom-cut foam.

Besides a tracking device, there was a small RFID blocker, useful for intercepting or shielding signals as needed; a network implant, for infiltrating local servers; a slim black torch, equipped with several light modes; a set of lockpicks, neatly folded into a leather pouch; a portable signal jammer, capable of disrupting local radio frequencies, cell signals, and even Wi-Fi; a miniature camera disguised as a pen; a multitool with various fold-out implements; and a vial of chemical solvent capable of dissolving adhesives or plastics without damaging the surface beneath.

Cooper took out the tracker, no larger than a coin. It was magnetic, with an adhesive backing. The device was linked to an app on his phone, capable of transmitting its location even in areas with low signal.

He closed the case and packed his bag. He needed to go and check out and then take the hire car back to the airport; he'd meet Milton after that and run through what they were going to do again. They had a measure of control at the moment, but, once they got started—and definitely once they arrived in Serbia—they would cede that control to the vicissitudes of fate and circumstance. They could plan for the outcome they wanted, but they had to accept the uncertainty that would arise. They'd need to rely on the quality of their plan to remove as much of the risk as they could.

59

Milton and Cooper arrived an hour before the time Valentina had said she would be leaving, and Milton scoped out a location for the dead drop. It had to offer a place where she could collect the tracker whilst also being surveilled from a decent vantage point. They knew that Valentina would be watched, but they needed to find somewhere where she could be unobserved for just a moment. In the end, they'd settled for the women's bathroom next to a row of luxury shops in the departures section of the airport. The area was laid out to allow clear sightlines from the balcony above where Milton had set up.

The airport was alive with the hum of activity: announcements, the muffled engines of departing jets, snippets of conversation in several languages. Milton's eyes flicked between his phone screen, where he could see Cooper's messages, and the seating area in front of him. The coffee he had bought sat untouched on the balcony.

Milton's gaze shifted to the right, scanning for Valentina. He spotted her stepping off the escalator. Her movements were deliberate but not hurried, her expression neutral but slightly wary.

"Eyes on," he said into the microphone.

"I got her," Cooper murmured through the earpiece. "What do you think?"

"She's on her own," Milton said. He paused. "Wrong—no, she isn't. Big guy, blue denim jacket and cargo pants, desert boots. Fifty feet behind her. He stopped when she stopped; now he's on his phone. Looks like he's coordinating. See him?"

"Not from my angle."

Valentina slowed her pace as she approached a Rolex concession, her gaze lingering on the timepieces beneath the glass counter.

"Got him," Cooper said.

The man stood near a vending machine, feigning disinterest but with his phone pressed to his ear and his eyes on Valentina.

"She stopped; he stopped," Milton said. "Watching her like a hawk, too."

"Anyone else?"

"No one obvious."

Valentina moved again, her pace leisurely as she passed by the rows of luxury shops: Burberry, Dior, a store selling overpriced perfume. Milton watched. The man in the denim jacket mirrored her path, his movements just out of sync enough to look natural to an untrained observer.

Milton stepped closer to the balcony as she drew nearer. He caught the briefest flicker of her eyes as she glanced around, perhaps looking for him. They'd given thought to whether Milton should meet her to deliver the tracker in person, but, as they'd sketched out the subsequent steps to the plan, it was obvious that that couldn't happen. It would be important that Niko and the men working for him did not have a photo of Milton or a better description than would have been provided by the man who had tailed him from the hotel. By the same token, it was important that they didn't recognise Cooper, either; hence his disguise.

The man in the denim jacket slowed his pace but didn't stop, his attention split between Valentina and his phone.

Milton watched as Valentina peeled off and aimed for the bathroom.

"Here she comes."

60

Valentina's heart pounded as she approached the bathroom in the far corner of the terminal. The man's instructions had been clear, but that didn't make it any easier. She scanned the area for anything out of the ordinary but saw nothing unusual.

The entrance to the bathroom was bright and airy, with a door to the right for the women and a door to the left for the men. A cleaner was fiddling with his cart in the entranceway; Valentina stepped around him and turned right.

She entered the bathroom, relieved to find it empty. Her heels clicked against the tiles as she made her way to the stall at the very end of the line. The space smelled of industrial cleaning products, and the faint hum of air conditioning masked the murmur of the terminal outside.

She slid the stall door shut and locked it, then stood for a moment. The man had called her and said the tracker would be taped behind the toilet. She closed the lid and looked, her eyes landing on the metal pipe running vertically behind the pan. Fixed to its base, out of easy sight, was a strip of black tape.

She reached down and peeled the tape away, seeing the small circular device that had adhered to the sticky side. She pried the tracker free, her fingers trembling, and slipped it into her handbag. She stood and adjusted herself in the mirror attached to the back of the stall door. Her reflection stared back, her eyes were wide, and despite her best efforts to maintain a little sangfroid, she looked as scared as she felt.

She stepped out of the stall and saw the bathroom attendant by the sinks. He was wiping the counter with a cloth, but his gaze lifted as she exited.

"Got it?" he asked.

She froze, her grip tightening on her handbag. The man had sandy brown hair tucked beneath his cap and wire-framed glasses. His features were ordinary—forgettable, even—but there was something about the way he held himself that felt off.

She nodded.

He looked dead straight at her. "Listen carefully," he said, his tone sharper now. "We don't have long, and if they ask, this conversation didn't happen. If Dragomir or Niko bring a man to you in Serbia, and they ask you if it's the same person who came to your hotel room in Rome, you tell them it is."

"Why?"

"Don't ask questions. Just do it. It's the only way you're getting out of this."

She opened her mouth to protest, but something in his tone stopped her. The calm authority, the air of someone who had done this before. He wasn't asking; he was telling.

She nodded, clutching her handbag tightly. "All right."

"What will you tell them?"

"That it's the same man."

"Good. Now get outside and tell them you have the tracker. Continue as if this never happened and try to relax. I know that's difficult, but you're in good hands. Okay?"

"Okay," she said.

The man nodded to the exit. "Go on—and good luck."

She stepped back outside, feeling a moment's disorientation as the noise and movement swept over her again. She set off, watching Peskov amble after her as she moved toward the gate.

～

Cooper watched her go. He'd left the call to Milton open, and now he adjusted the in-line microphone so it was closer to his mouth. "Did you hear all that?"

"I did," Milton replied. "What do you think?"

"She's frightened—but that's not surprising."

"Did she take the tracker?"

"She did. Give it a minute to update and then check your phone—you should have it."

Cooper went to the cart and pretended to busy himself, taking the opportunity to watch as Valentina continued away. He saw a man waiting for her at the junction that led down to the gates.

"See the guy who's waiting for her?"

"Yes," Milton said. "Niko?"

"Affirmative."

Cooper watched as Niko said something to Valentina before the two of them set off, turning the corner and disappearing from view.

"The tracker's working," Milton said.

"Copy that."

He felt about as confident as he could that the exchange had gone to plan. Niko clearly knew it was going down but shouldn't know the full extent of the plan Cooper and Milton had set in train. The most obvious vulnerability that Cooper could see was Valentina; she knew enough to be able to make things impossible if she buckled under the pressure, and if the tracker led them to Dragomir and the confrontation Milton intended, she'd need to be persuasive. She was an actress, Cooper reminded himself, and a good one, but she was also terrified. They needed her to overcome her fear because, if she didn't, things would go south very quickly indeed.

PART VII

BELGRADE

61

Milton stepped off the plane and onto the tarmac, the chill of the Serbian evening air hitting him like a slap after the warmth of the cabin. Belgrade's Nikola Tesla Airport sprawled ahead of him, glass and steel buildings all about function over form. He adjusted his jacket as he made his way toward the terminal. He felt the usual sense of mild unease that typically accompanied him whenever he arrived in a new place, particularly one that was home to people who would not be hospitable if they knew why he was there.

This was TrueCoin's base, the city in which it had been founded and from which its influence extended. The centre of the web. Milton had learned enough about the business to know that its reach was wide, but it started here.

He doubted he would find any friends.

Cooper had booked a seat on a plane that left Rome two hours later. There was no reason to suspect that they were being followed, nor any reason to think that Niko and Dragomir had any idea what Cooper looked like, but it didn't make any sense to risk anyone realising later that they had flown to Serbia on the same plane; better to pretend that they were independent of one another until they could meet in a location where they could be confident they wouldn't be seen together.

Niko would have a rough idea of what Milton looked like, but it was unlikely to extend beyond the impressions of the man who had tailed him from Valentina's hotel or a more detailed description from the man who had tried to kill him in Moretti's villa. That was the main issue with the plan Milton and Cooper had concocted; it was going to be important that Niko and Dragomir believed it was Cooper who had visited Valentina in Rome. If they realised it *wasn't* him… they would lose the benefit of surprise, and *that* would make things much more dangerous.

The airport was busier than Milton had expected for the time of night, passengers hurrying with luggage and travel documents in hand. He picked a path through the crowd, made his way into the terminal and followed the signs to the baggage claim area.

∼

THE HUM of traffic from the road that connected the airport to the city was punctuated by the occasional blare of a horn, and, as Milton looked up, tiny flakes of snow settled on his skin. Cooper had booked himself in a place near the old town while Milton had chosen a mid-range hotel that offered little in the way of charm but made up for it with anonymity.

The cab Milton flagged was old, with cracked vinyl seats and a dashboard cluttered with ornaments and lucky charms. The driver spoke enough English to understand the address and nothing more. Milton settled into the seat, the streetlights making patterns across his face as they drove. The city revealed itself: brutalist concrete hulks from the communist years loomed beside glass-fronted offices, harsh lines softened by the occasional colourful splash of graffiti. Stately Orthodox church spires pierced the skyline, their golden domes picked out by the glow of floodlights. The taxi wound its way toward the city centre, passing Kalemegdan Fortress perched high above the confluence of the Danube and Sava rivers. Milton caught a glimpse of the ancient walls, illuminated in soft amber light. The driver gestured toward it and muttered something in Serbian that Milton didn't catch. He nodded politely, his mind elsewhere.

The cab pulled up outside the hotel just off Kneza Mihaila Street, the city's main pedestrian thoroughfare. The area was bustling, even as the temperature dropped. The street was lined with cafés, restaurants, and shops, their bright displays contrasting with the dimly lit alleyways that branched off.

Milton paid the driver, took his bag, and stepped inside the hotel. The lobby was small but welcoming, with polished floors and warm lighting. A receptionist behind the desk greeted him in accented English, her smile professional but tired.

"Checking in?" she asked.

"Yes," Milton replied. "Eric Blair."

She tapped at her keyboard and, a moment later, handed him a key card. "Room 314. Third floor. Breakfast is served between seven and ten in the dining area to your right."

Milton nodded his thanks and made his way to the lift. He pressed the button for the third floor and leaned against the wall, letting out a slow breath as the doors closed. He had done this—or things very much like this—many times before, but it was always exhausting. His mind went back to his conversation with Valentina. Everything he did now would need to be precise. They were going to try to pull off a tricky misdirection, and a wrong step would not only blow his cover but also cost Valentina and Cooper their lives.

∼

Room 314 was small but clean, with a narrow bed, a desk, and a window that offered a view of the street below. Milton set his bag down and checked everything over. The wardrobe was empty save for a few hangers, the bathroom stocked with basic amenities. He looked for anything out of place, a habit from years of staying in rooms where surprises were rarely good. He found nothing and unpacked just what he would need, leaving the rest of his meagre belongings in his bag.

He undressed, showered in the cramped bathroom, and got into bed. He was asleep in moments.

62

Valentina was woken by the ringing of her phone. She was bleary-eyed, and as she reached for it, she knocked over the unfinished glass of wine from the bottle she'd taken from the minibar. The glass tumbled onto the floor, making a mess of the thick carpet. Valentina cursed, winced at her hangover, and—the phone still ringing—fumbled across the bedside table until she was able to pick it up and squint at the screen.

It was Peskov.

"What do you want?" she muttered. "It's..." She looked at the screen. "It's four in the morning."

"We're leaving in thirty minutes."

"What? I can't... I haven't even packed."

"Leave your things here. We'll be coming back. The room has been booked all week."

Valentina groaned, the weight of her headache making her feel like her head was being squeezed in a vice. She sat up, the sheets tangling around her legs, and ran a hand through her dishevelled hair. "Are you serious?"

"Be downstairs, ready to leave. And make sure you have the device."

The line went dead. She stared at the phone, sluggishly trying to process what he'd said. She swung her legs over the edge of the bed and sat there for a moment, trying to gather the energy to move. Her mouth was dry, her tongue thick with the taste of stale wine, and her stomach churned with nerves and too much alcohol.

She dragged herself to her feet. The minibar was still open, its door ajar to reveal the almost-empty bottle of wine she'd liberated last night. She kicked it shut and stumbled toward the bathroom, flicking on the light. The glare made her wince again, and she caught sight of her reflection in the mirror.

"Christ," she muttered, leaning closer. Her mascara was smudged, and her eyes were bloodshot, ringed with dark circles.

Thirty minutes? That was going to be pushing it if she wanted to look presentable.

She splashed cold water on her face, trying to wake herself up. The icy shock helped a little, though it did nothing for the throbbing in her head. She grabbed a flannel and scrubbed her face. What was Peskov playing at? What was so important that she was dragged out of bed before dawn? She knew Dragomir wanted to see her, but had assumed it would be somewhere in Belgrade. Was she wrong? She'd heard that he had other property—of *course* he did; he was a multimillionaire thanks to TrueCoin—but she didn't know where it was. She'd assumed he would invest in places with a more glamorous reputation than Serbia, but maybe not. Maybe he preferred the security he could find in a country he knew.

She forced herself to focus, tugged a sweater over her

head and threw on a pair of jeans. She stuffed her essentials into a small shoulder bag: wallet, phone, sunglasses, and a bottle of aspirin. She'd leave the rest of her things here.

She slipped into her shoes, grabbed her bag, and took one last look around the room. The bed was unmade, the wine stain spreading across the carpet next to the bedside table. Housekeeping would have to deal with it.

She went to the door, then remembered: the tracker. She went back to the bedside table and picked it up. It was a small, discreet device disguised as a keychain charm, an innocuous black pendant. She had no idea what was inside it, how long its battery would last or what kind of range it had. All she knew was that the man who had come to her room had asked her to take it with her and that Niko wanted her to bring it, too.

She knew that she was likely leading the man into a trap, but what else could she do? Niko knew everything, and he and Dragomir—*especially* Dragomir—terrified her. She had no choice.

She rode the lift down to the lobby, and when the doors opened, she saw Peskov waiting near the entrance, his arms crossed and his expression grim.

"I said thirty minutes," he said, his eyes narrowing as he took in her appearance.

"It's four in the morning," she shot back, tugging her bag higher on her shoulder. "What did you expect?"

"I expect you to be ready when you're told. Where is the tracker?"

She nodded down at her bag.

"Show me."

She swallowed down another curse, unzipped the bag and took out the device. "Happy?"

He took it, checked it, and gave it back. "Good," Peskov said. "Now move."

He turned and strode toward the exit. A black SUV idled at the curb, its engine rumbling softly in the quiet pre-dawn air. Valentina hesitated for a moment, then climbed into the back seat. Peskov got in after her, taking the seat beside her. The driver, a man she didn't recognise, glanced at them in the rear-view mirror before pulling away from the hotel.

"Where are we going?" she asked.

"To see Dragomir," Peskov said.

"Where?"

"In the mountains."

"Where's Niko?"

"He left last night. We will see him there."

His tone was final and suggested he was not interested in continuing the conversation.

Valentina leaned her head against the cool glass of the window, closing her eyes against the passing streetlights.

63

Milton woke to the faint light filtering through the thin curtains. The radiator beneath the window clicked as it fought to push back the chill. He lay still for a moment, listening to the muffled sounds of the city outside: a car engine turning over, footsteps crunching on snow, and the murmur of voices carried on the wind. His breath misted slightly in the cold air as he exhaled; the temperature waiting for him outside was not going to be pleasant.

He threw off the heavy duvet and swung his legs over the side of the bed. The wooden floor was cold underfoot as he went to the bathroom. The shower took a moment to warm up, and Milton stood under the spray, the steam slowly filling the room as the water eased the tension from his muscles. He let it run a little longer than usual, savouring the warmth.

He dried off and dressed; his first job this morning would be to pick up appropriate clothing for the weather. He went down to the restaurant. It was a small, unassuming space with half a dozen tables set up under warm lighting.

He was the first guest to arrive, and the waitress was sitting quietly with a coffee, scrolling through her phone.

The breakfast spread was simple but hearty, laid out on a table against the far wall. Milton served himself a plate of eggs, sausages, and warm, crusty bread, adding a small dish of *ajvar*: a smoky, tangy red pepper spread that was a Serbian staple. He poured himself a steaming cup of strong black coffee and took the table by the window. He ate methodically, his thoughts shifting to the day ahead. He needed to go shopping, and then he would touch base with Cooper.

His eyes flicked to the window, watching as a pair of bundled-up locals trudged through the snow-dusted street outside. The coffee was strong enough to jolt him properly awake, and he finished it quickly before heading back to the buffet for a second cup.

His phone buzzed. He took it out and saw he had a message from Cooper.

She's on the move.

64

Cooper arranged to pick Milton up in a couple of hours. That gave Milton the time to get the things they might need, so he packed his bag, checked out, and followed the route on his phone to the shopping district in Novi Beograd.

Valentina had said Dragomir had a place in the mountains to the south, and Cooper had confirmed that the tracker was heading in that direction. The forecast for the next week was for severe winter weather, so he found a store that specialised in outdoor and adventure clothing and equipment and filled a trolley with gear: a high-quality insulated jacket, waterproof trousers, thermal base layer, gloves, a hat, and thick wool socks. He added a pair of sturdy hiking boots with reinforced soles and lightweight crampons for extra traction, then moved to the equipment section and grabbed a compact sleeping bag rated for subzero temperatures, a lightweight tent, a rucksack and a portable camping stove with fuel cannisters. He took a torch with extra batteries, a multitool, a first-aid kit, and a small waterproof map case. Finally, he picked up a handful of energy bars and packets of dehydrated meals, aware that the next few days might demand more resources than he could anticipate.

He went to the checkout and paid in cash, avoiding the use of cards that could be traced, then carried the bags outside. He found a quiet corner in a nearby café to sort through his purchases, packing the essentials into his rucksack and leaving the rest neatly folded in secondary bags for Cooper to store in the car.

∼

MILTON HAD JUST FINISHED PACKING the rucksack when he spotted Cooper pulling up outside the café in a dark grey SUV. It wasn't flashy, but it looked solid and adaptable; ideal for the uncertain journey ahead. Cooper climbed out of the driver's seat and waved through the window before heading into the café.

"Been busy," Cooper said as he approached, nodding at the pile of bags near Milton's feet.

"Got kitted out. The forecast's not looking good."

The two men carried the bags out to the SUV. Milton took the passenger seat while Cooper stowed the gear in the back. Milton noticed Cooper had already brought along a map of the region, folded neatly on the dashboard, along with a thermos of coffee in the cup holder.

Cooper slid into the driver's seat and adjusted his mirrors. "Tracker's still heading south. That could mean a lot of places. Kopaonik, maybe?"

"Or Tara—there's a national park there," Milton said. "I looked it up—rugged terrain."

"Could be either." Cooper merged into the traffic. "We'll know more when the tracker stops moving."

65

They fell into a steady rhythm as they left the city behind. The buildings thinned out, giving way to open countryside blanketed in snow. Cooper navigated the roads with ease, the SUV humming beneath them as it ate up the distance.

Cooper's guess at their destination—the area around Kopaonik—was quickly discounted as they started to turn to the southwest rather than the southeast. Milton opened the map on his phone and watched as the tracker passed through Valjevo, then Zarožje and Crvica. It was around a hundred kilometres ahead of them, but it stopped twice—likely at service stations, according to the map—and, with a full tank and no need to refuel, Cooper and Milton were able to close to sixty kilometres behind them.

The SUV's heater worked overtime, keeping the chill at bay as they started to climb into the foothills. The occasional cluster of red-roofed houses dotted the landscape, smoke curling from chimneys into the overcast sky. They continued south, and the landscape grew more rugged, the hills rising into jagged peaks that loomed in the distance.

"It's Tara," Cooper said. "You were right."

Milton opened a new browser window and, on a whim, searched for Dragomir's name together with 'Tara' and 'TrueCoin.' None of the results were of any interest.

"He'll be careful," Cooper said, nodding down at the screen. "Won't buy anything that could be tracked back to him."

"I know," Milton said. "It'll be through a shell company."

Cooper clucked his tongue thoughtfully. "Try 'White Summit Holdings.' That's one of the companies we think he's been using. Registered out in Cayman."

Milton cleared the search and typed again, replacing Dragomir's name with the company Cooper had mentioned.

"Might have something."

The top search result displayed a headline in Serbian above a picture of a sprawling villa nestled against a backdrop of rugged, snow-covered peaks. The property's modern design contrasted with the wild beauty of the mountains; it stood out even in the small image preview.

Milton tapped the link. The article was a promotional piece from a high-end real estate website, showcasing the sale of the villa. He translated the page into English and read it out.

"'Exclusive mountain retreat in the Tara National Park built by an international investment group,'" he read. "'The villa, boasting over ten thousand square metres of living space, includes luxury features such as a helipad, an infinity pool, and a private security system designed to military standards.'" He scrolled further down. "'The property is owned by White Summit Holdings, a company connected to emerging markets in cryptocurrency and financial technologies.'"

Cooper tapped the wheel. "That's got to be it."

Milton tapped on the photo of the property to enlarge it. "It fits. Remote enough to stay off the radar and defensible enough for someone paranoid enough to expect trouble."

"Now we just need to find it. Tara's a big area."

Milton looked at the map that showed the tracker's location. "We'll leave that to her," he said. "She'll take us right to the front door."

66

Valentina stepped out of the car to stretch her legs on the forecourt of the service station while the driver refuelled the car. The air was crisp, carrying the scent of petrol and damp earth, and she wrapped her coat tighter around herself as a shiver went up and down her spine. The station was a lonely outpost halfway between Belgrade and the mountains; the satnav said it would take them another couple of hours to arrive.

She glanced over at Peskov. He stood by the car, arms crossed, staring back at her. He hadn't said anything, sitting next to her and playing video games on his phone. His presence was still oppressive, a reminder that she didn't have much choice about whether she wanted to go and see Dragomir or not. Niko had made it clear: Dragomir had summoned her, and that was that. No questions, no leeway, no flexibility. That alone was enough to set her nerves on edge.

"I'm going to get a drink," she said.

"Ten minutes," Peskov grunted, pulling a cigarette from his jacket and lighting it with the flick of a silver lighter.

She walked over to the café inside the station. A few tired-looking truck drivers nursed cups of coffee. She went to the counter and ordered a coffee, hungry but unsure whether she'd be able to keep any food down. The thought of meeting Dragomir made her stomach twist. She took her coffee and leaned against the counter as she drank it. Her reflection in the window wasn't flattering: dark circles beneath her eyes, lips pressed into a thin line.

She drained the coffee, took a deep breath and stepped back outside. Peskov flicked his cigarette to the ground and crushed it beneath his boot, motioning for her to get in the car. She hesitated for a fraction of a second, looking down the long road that stretched ahead of them.

No way out.

She slid into the back, and Peskov climbed in beside her. They pulled away from the station, the lights fading into the distance. Valentina stared out of the window, watching the mountains loom closer with every kilometre.

Not long now.

67

Milton watched on the map as the tracker slowed and then—finally—stopped. It had continued into the mountains, climbing steeply via a series of switchbacks that Cooper had just negotiated. The ascent had brought them up a thousand metres, and there had been moments when the drop off the side had been enough to make even Milton—who was stoic about such things—a little green around the gills. The road—labelled as the 403 on the map—now zigzagged left and right as it continued across the higher land, with small one-lane tracks feeding off it.

Milton zoomed the map as far as he could and saw that the dot was alongside a cluster of buildings. The article he had found online didn't give the address of the property that the holding company had purchased, but the orientation of the buildings from the top-down view matched the picture that had accompanied the piece.

"That's it," Milton said. "That's where they've gone."

"We're ten kilometres away from there," Cooper said. "What do you want to do?"

"Get to within five clicks."

They drove on for another fifteen minutes, following the road as it continued to climb. Cooper pointed to a cleared area at the side of the road.

"There?"

"That'll do," Milton said.

He turned off the road, and the SUV bumped over the pitted surface until Cooper brought them to a stop. He killed the engine, and they both got out, their breath immediately clouding in front of their faces.

The clearing overlooked a rugged landscape that seemed almost untouched by time. The ground fell away sharply, and, below, the Tara River carved a turquoise path through the valley, its meandering waters shining in the light like a ribbon of silk. Towering cliffs rose on either side, their craggy faces weathered by the wind and rain. The view stretched on endlessly, an expanse of forested slopes, the occasional isolated farm, and winding trails that disappeared into the horizon. The vantage point was framed by trees, and a wooden fence guarded the start of the drop. The air was crisp and carried the scent of pine and earth, while the faint rustle of leaves and the distant murmur of the river added to the serenity of the place.

"I can see why he'd buy a place here," Milton said.

Cooper went to the fence and rested his elbow on it as he looked down. "Beautiful."

Milton looked for the sun and then turned to look a little more to the south. "They're on the other side of that peak," he said.

"How far?"

Milton gauged it. "Five or six kilometres."

Cooper pointed to the fence. A trail led down to the

river, a hundred feet below. "Sure you don't want to change your mind?"

"No," Milton said. "That's the way to do it. Get down there, follow the river and climb the slope."

"I won't have the strength to get down there, let alone climb back up."

"Luckily we don't need you to do that," Milton said. "You get to take the car."

68

Marco sat on the sofa, his hands clasped tightly together. Chiara was beside him, her legs curled up under her, a blanket over her lap. The television was on, and Marco was almost sick with nerves.

Isobel had called earlier that afternoon. The interview was going out tonight and was being coordinated with a wave of newspaper articles detailing the scandal of True-Coin. The entire operation was coming under scrutiny, all at the same time, and Marco's story was a key part of it.

He glanced at the clock on the wall: five minutes to go.

"Do you think people will believe us?" he asked quietly.

"Why wouldn't they?"

He nodded again, his throat tight. Chiara had been right all along. They needed to speak out, not just for themselves, but for the thousands of others who had been caught in the same trap.

The channel switched to the familiar opening music of the news programme. Marco sat up straighter as the anchor introduced the segment.

"Tonight, an exclusive investigation into TrueCoin, the cryptocurrency investment that promised financial freedom but left thousands in ruin. Our special report features the voices of those affected, including Marco and Chiara Caruso, a family from Venice who lost everything."

Marco swallowed hard as they appeared on the screen. The camera panned to them seated across from the journalist. He watched himself speak, recounting their story: his cancer, Chiara's diagnosis, the money that they'd lost.

He could barely breathe. Next to him, Chiara squeezed his hand.

69

Cooper woke up to his alarm, and it took him a moment to work out where he was. He blinked away the sleep, saw the inside of the roof of the hire car and remembered that he'd parked up and slept here. He took out his phone and checked the time: eleven. He activated the torch and shone it around the cabin. The windows had frosted over, and the light shone back at him. He'd lowered the rear seats to open up the cargo space and, with that, had been able to stretch out all the way. The sleeping bag had kept him warm enough, and he'd managed a decent amount of sleep. He unzipped the sleeping bag, opened the rear door and got out.

There was a clear sky, and the moon shone down brightly, edging everything in silver and throwing thick black shadows across the terrain. The air was cold and crisp.

He opened the driver's side door, reached in and switched on the engine. He cranked the heating all the way up and closed the door to let the warmth gather, carefully making his way to the trees to relieve himself.

He gazed out over the valley. He could see the Tara River

winding through the valley like a glimmering thread, its surface catching the moonlight. Beyond the river, the terrain climbed steeply toward the dense, forested slopes, beyond which Dragomir's villa was hidden.

He couldn't help the buzz of nerves as he thought about what he had agreed to do. Cooper wasn't green and had years of experience in situations at least as dangerous as this promised to be, but he was operating alone, with no immediate backup, and it was the first time he had been in the field like this since his poisoning. Nerves were fine, though; he would have been more concerned if they had been absent. He was prepared, as much as he could be, and while the plan had been put together quickly, it was decent and maximised their advantages.

Niko and Dragomir would know that someone was coming, but they wouldn't know that Milton and Cooper *wanted* them to know. There'd be a surprise for them, and when that happened, there would be a moment when the balance swung in Cooper's favour; he would just have to be ready to exploit it.

70

Cooper got back into the car and drove carefully back to the road. The surface was slick with ice, and with a steep drop away to his left, he very gently increased his speed. He crested the ridge and gained the plateau before the road slowly dipped down again.

The moonlight revealed Dragomir's villa. It was perhaps another kilometre down the road and nestled against the edge of a sheer drop, its location evidently chosen for its seclusion and defensibility. Cooper could make out a cluster of buildings surrounded by a high perimeter fence, the dull grey of concrete blending into the rugged terrain. A large villa stood at the centre, and, around it, smaller structures were scattered: housing for guards or storage facilities. Beyond the walls, the terrain plunged into the valley, the river below sparkling faintly.

Cooper saw movement near the entrance: a pair of guards patrolling the main gate, rifles slung across their backs. A single track led from the villa to the road, the snow churned up by recent vehicle activity. Cooper saw a helipad to the right of the villa, currently empty, though it looked as if it had recently been cleared of snow.

He killed the engine and took out his phone again; there was still no signal. It would have been useful to know if Isobel had gone ahead and told the journalists to pull the trigger and publish the stories that they'd been working on; they'd collected powerful testimony from all the European markets in which TrueCoin was active, and the early indication from mainstream media—newspapers, radio and television—was that the stories would be picked up and amplified. Isobel had suggested it would be like pushing a boulder down a hill; once it started to roll and pick up momentum, it would be impossible for anyone to stop. The boulder would gather speed until it smashed a hole through everything that Dragomir and Niko had built. That would be bad enough, but then, with TrueCoin knocked off balance, the legal actions would be launched. Cooper knew that Dragomir was onto them, and had seen evidence that they were starting to fold things up so they could retreat with their millions—their billions, perhaps—but this would give them something serious to think about in the meantime. They were good, but they wouldn't have had to deal with anything like this before.

It was inevitable that they would take their eyes off the ball, if only for a moment.

Cooper was counting on that.

He would take advantage of it.

71

The track descended onto the plateau and then continued toward the villa. Trees lined up on either side, but, as Cooper reached the bottom of the track, they had been cleared to provide space for the buildings. The villa was surrounded by a fence and then a brick wall. The only way inside was to go through a gate in the fence and then, beyond that, a second gate in the wall. Both gates were shut and lit by overhead floodlights; the glow was enough for Cooper to see other lights that had been installed on tall posts between the fence and the wall, as well as a number of security cameras. Cooper had no doubt the villa was luxurious inside, but, from his vantage point, the focus was very much on security.

Some of the reports he'd accessed from an old contact in Six suggested that Dragomir's money had bought him friendly relationships with senior members of the government and law enforcement in Belgrade, but he would have known that when the tide turned and TrueCoin was exposed for the monumental scam it was, those contacts would be left with no choice but to turn their backs on him.

When that happened, Dragomir would want to ward against the possibility of his sudden arrest; a villa like this, with armed guards behind the wire, would give him all the time he needed to summon a helicopter and make his escape.

Cooper took another moment to brace himself. He knew both that he was taking a risk and that he was likely to receive some unpleasant treatment in the next few hours. But he accepted that, he'd been trained to be stoic, and his work in the Group had seen him suffer plenty of depredations over the years. This would be no different, and the payoff at the end—justice for the victims of Dragomir and Niko's scam—would be worth an hour or two of his discomfort.

He drove off, leaving the cover of the treeline and driving straight down the track. He saw the unblinking red status light of a security camera on a concrete post to the left and made no attempt to avoid its scrutiny. He tripped a motion sensor, and security lights snapped on to his left and right.

He reached the wire fence and the gate. A concrete pillar had been driven into the ground and an intercom fitted to it.

He got out of the car, went to the intercom and pressed the button.

There was a moment, and then a man grunted something in Serbian that Cooper couldn't understand.

"I'm here to see Dragomir Jovanović," he said.

72

Niko was with Dragomir when the first story broke. His phone buzzed with an incoming message, and as he took it out, he saw that it was from the public relations agent they had retained in Rome. The first message was just two words—CALL ME—followed by half a dozen additional messages, each containing links to newspaper sites: the *Times* in London, *El País* in Madrid, *Le Monde* in Paris, *Die Welt* in Berlin, the *New York Times* in the United States, and *Corriere della Sera* in Milan.

The links had been previewed, and Niko scrolled down, reading off the headlines as he did.

Scam Cryptocurrency Stole My Life Savings.

Global Ponzi Scheme: How TrueCoin Exploited Thousands Across Europe.

Billion-Dollar Crypto Fraud Traced to Shadowy Network.

Victims Speak Out: 'I Lost Everything to TrueCoin.'

UK Courts to Investigate Crypto Fraud Worth Billions.

He looked over at Dragomir and saw that he, too, was looking at his phone, his brows furrowed in confusion.

"What the fuck is going on?" Dragomir demanded, his voice sharp.

"You're seeing it?"

"Seeing what?" Dragomir snapped.

"The newspapers."

He frowned. "What newspapers?"

"Luigi hasn't messaged you?"

"No," Dragomir said. "The lawyers in London emailed me—you, too."

Niko felt a growing sense of panic as he closed the messaging app and opened his email. There were twenty or thirty unread messages. He scrolled down until he found the one from the law firm in London that Dragomir was referring to. He opened it and quickly scanned the contents. The partner in charge of their file reported that proceedings would be launched against TrueCoin in the High Court tomorrow, with a group action of thirty claimants seeking an injunction to freeze the company's assets until the case could be heard. They were claiming that the company had engaged in fraudulent misrepresentation, selling worthless tokens and diverting funds into offshore accounts under false pretences.

The lawyer also reported that he had been tipped off that the City of London Police were about to announce a criminal case against the company, with the likelihood that extradition proceedings would be included in an attempt to bring those responsible to the United Kingdom for questioning.

"Shit," Niko muttered under his breath.

"What did you mean?" Dragomir said. "You said newspapers. What newspapers?"

Niko forwarded the links to Dragomir and waited, his throat dry, as Dragomir opened them and began to read the stories. His expression darkened as he read before he threw his phone across the room.

"What the fuck," he muttered.

"This is coordinated," Niko said. "The media, the lawyers, the police—it's all coming down at once."

"It's Everett," Dragomir said. "It has to be him."

Niko's phone buzzed again with another message from Luigi.

RTS1 is running it now. Live.

Niko opened the link, the stream from Serbian TV loading just in time for them both to hear the anchor say, "... alleged cryptocurrency fraud spanning multiple continents, with victims in Europe, the United States, and beyond. Authorities believe the operation has siphoned billions of dollars from unsuspecting investors. A representative for the victims has called this 'one of the largest financial scams of the decade.'"

Niko turned the screen toward Dragomir. "It's everywhere."

"We should've paid him back," Dragomir said. "I *told* you we should've paid him back."

"It was thirty million," Niko reminded him, deciding not to mention that Dragomir had only recently brought it up. "It was early. We didn't have the money to pay him back—I explained it to you, Dragomir. I told you—"

Dragomir surged across the room, closing the distance between them before Niko could even raise his arms to defend himself. Dragomir tackled him and shoved him up against the wall, his hands going to Niko's throat and squeezing.

"What did you say?"

"I didn't mean it... like that," he gasped.

"If you'd done what I told you to do, we wouldn't be in this mess."

Niko could feel his eyes bulging. "Please," he managed. "You're... choking..."

Dragomir held on; Niko tried to work his forearms up between Dragomir's hands to free himself, but Dragomir—despite being years older—was far too strong for him. Niko heard the thud of his heart and felt the roar of his blood in his ears. The room started to darken at the edges, and as he caught a single thought—*he's going to kill me*—Dragomir released him and stood back.

"*Jobote!*" Dragomir yelled.

Dragomir threw a punch. It missed Niko's face by inches, his fist crunching into the wall and cracking the plaster.

Niko edged along the wall, putting a little distance between them, and rubbed his throat. He'd known Dragomir for years and had even allowed himself to entertain the thought that they might be friends. But he knew—and, if he was honest, he'd always known—that it was an illusion. Dragomir didn't have friends. He never had. The people he surrounded himself with were people he knew, and people he used to get the things that he wanted—Davor was one of them, and Niko was another—but no one was allowed to get close to him. Everyone and everything was disposable. He only cared about himself.

"That's it, then," Dragomir said. "We wind it all up."

There was no apology; Niko hadn't expected one.

"I agree," Niko said. "But all it means is we accelerate the timetable."

"Exactly," Dragomir said.

"I mean," Niko went on, "how much do we need? We've got enough to disappear."

Dragomir turned away and muttered, "I don't like leaving money on the table."

"We never need to do a day's work again."

"Shut up, Niko. Just shut up—I don't need your platitudes. I want you to do one thing for me—work with the office to move the money. Every last cent. Do you think you can do that? I don't know, Niko. It seems simple enough. I mean, so simple that it seems almost impossible for you to fuck it up."

Niko bit his tongue. Dragomir's ingratitude had taken him by surprise. The two of them had been equal partners. TrueCoin had been Niko's idea, and Dragomir's early investment had started things moving in the right direction. Niko wasn't naïve enough to think that he could've done even a fraction of what they'd achieved alone, but it would have been nice for Dragomir to at least acknowledge the fact that it was Niko's brilliance that had enabled them to make their fortunes.

"Leave it to me," he said.

He turned to leave but hadn't started toward the door when it was flung open. It was Peskov.

"Boss," he said, "you need to come and see this."

Dragomir turned, irritation on his face. "I'm busy. What is it?"

"A man drove up to the gate and said he wanted to speak to you."

"He drove up to the gate... *what*?"

"I know—it's weird. We've brought him inside."

"Who is he?"

"He says he'll only speak to you. He's English."

Niko's eyes went wide. The avalanche of bad news had distracted him, and he'd forgotten all about Valentina and the man who'd broken into her suite in Rome and the tracker she'd picked up in the airport.

"It's the man who gave Valentina the tracker," he said. "It has to be."

Dragomir's brows lowered in a baleful frown. If it was the same man—if he'd been stupid enough to follow the tracker out here and stupid enough to get caught—he was going to be in for a *very* unpleasant few hours.

"Where is he?" he asked.

"In the guardhouse. Stefan is with him."

73

The guardhouse was on the eastern side of the villa, between the wall and one of the buildings that looked as if it was used for accommodation. Cooper had been met at the gate by two guards, and, without preamble, both had aimed pistols at him and told him that he was to come inside. He didn't struggle or complain; he *wanted* to go inside. They had led him at gunpoint through the villa and brought him here, instructing him to sit in a wooden chair that faced the door. He'd taken a chance to assess the room and didn't see anything that would be of help if the situation veered away from the plan that he and Milton had crafted. The air was thick with the stale scent of cigarettes and sweat, and the light overhead buzzed faintly, casting long, twitching shadows across the bare concrete walls. Cooper kept his breathing slow and steady as he thought again of all the possible ways this could play out.

One of the guards—Cooper thought his name was Peskov—left the building. The second man—Stefan, he thought—was a slab of muscle with a face that looked like he had seen too many fights and won too few. He wasn't particularly alert, though; Cooper knew he didn't look like much, and he doubted the man would have considered him any sort of threat, especially with the pistol he held in his right hand. It didn't serve Cooper's agenda to disabuse him of his misapprehension yet, although that time might not be very far off. Cooper wasn't as strong as he had been before his poisoning, but, even with that considered, he was confident that his unthreatening appearance would be enough to give him a chance if he had to fight.

"What's happening?" he said.

Stefan glared at him, said something in Serbian and, when he realised that Cooper didn't understand, put a finger to his lips and said, in broken English and with a thick accent, "No talk."

He heard voices and the sound of feet. The door opened, and three men came inside: Peskov, Niko Petrović and an older man Cooper hadn't seen before.

The older man came up to stand in front of Cooper. He squatted down so that the two of them were at eye level and said, in English, "Who are you?"

"My name is Cooper. You must be Dragomir."

"I am," he said.

Cooper glanced over Dragomir's shoulder. Peskov had holstered his pistol, and Stefan was just doing the same. Niko was behind Dragomir; he was wearing his usual smirk, though Cooper didn't miss the tension in his shoulders.

"You've taken quite a risk coming here, Mr. Cooper."

"I would've made an appointment, but I doubt you would have taken my call."

The blow came hard and fast; Stefan's knuckles cracked against Cooper's cheek, sending a sharp jolt of pain through his jaw.

"What are you?" Dragomir said. "A comedian?"

Cooper leaned to the side and spat out a mouthful of blood. "That wasn't very friendly. Don't do it again."

Another blow, this time to his gut. Stefan's fist drove into him like a hammer, and Cooper coughed, doubling over before forcing himself back upright.

He gasped for breath. "Enough," he said. He didn't need to fake the wheezing. "Stop—you don't need to beat me up. I want to help."

"Answer the question," Dragomir said. "Why are you here?"

"I'm an investigator," Cooper said. "I work for someone you know."

"Go on."

"Nick Everett. You know who he is, don't you?"

There was no point in pretending the name was unknown, and Dragomir did not. "We know him. He's the cause of a lot of…" He paused, looking for the right word.

"Annoyance," Niko offered from the back of the room.

"A lot of trouble," Dragomir said.

"I'm sure he is," Cooper said. "And I'm afraid the work I've been doing will have contributed to that trouble." He reached up unselfconsciously to dab his fingertips against his cheek. "He didn't instruct me directly. That was the lawyers. They hired my firm to find out as much about you as we could. I won't say it was easy, but we've found enough information to give them the ammunition they need to launch legal claims against you."

"I know all that," Dragomir said.

"Actually, you don't. You don't know everything. That's why I'm here. *I* know everything, and I can give it to you. I can give you everything you need to defend yourself against the claims Everett is going to bring."

"But you wouldn't be doing that out of the goodness of your heart, would you?"

"Of course not," Cooper said. "You'll have to pay me, and it'll be a lot. That's why I came. I want you to take me seriously, and I thought the best way to do that was for you to see that I'm prepared to put myself at considerable personal risk to make you my offer."

Dragomir eyed him shrewdly. "How did you find me?"

Cooper knew that Dragomir and Niko were aware of the tracker Valentina was carrying, but it didn't serve Cooper's purposes for them to know that he was a step ahead of them.

"I went to see Valentina Rossi—I'm sorry, I mean Giordano—in Rome. I gave her a device to bring with her. It's a tracker—I flew to Belgrade yesterday, and I followed the tracker here." He shrugged. "Ask her if you don't believe me."

Dragomir smiled. "I think we will." He turned to Peskov. "Go and get her. We'll see what she has to say."

74

Valentina shut the door to her room, leaning her back against it as she exhaled a shaky breath. Her hands trembled as she reached for the lock, twisting the key into place. She pressed her palms against her temples, trying to steady herself, but the weight of the situation pressed down on her like a stone.

She crossed the room to the small desk by the window, her feet silent against the hardwood floor. The curtains were drawn, and she pulled them back slightly, glancing out at the rugged mountains beyond the villa. Once upon a time, she would have considered the moonlit view to be beautiful; now, though, the mountains all around her felt like a prison.

She closed her eyes and let her head fall forwards.

Africa.

She'd hoped Dragomir and Niko might have changed their minds, but that was stupid. Of course they wouldn't. It was a chance to make even more money, and they were never going to turn that down. The thought of it made her stomach churn. More events, more lies, more people to deceive and rob. She sank into the chair by the desk. The thought of what she would have to do made her feel sick. She could hear the applause and see the faces of people desperate to believe in the dream she was selling.

How had her life changed into a nightmare that she couldn't wake from?

Every morning, she told herself she'd find a way out; every night, she realised she was sinking deeper.

Her thoughts were interrupted by a knock at the door. She pressed her fingers against her lips, willing herself to stay calm. She stood and crossed the room. Her hand hesitated on the lock.

"Who is it?" she called, trying to keep the tremor from her voice.

"Dragomir wants you," a gruff voice replied.

Her heart sank. "What for?"

"Just come," he said, his tone leaving no room for argument.

Valentina unlocked the door and opened it, finding Peskov towering over her. He stepped back to let her pass and then followed her down the hallway.

"Where are we going?"

"The guardhouse," he said.

They exited the main villa and crossed the courtyard, the chill of the mountain air causing her to draw breath. Peskov didn't speak, and Valentina didn't dare ask questions.

They reached the guardhouse.

Peskov opened the door and gestured for her to enter.

Niko and Dragomir were waiting. Niko was leaning against a table, his arms crossed over his chest, while Dragomir paced.

A man sat in a chair in the middle of the room, his head slumped forward.

"*There* she is," Niko said, his voice dripping with mock sweetness.

Dragomir turned to face her, then pointed down at the man in the chair. "Look at him."

She did.

"Do you recognise him?"

Valentina swallowed hard. The man's face was bruised, and there was a small cut above his eyebrow, but his eyes were alert, and he was watching her.

"Yes," she said.

Dragomir's expression didn't change. "Who is he?"

"The man who came to my hotel."

Niko's eyes narrowed. "The man who gave you the tracker?"

She nodded. "Yes," she said, a catch in her voice. "That's him."

Dragomir was watching her carefully. "Are you sure, Valentina? You don't sound sure."

"I am. It's him."

The man didn't say anything, his gaze fixed on Valentina. She looked away, focusing instead on the floor. Her palms were clammy, and she clasped them together to stop them from shaking.

"Good," Dragomir said. He turned back to the man. "There is a line between bravery and stupidity. I admire someone who will take a risk, but you have been unlucky. You're too late. Everett has been running his campaign against us for months, and now he has filed his claims. Have you seen the stories on the internet?"

The man shook his head. "What stories?"

"Articles in big newspapers all across Europe," Niko said. "They've really gone to town. Of course, the stories have been picked up and repeated. It's everywhere. We've been getting ready to wind everything up, but what he did tonight has accelerated things."

"You don't have anything that we need," Dragomir said. "We're not interested in fighting. We have what we require. We'll just disappear, and he'll never see us again."

"What does that mean?" Valentina said.

"It means it's done," Dragomir said.

She turned to Niko. "Done?"

"It's all over," he said. "The Italian police have been looking into it, too. They'll be coming after us soon. Obviously, we're not there, in Italy, but that won't stop them. They'll know where we are, and they'll try to force us to go back."

She felt the blood running from her face. "And me?"

Dragomir frowned, as if she had just said something so stupid that he needed to think to understand it. "And you?"

"I mean," she stammered, "they'll want me, too, won't they?"

"You're the face of TrueCoin," he said with a bemused laugh. "You'll be the first name on their list."

She'd known that would be the case but had tried to make herself wilfully blind to it. It was only bad when she thought about it, and she'd found ways—exercise, chiefly, and sometimes booze—to forget about it. But as was increasingly common these days, it was harder to do that when she dreamed about what she had done and what it might mean for her future.

"You look surprised," Dragomir said.

She realised, too late, that she was in danger. She was in an isolated place, with people who were not—and had never been—her friends, and they might well decide she knew things about them and their business that she could be tempted to exchange in return for lenient treatment. It wasn't me, she might say. I was just given the lines to read. It was Dragomir and Niko—they were behind it, they scammed all those people, they made all the money…

And if *they* thought *that*…

"I'm not surprised. I knew what I was getting into when I took the job."

"That's good to hear." He turned to Niko. "Good to hear, isn't it?"

"Very good."

Dragomir exhaled theatrically. "Problem is, you might be looking at years in prison. The articles in the newspapers really lay it on thick about how much money you've made and how much misery you've caused. They'll throw the book at you. I'm going to disappear into the mountains. They won't find me there, but it's going to be a few years without the luxury we've all come to enjoy. I can do that—I lived that way for years, and then the war made it worse. But I don't know if you're cut out for that kind of life, Valentina. No fancy restaurants. No hotels. The money will still be there, but you won't be able to spend it—not for years. Are you cut out for that kind of life?"

"I can do it," she said, trying not to sound desperate. "I *will* do it. I don't have anyone waiting for me. I don't have a husband or kids. I don't have any ties. I'll go somewhere they'll never find me."

"What if they do find you?"

"They won't," she said.

"Humour me," he said. "*What* if they do? What if they said you'll get twenty years if you don't cooperate and two years if you do? What—"

"I wouldn't say a word," she cut over him.

He bit his lip and shook his head. "Really?" He turned to Niko. "Really?"

She turned to look at Niko. It was clear he could see where the conversation was going, and, although she doubted Niko would have approved of what Dragomir was implying, she knew he was scared of him, and if it came to a question of standing up for her or protecting himself, Niko would wash his hands of her every time.

The man in the chair could see it, too. "There's no need to hurt her," he said.

Dragomir didn't even look at him: he backhanded him across the face, his knuckles cracking against the man's cheekbone and nose, drawing more blood.

Dragomir turned to her and smiled; there was no friendliness there.

All she could see was death.

"I'm sorry," he said. "We can't take the chance."

He turned to Peskov and held his hand out. The big man opened his jacket and reached inside, taking a pistol from a shoulder holster and extending it, handle first, for Dragomir to take.

"Please," Valentina said.

"You don't have to do that," the man in the chair said.

Dragomir pistol-whipped him, cracking the frame of the pistol against the side of his head, then spoke as if he hadn't just struck him. "You're right," he said. "I don't." He held the gun out for Niko. "She's your responsibility," he said.

Niko stood with his mouth open. "I... I..."

"Take it," Dragomir insisted, and Niko did. Dragomir turned away. "Do them both and then get ready to leave. The helicopter will be here in half an hour."

He left the guardhouse with Peskov, leaving Valentina with Niko and Stefan and the man in the chair.

Niko looked down at the pistol.

"Please," Valentina said. "Niko, *please*—I'd never say a

thing. You know me better than he does. Tell him you believe me. Tell him. Please, Niko. *Please.*"

Niko stared at the pistol in his hand, his jaw clenching and unclenching.

He reached up with his spare hand and massaged his forehead, then raised the pistol and aimed it at the head of the man in the chair.

The lights went out, and the room went dark.

75

Milton yanked down on the large red lever marked "OFF" to kill the generator, then reached over to the identical backup unit and did the same again. Both generators sputtered and groaned before falling silent, leaving only the faint hum of residual power winding down in the cables. The air around him quickly became still, heavier without the constant mechanical thrum.

The structure housing the generators was a small reinforced concrete building tucked into the back corner of the grounds, partially obscured by shrubs and shadowed by a steep slope rising behind it. Milton had found it in his reconnaissance, its location betrayed by the faint hum and the smell of diesel in the cold air. The shed had been secured with a padlock, but a few seconds with his multitool had allowed him to open the door and get to the equipment inside.

The shed was cramped, the air thick with the acrid tang of oil and exhaust fumes. The two generators dominated the space, their hulking, industrial frames bolted to the concrete floor. Each was painted a faded yellow, the manufacturer's name—Kohler Power Systems—barely visible beneath layers of grime and oil stains. Heavy-duty cabling snaked out from each unit, disappearing through a hole in the wall that Milton guessed led to the villa's main electrical junction.

He unscrewed the access panels on both generators. He turned off the fuel valves and then cut the fuel lines with his bolt cutter, starving the engines. A repair would take hours.

He scanned the small room for anything that might serve as a backup to the backup. It wouldn't have surprised him to find a facility as remote as this with portable generators or UPS units for critical systems. He saw nothing more than spare fuel drums and a stack of tools in the corner and was confident the villa would be dark for at least the next few hours.

He went back outside. It was freezing cold, the kind of bitter air that turned every breath into vapour. Despite the chill, he was sweating inside his insulated jacket. He'd been on the move for four hours, trekking through terrain that had proven to be even more challenging than he'd anticipated. He'd followed the slope down into the valley and reached the river, dark and fast-moving. He'd identified a ford during his inspection of Google's satellite imagery: a narrow section where the water spread more thinly over the rocky bed and stepping stones had been left across its width. When he reached it, he found the stones slick with ice, each step a careful negotiation to keep from plunging into the frigid current. His waterproof boots held up as well as could be expected, though the chill had seeped into his toes by the time he was across.

The climb on the other side up to the plateau had been gruelling. The path wasn't marked, and Milton relied on the faint last light of dusk filtering through the canopy above him. He clipped the lightweight crampons onto his boots when the incline became treacherous with patches of frozen soil and loose gravel. He'd paused every so often to listen to the wind for any sounds of movement. The silence of the wilderness was deceptive; he knew security patrols might easily be posted beyond the villa's perimeter although he hoped that the isolation out here, and the difficulty of getting to this side of the grounds, might mean security was focused elsewhere. That had been the case, but he knew the power going out would tell them something was afoot.

He edged around to the corner of the shed and scanned left and right. The chain-link perimeter fence topped with coils of razor wire was behind him; he'd used bolt cutters to get through it, their blades wrapped in tape to muffle the sound. Before slipping inside, he'd secured the severed links with a piece of black cord to keep the gap from being immediately obvious to anyone passing by.

He looked over to the main building. The windows that had glowed with light moments before were now dark, and faint voices carried over the night air: confused, agitated. The shadows of men carrying torches danced along the perimeter, and he could hear the sharp bark of orders in Serbian.

The distraction would only be temporary, however, and he had a lot to achieve before the guards had had a chance to recover.

He ducked down low and moved.

76

It was dark, with just a little moonlight filtering in through the window.

For a moment, nobody moved.

Stefan cursed, and Niko muttered something panicky in Serbian.

Cooper ignored it all and made his move.

Two targets.

Niko: armed, but soft.

Stefan: unarmed, but big and nasty.

Niko first.

He lunged from the chair. Niko yelped in surprise, but Cooper's shoulder collided with his midsection, driving him backward into the wall. The gun clattered to the floor, the metallic clang ringing through the room.

Cooper glanced down, couldn't get to it, put it out of his mind.

He pivoted, keeping his weight low as Niko crumpled against the wall. Stefan moved, his boots scraping against the concrete floor. Cooper could feel him coming even though the darkness made it impossible to see and shifted just in time, avoiding a wild swing aimed at his head.

Stefan cursed, and Cooper used the sound to orient himself. He lashed out with a kick, his boot connecting with the man's shin. It wasn't enough to drop him, but it bought Cooper a moment to reset. He needed to take control before the two of them regrouped.

Niko groaned, somewhere to Cooper's right; Cooper stepped in and drove an elbow into his jaw, sending him slumping to the floor.

He turned back to Stefan. He was advancing on him. Cooper ducked under another wide swing and drove his shoulder into the man's stomach. It was like hitting a wall, but the impact knocked Stefan off balance, sending him stumbling backward. Cooper followed up with rights and lefts into his ribs. Stefan grunted in pain, but still didn't go down.

Stefan swung again, this time connecting with Cooper's side. Pain lanced through his ribs, but he gritted his teeth and twisted away, using the momentum to deliver a kick to the side of the man's knee. The joint buckled, and he went down with a heavy thud.

Cooper turned back to Niko; he'd crawled toward the centre of the room, trying for the gun. Cooper kicked it away, sending it skittering into the corner.

Niko cursed and, desperate, tackled Cooper and took him to the ground. He somehow managed to get behind Cooper and wrapped his legs around Cooper's knees, locking his ankles one over the other, and then forced his arm around so that Cooper's throat was in the crook of his right elbow. He started to squeeze.

Cooper heard a grunt and saw the shadow of movement as Stefan got up.

Cooper started to find it difficult to breathe. Niko might have been soft, but he was desperate. And, while Cooper would have been able to handle him easily before, the poisoning had weakened him even more than he'd feared.

Niko reached around with his left hand and locked it around his right wrist, pulling hard to increase the torque even more.

Cooper gasped for breath.

This wasn't how he thought he'd go out.

77

Milton slipped back into the cover of the trees, his path carefully plotted in advance to avoid any approaching guards. The blackout would create just enough chaos and confusion to give him the window he needed, but it wouldn't be open forever.

He had to move quickly.

He checked his watch: a minute past midnight. He'd agreed with Cooper that he'd cut the power at midnight, and that would be the signal for them to begin to execute the plan.

The villa lay ahead, obscured by dense pine trees. He saw the silhouette of the main building and a scattering of smaller structures. He crouched behind a cluster of bushes and looked for guards.

Still nothing.

Time to move.

Milton set off, low and fast, keeping to the shadows. He avoided the open spaces, sticking to the tree line and using the scattered equipment around the grounds as cover.

78

Niko squeezed tighter.

"Stop!" Valentina's voice cracked.

Cooper's vision started to go dark.

"*Stop!*"

Niko grunted and squeezed tighter still.

There was a sudden flash and then, a fraction of an instant later, the boom of an explosion.

Stefan jerked as the bullet struck his chest. He stared at Valentina, wide-eyed and disbelieving, before collapsing backward against the wall. He slid down to the floor, his bulk crumpling with a final thud.

Niko froze. His hands slackened on Cooper's neck, and Cooper gasped, choking for air.

"Valentina..." Niko started, his voice thin and desperate.

"Shut up!" she shouted, her voice trembling with fear and rage.

"Think about what you're doing," Niko said.

"You were going to kill me."

"That was Dragomir, not me."

"Liar," she spat.

She fired again. The gunshot echoed as the bullet struck him in the throat.

The pistol slipped from Valentina's fingers and clattered to the floor.

Cooper coughed and struggled out from underneath Niko's twitching body. He got to his feet, rubbing his throat.

"You okay?" he rasped, his voice hoarse.

Valentina shook her head and sobbed.

"You had no choice. You would've been next."

He reached down for the gun and tucked it into his waistband. He glanced at the door, listening for any signs that the two shots had attracted attention. The villa was still dark, and the silence suggested that, for now, they were safe; that couldn't last.

"Who are you?" she said.

"I'm with the man you met in Rome. I'm going to help get you out."

She stifled a sob.

"Stay behind me," he said. "We have to leave now."

79

Milton heard the crunch of footsteps running across gravel. He ducked into cover as a lone guard hustled in the direction of the generators. The man held an automatic rifle in both hands.

Milton waited as the guard went by and then followed, staying low and in cover, using the terrain to mask his approach. The guard arrived at the generators, saw that the door had been forced and reached for the radio clipped to his belt, no doubt to report what he'd found.

Milton didn't give him the chance.

He closed in and pounced, looping an arm around the guard's neck and cutting off his air supply. He clamped his other hand over the man's mouth to stifle any noise and held it there as the guard struggled, his movements increasingly frantic. Milton's grip was firm, and he had no intention of relenting, and, within seconds, the guard's body went limp.

Milton lowered him to the ground and relieved him of his rifle, sidearm and radio.

The rifle felt familiar in his hands. He checked the magazine, chambered a round, and moved on.

He needed to find Cooper.

Milton hadn't got far when he heard the sound of a gunshot and, moments later, a second.

He turned: the shots had come from a building to his right, up close to the fence.

He waited in cover until a guard with an unholstered pistol went by, and then carefully made his way toward the building. It took him a minute to arrive.

The building was small and utilitarian; everything was dark.

Milton approached the door, listening for movement inside.

He thought of the shots and feared the worst; they'd known it was a gamble, that they'd both be in considerable danger, but they'd concluded that Cooper needed to keep his mouth shut just long enough for Milton to reach him. Cooper had received the same anti-interrogation training as Milton, and his likely captors—local thugs, they assumed—wouldn't have had the wherewithal to go beyond the most brutish of questioning. Cooper might take a beating, but he would be able to withstand that.

But if they'd been wrong?

What if they'd decided he wasn't worth the effort and put a bullet in him?

Milton used the muzzle of the rifle to ease the door open just enough to see inside. The moonlight revealed two bodies. One large man was sprawled on the floor—Milton didn't recognise him—but the man slumped against the wall was familiar. It was Niko, and his face was a mask of shock and disbelief. Blood pooled beneath both of them, dark on the concrete floor.

Milton turned. Valentina stood in the corner; her face was pale. Cooper stood near her, his face bloodied.

Cooper looked over at Milton. "You're a bit late."

"Sorry," Milton said. "You okay?"

"Fine."

"Not as pretty as you were."

"All your fault." Cooper nodded over at Valentina. "Would've been a different story without her."

Milton gestured down at the bodies. "She did that?"

"They were going to shoot us both."

Milton looked at Valentina and nodded; he wouldn't have suspected she had it in her to shoot a man, never mind two, but he'd been wrong about things like that before, and desperate times required desperate measures.

Cooper turned to Valentina now. "Do you know where they keep their servers?"

She tilted her head in confusion; Milton wondered whether she understood what she'd been asked.

"It'll be a room with lots of computers," Cooper said, "probably in racks."

"I saw it when I got here," she said. "It's on the way to the accommodation."

"Can you take us there?"

She was reluctant. "You said we were going to leave."

"We will," Milton said. "But we need to do something else first. It's important."

Valentina hesitated.

"I know you probably never imagined what you did would affect so many people—but you know now, and you have to help us put it right."

She nodded and led them out of the guardhouse and across the courtyard, keeping close to the shadows. The main building loomed ahead, its windows darkened by the power outage. The silence was unnerving, broken only by the distant shouts of guards scrambling to restore order. Milton scanned their surroundings, his rifle at the ready. Valentina hesitated for a moment, her breath visible in the cold night air, then continued forward. The group stayed low, slipping between a stack of crates and two parked Land Rovers.

The entrance to the main building came into view: a heavy metal door propped ajar, its security system disabled by the blackout. Milton stepped up, easing the door open a fraction further, and scanned the dim interior.

The corridor beyond was empty.

He motioned for Valentina to go first, and she slipped inside, Milton and Cooper close behind.

The building was a maze of corridors and unmarked doors, the occasional emergency light emitting a faint glow. Valentina's steps quickened as she led them left and then right. They met no guards, a small mercy Milton attributed to the confusion caused by the power going out.

They reached the server room without incident. The door was unlocked, and they went inside. Rows of servers lined the walls; their indicator lights were all off, more victims of the power cut.

Cooper turned to Milton. "Do you have it?"

Milton took the device from his pocket and gave it to Cooper. He'd described it as a network implant—a device no larger than a deck of cards—and said that he'd been given it by the man who had come to work for him after leaving Group Two. Cooper located an open port and plugged in the device, securing it in place with a small adhesive strip.

"Done," Cooper said. "It'll go live when the power comes back up."

"That's it?" Valentina said.

"That's it."

"Please can we go now?"

Milton said that they could. They retraced their steps. Voices echoed through the corridors now, and the sound of footsteps on gravel grew louder. They kept to the shadows as they moved through the dimly lit corridor. They passed an open doorway, and something inside caught his eye. He stopped, peering into the room. It was a small office, cluttered with papers and electronic equipment, but what drew his attention was the stack of cash piled neatly on a metal desk. Bundles of banknotes, tightly wrapped in plastic bands, were lined up in rows across the surface. Euros, dollars, pounds... and millions of them, by the look of it. Milton's gaze flicked to Cooper; he gave a slight nod, understanding immediately.

"Make it quick," Cooper whispered, keeping watch at the door while Valentina shifted nervously behind him.

Milton stepped inside, pulling his rucksack from his back and unzipping it. He swept several stacks of cash into the bag, working fast but careful not to disturb the rest of the room. He reached for one final bundle, dropped it into the bag and zipped it closed. He slung it back over his shoulders.

Valentina's eyes were wide when he rejoined them. "You're robbing them now?" she whispered.

"It's not for us," Milton muttered.

80

They kept close to the perimeter, avoiding the open spaces where they'd be more visible. Milton heard movement and signalled for them to pause behind a low wall; a pair of guards emerged from one of the side buildings, their torches cutting through the darkness as they moved in the opposite direction. Milton waited until they disappeared around a corner, then motioned for Valentina and Cooper to follow.

The path to the garage led between storage sheds. Milton kept them moving steadily. Valentina stumbled once, a loose stone shifting underfoot, but Cooper steadied her before she could make any more noise. They froze as another shout echoed from somewhere nearby, but the sound grew fainter, and they pressed on.

Milton had already identified the garage, and, finally, it came into view: a large structure with a corrugated metal roof, its bay doors partially open. Several vehicles were parked inside. Milton gestured for them to wait and crouched low, scanning for movement. It was clear; he signalled them forward and led them to the nearest vehicle.

He stopped and looked up. He heard the thrum of an aircraft approaching from the south.

It was a helicopter. He saw the aircraft descending toward the villa, its spotlight sweeping over the terrain.

Milton saw three men running to the helipad.

"Dragomir," Cooper said.

The helicopter landed, its rotors still spinning as Dragomir climbed aboard.

Milton cursed under his breath.

"Let him go," Cooper muttered. "We've done what we came here to do."

Milton clenched his jaw, forcing himself to think logically. He weighed the options. Taking Dragomir out would be satisfying, but it would also be dangerous. They'd done what they had come here to do, as Cooper had said, and would leave with a bag full of cash and Valentina removed safely and the prospect of evidence once the device powered up. The risk of getting caught in a firefight with the remaining guards wasn't worth it. And Cooper wasn't fit enough to get clear with Valentina without his help.

Too risky.

Dragomir could wait. Milton wouldn't forget.

He nodded. "Let's get out of here."

Cooper nodded in reply and moved toward the SUV closest to the exit. Milton helped Valentina into the back seat and then climbed into the front passenger seat, while Cooper slid behind the wheel. Milton took one last look at the helicopter now rising into the night sky, its navigation lights winking in the darkness. He hated leaving loose ends, but they'd done enough for now.

"Keys," Cooper whispered urgently.

Milton reached into the glove compartment and found a set. Cooper took them, and the engine growled to life, the sound muffled by the whine of the helicopter's engine overhead. Cooper put the SUV into gear, easing it forward through the garage doors and out onto the dirt track leading away from the villa.

Milton watched the villa in the wing mirror as they carefully descended the winding road, headlights off. Figures scrambled in the distance, some waving torches, but they were too slow to react.

The SUV bounced over the uneven terrain as they descended the mountain. Milton leaned back in his seat, allowing himself a moment to breathe.

EPILOGUE

Valentina Giordano had been back in the country for three days. She had flown out of Serbia with the two men who had followed her to Dragomir's villa; they had taken charge, heading straight for the airport and booking three seats on the next flight to Rome. She had sat next to the one with the blue eyes—he said his name was John—and asked him what he thought she should do. He had been brusque—not unfriendly, but businesslike—and had told her that she would need to hand herself into the authorities. Valentina hadn't protested; she had already decided that was what she was going to do. She believed she had been taken advantage of by Niko and Dragomir, but she had allowed herself to be put into that position and had ignored a number of opportunities to get away from them. John had told her she was culpable, and she found she didn't have the heart to argue with him.

She agreed: she was.

He had said that her best course of action was to cooperate with the authorities, and with that in mind, she had returned to her flat in Rome for the first time in months, packed a bag and taken a taxi to Via Nomentana and the headquarters of the Guardia di Finanza.

She was outside the building now. It loomed above her, eight storeys high and with flagpoles over the entrance bearing the flags of Italy and the European Union. The prospect of coming here and confessing suddenly seemed a lot more real than it had when she had agreed to it during the flight. She clasped her bag in her right hand and a folder under her left arm. The folder contained printouts of everything she thought might help the investigators looking into TrueCoin. She'd give them access to her emails, too, and was prepared to answer all of their questions.

She had asked John whether she should tell them about what she had done in Serbia, and, after considering it, he had said she should tell them she'd been to the villa and believed Dragomir had shot and killed Niko before disappearing. The other man—his name was Charlie—had said that he'd corroborate her story. Charlie would also testify that he'd given her the tracking device and that he'd been captured outside Dragomir's villa before breaking himself and Valentina out. John had asked only that his own name be left out; she didn't ask why but agreed.

She crossed the road and approached the steps that led up to the entrance. Two officers—a man and a woman—came out and passed her on the stairs. Valentina smiled at them, convinced that her guilt must have been written over her face, and almost turned back. She stopped, her hand on the rail, and closed her eyes. The same memories came back to her: hundreds of events in dozens of cities, thousands of people who had been persuaded to invest their money in a worthless coin, a scam that had made millions.

She remembered what John had said.

She had known what was happening.

She had to accept her responsibility for it.

And she would.

She reached for the door, opened it, and went inside.

∼

MARCO AND CHIARA had watched the story unfold with a mixture of emotions: relief, that they had done what they both knew they had to do; hope, that perhaps now there might be the slightest chance for them to get out of the hole into which they had fallen; and something close to fear, as the story they had told ran away from them and gathered momentum. They had had a degree of choice before, but not now. The genie was out of the bottle, and there was nothing they, or anyone else, could do to put it back.

The story had been picked up by all of the other newspapers and TV stations. There were podcasts, too, and online articles. It had come to be referred to as the TrueCoin Scandal, and, despite the occasional troll who blamed those who were scammed for their greed and credulity, the great majority of comments on social media were sympathetic.

They had been contacted by other journalists, and, at Isobel's suggestion, they had politely refused to comment. One of them had found their address and had pressed the intercom in an effort to win an invitation inside; Marco had told them he wasn't interested. The woman had waited for him on the street and had followed him as he went to the nearest *alimentare*; he had smiled and thanked her for her interest, but had politely declined for a second time, and after following him back to the apartment and waiting for an hour, she had got the message and left.

They had escaped to Chiara's mother's house for a couple of days but had returned to their apartment. "We've done nothing wrong," Chiara said. "We shouldn't have to feel we need to move out."

They had just finished lunch when the intercom buzzed.

Chiara looked up at him. "Are you expecting anyone?"

"No," he said. "I don't think so."

"It's probably the press again," she muttered. "Leave it."

"I'd better check."

He went to the intercom and lifted the handset. "Hello?"

"Delivery," a man said. He spoke Italian, but it was with an awkward accent.

Marco looked to his wife. "Have you ordered something?"

"No."

"It's a delivery."

"Not me."

"I'll go and see."

He opened the door and went down the stairs. He expected to find a delivery driver outside the front door, but, when he opened it, there was no one there. He looked left and right and saw nothing; he looked down and, to his surprise, saw a large holdall had been left on the step. He crouched down and noticed that an envelope had been fastened to the top of the bag with a strip of tape. He took the envelope and pulled it away from the bag, sliding his finger inside it, opening it and taking out the card that had been sealed inside. He held it up: the front of the card had a picture of a vase of flowers and, above it, 'Buona Fortuna.'

He opened the card, read the message that had been written inside and then, barely able to control his curiosity, unzipped the bag.

He went back upstairs and into the flat. He closed the door and locked it.

Chiara must have seen the confusion in his face. "What is it?"

"You're not going to believe this."

He dumped the bag on the sofa and gestured down to it. "That was waiting for me outside the front door. This was stuck to the outside."

He handed over the card; Chiara opened it and read. "'Please take what you need and split the rest with the others. Good luck. I hope it helps.'" She looked up at him and frowned. "I don't understand."

He pointed to the bag; his hand was shaking. "Open it."

She took the zip, pulled it back and splayed the bag open.

"Fanculo!"

Chiara never swore, but, this time, it was warranted. She reached inside and took out a thick bundle of euros. She held it up; the notes were all fifties, sealed with a paper band, in a wad maybe two inches thick. The bag was stuffed full of more of them. She pulled the opening as wide as it would go and upended the bag; the thick wads tumbled out; some of them stayed on the sofa; others bounced off and fell to the floor.

"My God," she said. "How much is this?"

Marco picked up one of the bundles and riffled the edge. He thumbed through the notes. His fingers started to tremble when he reached the first hundred; he felt a weakness all the way up his arm when he reached two hundred.

"Ten thousand," he mumbled.

He'd never seen so much money before.

Chiara quickly counted the number of bundles that had fallen out of the bag. "There are one hundred of them. A hundred times ten thousand is..."

"A million euros," Marco finished for her.

Chiara got up and went to the window. "There's no one there," she said.

"I know."

"Who'd leave this much money like that?"

"I have no idea."

"What do we do with it?"

"I don't know," he admitted.

"I mean... do we tell the police?"

He bit down on his lip. "Why?"

"Because..." She stopped, then started again. "What if it's stolen?"

"And then given to us? Why would someone do that?" He ran his fingers over the note at the top of the bundle. "It's TrueCoin."

"You think someone saw us on TV and this is them trying to help?"

Marco knew that was a stretch, but he was looking for a reason to be able to keep the money, and he was prepared to accept anything, regardless of how unlikely it was. They needed the money. They were desperate for it. And if someone wanted to help, who were they to question it?

"Maybe," he said.

"That's got to be it," Chiara said.

Marco looked at her and could see that she knew it was unlikely, too, but knew as well as he did how much they needed the money. They were both prepared to close their eyes to its provenance.

Marco crouched down, gathered up the bundles and put them all back in the bag. He zipped it closed, and, with Chiara following behind, he took it into the bedroom and opened the doors to their wardrobe. He cleared out the shoeboxes that were stacked beneath their clothes and put the bag inside, then piled the boxes back until the bag was hidden.

"I need to speak to Carlo," he said.

"Isn't there a meeting this afternoon?"

"Yes," he said. "Isobel wanted to give us an update on the legal case. Are you okay if I go?"

"You should definitely go," she said. She nodded down to the wardrobe. "What are you going to say about that?"

"The truth. We'll need to work out how to distribute it. Carlo will know what to do."

She shook her head, still stunned. "He won't believe it."

"None of them will," Marco said.

∽

MILTON WAITED OUTSIDE until a minute before the meeting was due to begin and then went inside. It was in the same building as the first one that he had attended. Isobel Turner had sent an email to him last night, and to everyone else who'd provided her with their details, telling them that she was going back to London, but, before she did, she wanted to update everyone on the progress of the case that had been filed against TrueCoin. She also said, a little cryptically, that she would be bringing someone 'important' who wanted to thank them for what they had done. Milton had stared at the email and wondered who that might be and hadn't been able to come up with a satisfactory answer. But, seeing as he was in Venice anyway, he didn't think it would do any harm to go along.

The room was as busy as it had been the first time. Milton took the same seat at the back and watched as Marco and Carlo shared a conversation at the front of the room. Marco's body language was urgent; he spoke quickly and quietly, bursting with an obvious excitement so electric that his hands were quivering.

Milton couldn't make out what they were saying and, since they were using Italian, wouldn't have understood anyway, but he had a pretty good guess.

He'd found a spot near Marco's apartment building where he could watch the door without being seen and, after leaving the bag on the doorstep and announcing that a delivery had arrived, had retreated there. Milton had watched as Marco had opened the door, and after he'd looked up and down the street for the delivery driver, Milton waited for him to notice the bag. Marco's expression went from confusion as he opened the envelope and read the card to stupefaction as he opened the bag and looked at the money inside. Milton hoped he'd realise it was safe to keep the money and had been relieved when he'd picked up the bag and taken it up to the apartment.

What happened to the cash now was up to him. Milton supposed there was a chance that he would feel the need to contact the police, but he hoped not. He had been pleased to find that he'd confiscated enough money from the villa to make Marco and Chiara whole, with enough to spare to help the others who had spoken at the meeting. He had kept a thousand for himself so that he could afford a flight out of the country and would have enough to get by while he found himself a job wherever he decided to go.

Carlo reached out and hugged Marco, with both of them wiping away tears. Milton couldn't help his smile; he knew that TrueCoin's victims numbered in the thousands or even tens of thousands, and that it was beyond him to help all of them. But he *could* help *these* people, and he and Cooper had accelerated the end of the scam with what they had done in Serbia. The business had been detonated, and no one else would be affected by it.

Isobel arrived with a man Milton hadn't seen before. He looked to be in his late forties or early fifties, dressed casually in jeans and a royal blue turtleneck. He looked perfectly ordinary save for the chunky watch on his wrist. Milton was no expert, but he knew enough to recognise an expensive timepiece; this one, he thought, looked as if it might have cost six figures.

Isobel met Carlo at the front of the room, and then Carlo brought the meeting to order.

"Thank you," he said. "Thank you for coming—we should get started. There's a lot to discuss." He waited for the room to quieten down. "Many of you will remember Isobel from before—she wanted to come and say a few words before she flies back to London, so if it's all right, I'll hand over to her now."

Carlo stepped aside, and Isobel stood. The room applauded, and there were several loud calls of 'bravo' and 'grazie.' Isobel looked a little bemused by the reception but smiled, waited for the applause to die down and, when it didn't, encouraged it to stop by holding up her hands.

"Thank you," she said. "I'm delighted to have been able to help, but I don't think I deserve that. If you want to applaud, I think you should applaud yourselves—and if there's one person in particular, I'd suggest Marco."

She pointed to where Marco was sitting, and this time, the applause was lusty and long and accompanied by the stamping of feet and whoops of approval. Isobel let it continue for a whole minute before once again raising her palms; the applause stopped, and with a broad smile, she continued.

"I wanted to give you a quick update. As you know, we

filed claims against TrueCoin across Europe last week. The legal action was timed to coincide with the press activity that you would all have seen—including the extraordinarily powerful interview from Marco and Chiara. Now—the good news. We've applied for *procedimento sommario di cognizione*. It's designed for cases where the facts are straightforward and supported by documentary evidence. It allows the court to make a swift decision without the need for a full trial, and we've been told that we can expect a positive response when the court sits today. We'll back that up with an injunction against any bank holding TrueCoin funds. We've found some and will freeze everything until the money can be returned to those from whom it was stolen."

More applause; Isobel grinned, then gestured for quiet.

"And as of yesterday, the police in Rome have opened an investigation into TrueCoin. We've come into possession of three terabytes of data on TrueCoin's operations—that includes personnel and, most importantly, bank accounts. We believe TrueCoin staff have been engaged in moving money to jurisdictions where it will be harder to recover, but you have my word that we won't give up until we have clawed back every cent of the money they've stolen.

"And more good news—I've been told that Valentina Rossi has handed herself in and is prepared to cooperate with the investigation. Valentina's real name is Giordano, and we've been told that she has already provided valuable information, including the news that one of the men behind the scam—Nikolai Petrović—was shot dead in Serbia by his co-conspirator, a man called Dragomir Jovanović. We believe Jovanović has fled the country, but we have a number of leads on his location, and we are working with Interpol to find him. And we will."

The door at the back of the room opened, and a latecomer came inside; Milton turned to see who it was, but his view was blocked by a couple who were standing in the absence of any chairs where they could sit.

"I said there were two things I wanted to do today," Isobel said. "I've given you the update, so I'll move on to the second thing. I'd like to introduce you to someone who has been involved in the fight against TrueCoin from the very beginning. You'll all have heard of him before, and he wanted to come and say a few words." She pointed to the man sitting next to her. "Ladies and gentlemen, please let me introduce my client, Nick Everett."

Milton recognised the name and saw that the others did, too. There was more applause as the man got to his feet and smiled out at the crowd.

"Thank you," he said. "I don't know how much Isobel has told you about me, but I've been responsible for funding a series of claims against TrueCoin across Europe. I'm based in London, and I'm afraid I was foolish enough—perhaps even greedy enough—to fall for the same lies that Valentina told to all of you. I lost many millions of pounds to TrueCoin, but I'm fortunate that I have enough money to go after them. It wasn't so much the money—I'm afraid I've probably lost that—as the principle. I have enough wealth that a loss like that isn't the end of me, but I could see others without my good fortune being scammed, just the same, and losing everything. I wasn't prepared to accept it, and that's why I've had a bit of a personal crusade against them." He smiled. "And it's also why I was absolutely delighted to hear the good news that Isobel has just given you. Now—I can't promise that your money will be returned, but I *can* promise that I'll do everything I can to try to make it happen."

The room applauded again. Milton joined in but then

stopped; he heard something from behind him that sounded out of place, and as he turned, he saw someone edging around those standing at the back. The atmosphere changed, just a little; Milton felt a shiver of apprehension.

"And," Everett said, "I just want to tell you how much I appreciate what you've done. I know how difficult it can be to admit that you've been tricked by people like this. I'm as embarrassed as anyone. Everyone involved in this has been incredibly brave—especially Marco and his wife." He turned to address them directly. "I wanted to tell you, in particular, that what you've done has made an enormous impact and—"

There was a shout from the back.

It was in Italian—Milton didn't understand it—but it sounded like a warning.

Everyone turned in that direction.

Everett stopped speaking.

Milton stood.

He saw the gun, held in a careful two-handed grip.

The man holding the gun was obscured by those standing, but Milton knew who it was.

There was a scream and then another, and someone yelled out, 'Pistola!'

The gun fired.

Everett staggered.

People ran.

Milton shoved the chair out of the way.

The gun fired again.

Everett threw his arms up and fell behind the table, out of sight.

The shooter turned and headed for the door.

Milton followed.

THE SHOOTER WAS ALREADY on his way out of the building, but Milton recognised him; it was the man who'd battered him at Moretti's villa. He remembered what Cooper had told him: his name was Vuković, and he was one of Dragomir's men.

Vuković emerged on the path next to the canal and turned south. Milton was acutely aware that Vuković had already proven to be more than he could handle. On top of that, he'd just shot a man in front of an audience. He had operated with a little more discretion before, but now—with TrueCoin circling the drain—perhaps he felt as if discretion was unnecessary. Everett had conducted a vendetta against the scammers, and now, with them scurrying like rats into the shadows, it might have been that Everett was Vuković's final target. If that was right—if he was planning to disappear, too—this might be Milton's only opportunity to serve him with the justice he deserved.

The path here was narrow, with the canal on the left and buildings on the right. Vuković continued south, reaching a bridge that crossed over onto the opposite side of the canal. He crossed it and headed east. Milton stayed well back, assuming that Vuković would be savvy enough to check that he was not being followed and knowing that, if he did, there was a chance that he would recognise Milton from before.

Vuković turned left and headed north, following a wider canal in the direction of the Grand Canal and the Ponte dell'Accademia.

Milton looked at his phone again: if Vuković was on his way out of the city, it seemed likely that he'd find transport on the Grand Canal. It seemed much less likely that he would divert east or west and, with that in mind, Milton decided to gamble. He waited until Vuković ignored the first bridge over the canal and then took it himself. There was a steakhouse just north of the bridge; he stopped beside the railing enclosing the outdoor dining area, feigning a loose shoelace, and, when the waiter turned, he took a serrated knife from the closest table. He set off again, slowing as he passed a shop selling overpriced junk to tourists, and took an I LOVE VENICE baseball cap from a rotating rack. The owner looked at him with a quizzical expression; Milton added a pair of cheap sunglasses, pressed a twenty-euro note into the man's hand, put the cap and glasses on and hurried to catch up.

Vuković reached the Ponte de le Maravegie and carried on. Milton took it, crossing over onto the same side of the canal again. He checked his map and saw that there was no easy way to reach the Grand Canal from here; he'd just concluded that when Vuković followed the path up to a gate with a sign—Pensione Accademia—above it.

A hotel? Milton wondered whether Vuković had taken a room there.

It didn't much matter; he quickly saw that the courtyard beyond the gate was empty and picked up his pace to a brisk walk. The space was wide and shielded from the sun by two large canvas parasols.

Milton closed the distance between them and took out the knife from his pocket.

Vuković must have heard something; he turned.

Milton lashed out.

Vuković's reflexes were fast, even faster than Milton remembered. He twisted away at the last second, the serrated edge of the knife grazing his side instead of burying deep. He grunted, his hand shooting to Milton's wrist and grabbing it tightly. Milton felt the power behind it, the same brute strength that had been too much for him before.

He drove his shoulder forward, crashing into Vuković's chest and forcing him back a step. The surprise had bought him an opening, and he twisted his wrist violently, breaking free of Vuković's grip just enough to slice again, this time aiming for the thigh.

The blade found its mark, cutting through fabric and drawing blood. Vuković grunted again, stumbling, but still came on. He lashed out with his other hand, striking Milton in the ribs with enough force to send him staggering sideways into one of the parasol posts.

Vuković reached into his jacket for his gun. Milton intervened before he could get to it, feinting right and lunging left.

Vuković reacted quickly, sidestepping Milton's attack and catching his wrist for a second time. He wrenched it to the side, forcing the knife from Milton's grasp. It clattered to the ground, sliding out of reach.

Vuković slid around him, wrapping an arm around his neck and pulling him into a choke. Milton gasped, his vision narrowing as the pressure built. Vuković's strength was overwhelming, and Milton felt himself being dragged backward, his feet barely scraping against the stone courtyard floor.

The cap was jostled off Milton's head. He clawed at the arm around his throat, his pulse hammering in his ears, but Vuković held firm. Spots danced in Milton's vision, and he could feel his strength waning. He focused on the weight pressed against him—the point of his shoulder, the broad chest—then he felt it.

Vuković's pistol, tucked into a shoulder holster under his jacket.

Milton pushed back, driving them both into the wall of

the building. Vuković held on, but the impact had jarred open enough of a gap between his chest and Milton's back for Milton to be able to reach around with his left hand, his fingers scrabbling at the edge of the holster. He felt cold metal, and, with one last effort, he gripped the pistol's handle and yanked it free.

Vuković realised what was happening a second too late.

Milton twisted his body just enough to aim blindly behind him and squeezed the trigger.

The shot cracked through the courtyard, loud in the enclosed space.

Vuković's grip loosened instantly.

Milton felt the weight shift and staggered forward as the younger man stumbled back, clutching his side. Vuković's eyes were wide with shock, his mouth opening and closing without sound. He took an unsteady step toward Milton, but his knees buckled, and he crumpled to his knees, blood seeping through his fingers.

Milton stared down at Vuković, aimed the pistol and fired for a second time.

Headshot.

A woman screamed.

Milton looked up, saw a woman in the doorway of the hotel, and knew it was time to move. He grabbed the cap and put it on again, then retraced his steps, heading back to the south until he reached a narrow passageway between buildings. He took it, taking off the cap and glasses and dropping them into a rubbish bin. The passageway was tight, with just enough space for two people to walk abreast. There were shops on the right and the bare wall of a building being renovated to the left, with temporary screening overhead to protect passers-by from anything that the workmen might drop.

Milton walked as fast as he could without drawing attention to himself, eventually reaching the Rio del Malpaga. A water taxi was waiting, and Milton clambered aboard and went to sit at the front, shielded from the pilot by the wheelhouse. Milton told the man to take him as near to the Basilica as he could, and as they pushed off and moved north, Milton took the pistol from his pocket. When he was sure no one would see him, he dropped it overboard.

∼

DRAGOMIR JOVANOVIĆ STEPPED out of the cool, air-conditioned interior of the private bank and into the humidity of midday. He paused for a moment, adjusting his sunglasses against the glare of the sun, and allowed himself a smile. The funds were secure, spread across a web of accounts and shell companies so intricate that even the most dogged investigators would find themselves lost in the labyrinth. He had been worried that they had been too slow in moving the money, but evidently not; only a little had been frozen before it could be remitted.

George Town was spectacular. He inhaled the salty breeze, tinged with the faintest trace of diesel from the yachts bobbing in the marina. He'd done it. He'd escaped, slipping out of the country before anyone could do anything to stop him. The villa had been compromised, but that didn't matter. He was here now, thousands of miles away on Grand Cayman, and untouchable.

He'd been updated on what had happened as soon as he had landed. Valentina had handed herself into the police in Rome; that was unfortunate, but not unexpected. She'd been a useful tool in the beginning, but the pressure that came with her status had buckled her nerves. It was inevitable that she would crack. And Niko—poor, naïve Niko—was dead. He had been shot. Dragomir felt nothing. Niko, like Valentina, had served a purpose, and his death only solidified the reality that their operation was finished. A fitting end for someone who'd started to believe he was more than just a cog in Dragomir's machine.

He strolled along the waterfront, enjoying the gentle lap of waves against the docks. The island was a paradise, offering him peace and safety and a lifestyle that he fully intended to indulge in. He'd been working for too long, and now it was time to enjoy the fruits of his labour.

A celebration was in order. He found a quiet bar nestled between luxury boutiques, its shaded terrace offering a perfect view of the marina. He settled into a chair, ordered a whisky, and let his mind drift as he waited. He thought of the years spent building TrueCoin. He'd known it would eventually unravel, but he'd sucked up more than he could ever have thought possible. The manager of the bank had slipped him a statement inside an embossed leather portfolio, and the number at the bottom had eight zeroes.

His drink arrived, and he lifted the glass, watching the liquid swirl. He glanced across the bar, his gaze lingering briefly on a woman at the far end. She was attractive in an understated way, dark hair pulled into a bun, dressed in a fashion that suggested money but not ostentation. Class. She caught his gaze and smiled. He raised his glass, and she raised hers.

He might have been tempted to go over and take the stool next to her, but he had an appointment with a second bank in an hour, and he didn't want to be late. There would be plenty of time for rest and relaxation once he was sure that everything was exactly as it ought to be.

He took a moment to glance across the street. The palm-lined boulevard was peaceful, with just a few tourists idling along the pavement. A black Audi SUV idled near the curb, but he dismissed it; the police couldn't know that he was here, not yet, and he would be moving on soon. He didn't know where; he had a list of countries where he would be safe from extradition and had picked out a few possibilities: Russia was an option, as was China. He would be safe in either, but he wanted somewhere with a warm climate and had tentatively settled on Vietnam.

The woman from the bar had been watching him, and now he saw she was coming over.

"Do you mind if I sit down?" the woman asked.

He waved a hand and allowed her a smile. "Please."

Perhaps he could stay awhile.

"What's your name?"

"Nikolai," he said, using the first name that came to mind. "Call me Niko."

"Hello, Niko. Would you like to buy me a drink?"

A flash of movement caught his eye just as the woman pulled out the chair.

CRACK. CRACK.

The woman screamed.

It felt like a punch in the chest and another in the shoulder. A dull pain, and then more.

Gunfire.

Dragomir fell sideways off his chair and looked up. The woman was still screaming. Her blouse had been splashed with red.

He heard the screech of rubber and saw a blur of black as the SUV raced away.

The woman screamed and called for help.

He gasped, his hands clutching at his chest, his fingers slick with blood.

The woman screamed again, but Dragomir couldn't see her.

He sprawled on the terrace, choking for breath; none came.

His vision blurred, the sounds around him dulling into a drone that then started to fade. He tried to move but couldn't.

The drone faded out completely.

He looked up, blinking into the endless blue sky.

The woman was looking down at him, and then she wasn't.

~

CHARLIE COOPER DROVE out of George Town and pulled over to where Nathan Wiley was waiting to collect him. Nathan was Cooper's specialist, plucked from Group Two when Cooper decided to set up Veritas. The afternoon was still, and the only thing he could hear was the sound of the waves breaking on the rocks. Cooper stepped out of the car and slipped into the back of the Hyundai.

"Go," he said, tapping the back of the driver's seat.

Wiley put his foot down, and the Hyundai raced away.

"All done?"

"All done," Cooper said. "Put two shots into him. That ought to do it."

"I'll check with the police when we get to the airport," Wiley said.

It was far from the first time that Cooper had drawn blood, but it was the first time since he had left the Group. Veritas was involved in the collection of intelligence, not the martial work that Cooper had done for the government. But he'd decided to make an exception in this case. Dragomir had been able to evade the attention of the Italian police, but Cooper was damned if he was going to let him evade justice. A man with his resources would have been able to melt away into nothingness, and that was something that didn't sit well with Cooper. Milton had offered to do it, but the murder of Nick Everett in Venice had changed Cooper's view on things. He'd liked Everett, and, besides, Milton had already dealt with Vuković. It was Cooper's turn.

"Slow down," Cooper said as they reached a curve in the road.

The sea was on the other side of the barrier. Nathan slowed. Cooper opened the window and tossed the gun. He peeled off the gloves he had been wearing to ensure he didn't leave prints.

Wiley accelerated away again. "What's next?"

Cooper breathed in and then out, wondering about that. He'd given some thought to asking Milton whether he'd like to earn a little extra by taking on the odd job for him but had decided against it. It was clear that Milton wasn't in the employment market, and that all he wanted to do was disappear once more. There was something about the itinerant lifestyle he'd chosen that was attractive, although Cooper was happy with continuing to develop Veritas. News of his involvement in the case against TrueCoin had already leaked out, and he'd had an email from a lawyer investigating a Nigerian scammer who was alleged to have extorted money from hundreds of men, with two of them taking their own lives. That sounded like something Cooper could get his teeth into.

"The airport," he said, "then London. I've got work to do."

John Milton will return in The Butcher. You can preorder now so that you have it the moment it is released - Amazon will say it will be out in 2026, but it's more likely to be late summer 2025.

Preorder it here.

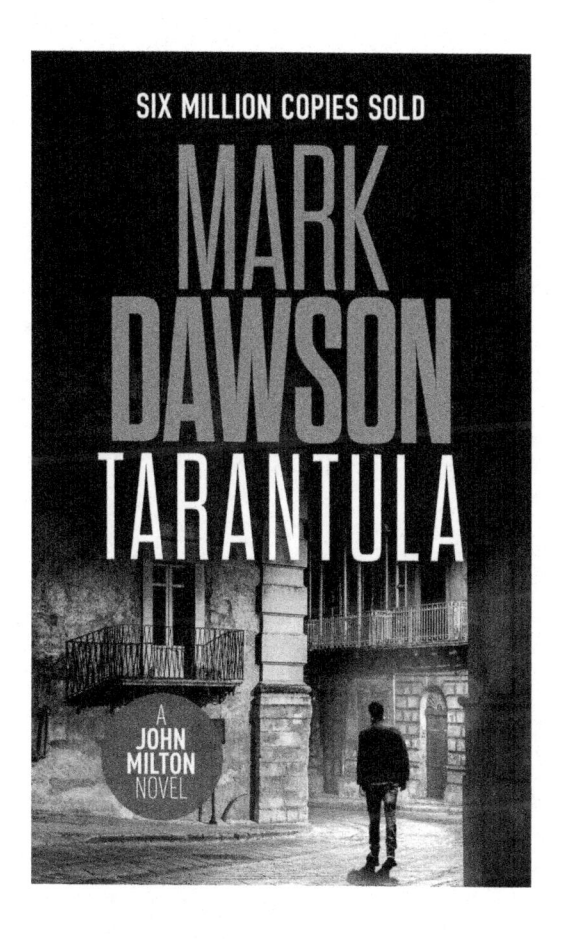

Building a relationship with my readers is the very best thing about writing. Join my Reader Club for information on new books and deals plus a free copy of Milton's battle with the Mafia and an assassin called Tarantula.

You can get your content **for free**, by signing up at my website.

Just visit www.markjdawson.com.

ALSO BY MARK DAWSON

IN THE JOHN MILTON SERIES

The Cleaner

Sharon Warriner is a single mother in the East End of London, fearful that she's lost her young son to a life in the gangs. After John Milton saves her life, he promises to help. But the gang, and the charismatic rapper who leads it, is not about to cooperate with him.

Buy The Cleaner

Saint Death

John Milton has been off the grid for six months. He surfaces in Ciudad Juárez, Mexico, and immediately finds himself drawn into a vicious battle with the narco-gangs that control the borderlands.

Buy Saint Death

The Driver

When a girl he drives to a party goes missing, John Milton is worried. Especially when two dead bodies are discovered and the police start treating him as their prime suspect.

Buy The Driver

Ghosts

John Milton is blackmailed into finding his predecessor as Number One. But she's a ghost, too, and just as dangerous as him. He finds himself in deep trouble, playing the Russians against the British in a desperate attempt to save the life of his oldest friend.

Buy Ghosts

The Sword of God

On the run from his own demons, John Milton treks through the Michigan wilderness into the town of Truth. He's not looking for trouble, but trouble's looking for him. He finds himself up against a small-town cop who has no idea with whom he is dealing, and no idea how dangerous he is.

Buy The Sword of God

Salvation Row

Milton finds himself in New Orleans, returning a favour that saved his life during Katrina. When a lethal adversary from his past takes an interest in his business, there's going to be hell to pay.

[Buy Salvation Row]()

Headhunters

Milton barely escaped from Avi Bachman with his life. But when the Mossad's most dangerous renegade agent breaks out of a maximum security prison, their second fight will be to the finish.

[Buy Headhunters]()

The Ninth Step

Milton's attempted good deed becomes a quest to unveil corruption at the highest levels of government and murder at the dark heart of the criminal underworld. Milton is pulled back into the game, and that's going to have serious consequences for everyone who crosses his path.

[Buy The Ninth Step]()

The Jungle

John Milton is no stranger to the world's seedy underbelly. But when the former British Secret Service agent comes up against a ruthless human trafficking ring, he'll have to fight harder than ever to conquer the evil in his path.

[Buy The Jungle]()

Blackout

A message from Milton's past leads him to Manila and a

confrontation with an adversary he thought he would never meet again. Milton finds himself accused of murder and imprisoned inside a brutal Filipino jail can he escape, uncover the truth and gain vengeance for his friend?

Buy Blackout

The Alamo

A young boy witnesses a murder in a New York subway restroom. Milton finds him, and protects him from corrupt cops and the ruthless boss of a local gang.

Buy The Alamo

Redeemer

Milton is in Brazil, helping out an old friend with a close protection business. When a young girl is kidnapped, he finds himself battling a local crime lord to get her back.

Buy Redeemer

Sleepers

A sleepy English town. A murdered Russian spy. Milton and Michael Pope find themselves chasing the assassins to Moscow.

Buy Sleepers

Twelve Days

Milton checks back in with Elijah Warriner, but finds himself caught up in a fight to save him from a jealous and dangerous former friend.

[Buy Twelve Days]()

Bright Lights

All Milton wants to do is take his classic GTO on a coast-to-coast road trip. But he can't ignore the woman on the side of the road in need of help. The decision to get involved leads to a tussle with a murderous cartel that he thought he had put behind him.

Buy Bright Lights

The Man Who Never Was

John Milton is used to operating in the shadows, weaving his way through dangerous places behind a fake identity. Now, to avenge the death of a close friend, he must wear his mask of deception once more.

Buy The Man Who Never Was

Killa City

John Milton has a nose for trouble. He can smell it a mile away. And when he witnesses a suspicious altercation between a young man and two thugs in a car auction parking lot, he can't resist getting involved.

Buy Killa City

Ronin

Milton travels to Bali in search of a new identity. He meets a young woman who has been forced to work for the Yakuza in Japan, and finds himself drawn into danger in an attempt to keep her safe.

Buy Ronin

Never Let Me Down Again

A human rights activist has vanished without a trace and his dying mother is desperate to know the truth. When the mysterious disappearance leads Milton all the way to the Western Isles of Scotland, he sees an opportunity to find an old friend and finally make amends for a mistake that cost him dearly. Milton is determined to track both men down, wherever his search may lead.

Buy Never Let Me Down Again

Bulletproof

Captured and imprisoned by the organisation he once worked for, Milton must do one last job in exchange for his freedom. Bullheaded billionaire fixer Tristan Huxley is brokering a weapons deal between Russia and India. He needs protection and he wants Milton by his side. Huxley has trusted Milton with his life before but these days his world is more decadent and his enemies more dangerous, in ways that nobody could ever have suspected.

Buy Bulletproof

Uppercut

John Milton is on the run again. Chasing clues to help him understand the new risks he faces, he finds himself in Dublin. Before he knows it, he is involved with a woman who has fallen foul of a dangerous local family.

Buy Uppercut

Bloodlands

John Milton is on a mission that will bring him face-to-face with enemies old and new. When his friend, Alex Hicks, finds himself pursued by mysterious adversaries, the two men are thrust back into the web of international espionage.

Buy Bloodlands

IN THE BEATRIX ROSE SERIES

In Cold Blood

Beatrix Rose was the most dangerous assassin in an off-the-books government kill squad until her former boss betrayed her. A decade later, she emerges from the Hong Kong underworld with payback on her mind. They gunned down her husband and kidnapped her daughter, and now the debt needs to be repaid. It's a blood feud she didn't start but she is going to finish.

Buy In Cold Blood

Blood Moon Rising

There were six names on Beatrix's Death List and now there are four. She's going to account for the others, one by one, even if it kills her. She has returned from Somalia with another target in her sights. Bryan Duffy is in Iraq, surrounded by mercenaries, with no easy way to get to him and no easy way to get out. And Beatrix has other issues that need to be addressed. Will Duffy prove to be one kill too far?

Buy Blood Moon Rising

Blood and Roses

Beatrix Rose has worked her way through her Kill List. Four are dead, just two are left. But now her foes know she has them in her sights and the hunter has become the hunted.

Buy Blood and Roses

The Dragon and the Ghost

Beatrix Rose flees to Hong Kong after the murder of her husband and the kidnapping of her child. She needs money. The local triads have it. What could possibly go wrong?

Buy The Dragon and the Ghost

Tempest

Two people adrift in a foreign land, Beatrix Rose and Danny Nakamura need all the help they can get. A storm is coming. Can they help each other survive it and find their children before time runs out for both of them?

Buy Tempest

Phoenix

She does Britain's dirty work, but this time she needs help. Beatrix Rose, meet John Milton...

[Buy Phoenix](#)

IN THE ISABELLA ROSE SERIES

The Angel

Isabella Rose is recruited by British intelligence after a terrorist attack on Westminster.

Buy The Angel

The Asset

Isabella Rose, the Angel, is used to surprises, but being abducted is an unwelcome novelty. She's relying on Michael Pope, the head of the top-secret Group Fifteen, to get her back.

Buy The Asset

The Agent

Isabella Rose is on the run, hunted by the very people she had been hired to work for. Trained killer Isabella and former handler Michael Pope are forced into hiding in India and, when a mysterious informer passes them clues on the whereabouts of Pope's family, the prey see an opportunity to become the predators.

[Buy The Agent](#)

The Assassin

Ciudad Juárez, Mexico, is the most dangerous city in the world. And when a mission to break the local cartel's grip goes wrong, Isabella Rose, the Angel, finds herself on the wrong side of prison bars. Fearing the worst, Isabella plays her only remaining card...

[Buy The Assassin](#)

The Avenger

Living under new identities in rural France, Isabella Rose and Michael Pope are trying to lay low. Tired of hiding, all Isabella wants is the chance to live an ordinary life. But Isabella is an extraordinary young woman and the people pursuing her will never, ever, give up. Her unique abilities have attracted the attention of the Academy of Military Science in Beijing. And it's not only Isabella who needs to stay in the shadows. Pope has his fair share of enemies and a family that he's desperate to protect.

[Buy The Avenger](#)

Pretty Face

Isabella is building a new life in Marrakesh, supporting herself with contract work and finally looking to put down roots. But when one of her contracts isn't quite what it seems, things quickly descend into chaos.

[Buy Pretty Face](#)

IN THE CHARLIE COOPER SERIES

Sandstorm

Group Fifteen operative and ex-MI6 officer Charlie Cooper is working undercover as a political negotiator. Attending a conference surrounded by diplomats, businessmen and lobbyists, nobody would suspect what he really does for a living. Also in their midst is Aisha, a Saudi activist whose protests against human rights abuses have made her an enemy of her country's regime.

Buy Sandstorm

The Chameleon

Masquerading as an analyst, Cooper manipulates his way into the company and soon finds himself en route to Istanbul. The stage is set for a high-octane showdown on Sidorov's private island. With geopolitical tensions on a knife's edge, Cooper must navigate a labyrinth of deception and danger to complete his mission.

Buy The Chameleon

Blood Brothers

Cooper travels to Israel to find his estranged half-brother, Freddy, who has mysteriously disappeared. Freddy's ties to NetGuardian, a cybersecurity firm implicated in dubious activities, propel Cooper into a dangerous web of corporate espionage, state-of-the-art surveillance technology, and the ruthless world of intelligence.

Buy Blood Brothers

Dead of Winter

Charlie Cooper is sent to Prague to investigate - and eliminate - the leader of a group of far right hooligans guilty of the murder of an Interpol agent. Cooper is on his final warning and is expected to get in and out with minimal fuss, leaving just the body of his target in his wake.

Buy Dead of Winter

Code Blue

Cooper is thrust into a high-stakes mission when a fellow operative, codenamed NORTH STAR, vanishes in Macao. The trail leads to a shadowy team of Russian mercenaries with a chilling agenda: to expose Group Fifteen, the clandestine organisation that operates beyond the reach of conventional intelligence agencies.

Buy Code Blue

North Star

After barely escaping an assassination attempt in Iceland, NORTH STAR, a former Group Fifteen operative turned Russian asset, vanishes. Driven by guilt and a thirst for revenge, Control tasks Charlie Cooper with tracking him down.

Buy North Star

IN THE ATTICUS PRIEST SERIES

The House in the Woods

Disgraced detective Atticus Priest investigates the murder of a family on Christmas Eve. He's been employed to demolish the police case against his client, but things get complicated when the officer responsible for the case is his former girlfriend.

Buy The House in the Woods

A Place to Bury Strangers

A dog walker finds a human bone on lonely Salisbury Plain. DCI Mackenzie Jones investigates the grisly discovery but cannot explain how it ended up there. She contacts Atticus Priest and the two of them trace the bone to a graveyard in the nearby village of Imber. But the village was abandoned after it was purchased by the Ministry of Defence to train the army, so why have bodies been buried in the graveyard since the church was closed?

Buy A Place to Bury Strangers

The Red Room

When a man's fatal fall from Salisbury Cathedral spirals into a scandalous case involving the victims of a sex ring, Atticus Priest and Mackenzie Jones uncover more bodies and incriminating videos. Racing against the clock, they confront personal demons and tangled emotions as they try to catch the murderer before he can strike again.

Buy The Red Room

All the Devils Are Here

Atticus Priest is employed by an estranged husband to dig up dirt on his wife. But when she goes missing after swimming in the River Avon, Atticus uncovers a conspiracy between five lifelong friends that goes back years.

Buy All The Devils Are Here

ABOUT MARK DAWSON

Mark Dawson is the author of the John Milton, Beatrix and Isabella Rose and Atticus Priest series.

For more information:
www.markjdawson.com
mark@markjdawson.com

AN UNPUTDOWNABLE ebook.
First published in Great Britain in 2025 by UNPUTDOWNABLE LIMITED
Copyright © UNPUTDOWNABLE LIMITED 2025

The moral right of Mark Dawson to be identified as the author of this work has been asserted by him in accordance with the Copyright, Designs and Patents Act 1988.

All the characters in this book are fictitious, and any resemblance to actual persons living or dead is purely coincidental.

All rights reserved. No part of this publication may be reproduced, stored in a retrieval system or transmitted in any form or by any means, without the prior permission in writing of the publisher, nor to be otherwise circulated in any form of binding or cover other than that in which it is published without a similar condition, including this condition, being imposed on the subsequent purchaser.

Printed in Great Britain
by Amazon